RAWHIDE RIVER

Cliff Farrell was born in Zanesville, Ohio, where earlier Zane Grey had been born. Following graduation from high school, Farrell became a newspaper reporter. Over the next decade he worked his way west by means of a string of newspaper jobs and for thirty-one years was employed, mostly as sports editor, for the *Los Angeles Examiner*. He would later claim that he began writing for pulp magazines because he grew bored with journalism. His first Western stories were written for *Cowboy Stories* in 1926 and his byline was A. Clifford Farrell. By 1928 this byline was abbreviated to Cliff Farrell, and this it remained for the rest of his career. In 1933 Farrell was invited to contribute a story for the first issue of *Dime Western*. He soon became a regular contributor to this magazine and to *Star Western* as well. In fact, many months he would have a short novel in both magazines. Farrell became such a staple at Popular Publications that by the end of the 1930s he was contributing as much as 400,000 words a year to their various Western magazines. In all, Farrell wrote nearly 600 stories for the magazine market. His earliest Western fiction tended to stress action and gun play, but increasingly his stories began to focus on characters in historical situations and the problems faced by those characters. *Follow the New Grass* (1954) was Farrell's first Western novel, a story concerned with a desperate battle over grazing rights in the Cheyenne Indian reserve. It was followed by *West with the Missouri* (1955), an exciting story of riverboats, gamblers, and gunmen. *Fort Deception* (1960), *Ride the Wild Country* (1963), *The Renegade* (1970), and *The Devil's Playground* (1976) are among the best of Farrell's later Western novels. *Desperate Journey*, a first collection of Cliff Farrell's Western short stories, has also been published.

RAWHIDE RIVER

Cliff Farrell

GUNSMOKE

First published in the UK by Random House

This hardback edition 2009
by BBC Audiobooks Ltd
by arrangement with
Golden West Literary Agency

ISBN 978 1 408 46236 2

British Library Cataloguing in Publication Data available.

TO MILDRED K.

Printed and bound in Great Britain by
CPI Antony Rowe, Chippenham and Eastbourne

CHAPTER 1

Standing on the crowded main deck, Britt Cahill watched St. Louis spread a fanfare of glittering lights along the black Mississippi shore, as the steamboat *Aurora* rounded to in the stream, sounded her whistle, and groped her way through the misty, early darkness of the spring nightfall toward the levee.

He could see that St. Louis had changed mightily in the three years since he had fled from it with death at his heels. Appomattox was six years in the past now, and a nation, exhausted by civil war, had lifted from its knees at last, and was turning its face westward toward the virgin prairies and plains that were to be its salvation.

St. Louis was a gateway to this destiny. The life artery of an empire now coursed through its streets and over its levees. Its lights were bright and beckoning—like the promise in a passionate woman's eyes. It had grown into a teeming city. Its old, shaggy frontier aspect was nearly gone.

Britt Cahill had changed, too, in those three years, but not that much. He knew he was risking the gallows by showing his face in St. Louis again. It meant his life if he was recognized by anyone from the past. And the worst of it was that the purpose that had brought him here was such a long gamble that he had hardly a chance in ten of succeeding. But these three years had hardened him to gambling with his life against odds.

The reversed wheel kicked a boil of muddy water along the *Aurora's* counter as she eased her way to her berth at the crowded levee. A few rotting ice floes, last of the breakup that the steamboat had followed down the Missouri River, grumbled against her hull. The mist of the river came up to mingle with the smoky glare of the torch baskets that hung from poles above the poised gangplank.

The torches laid a sooty half-light over the mass of impatient men who jammed the deck around Britt, anxious to plant their feet once again on solid land.

The *Aurora*, first passenger boat of the season from the upper Missouri, had started her trip from Fort Benton, more than two thousand miles away in far Montana, nearly four weeks earlier. Now she had reached her destination.

She wore a pair of buffalo horns on her verge staff, and a grizzly-bear hide was nailed to the wall of the captain's cabin on the top-deck structure known to rivermen as the texas. A Brule arrow, driven by the bow of some defiant warrior up near the Musselshell, jutted from the pilothouse. Bullet holes, made by Indian rifles, starred the windows on the passenger deck.

Britt Cahill had taken his place on the main deck, handy to the stage plank. He stood with his back to a stanchion for safety's sake. His possible sack was slung over his shoulder, and his right hand hung close to the holstered six-shooter under the skirt of his weather-stained, canvas brush coat.

He laid a narrow and probing attention on every man within reach, pushing them clear with a thrust of his shoulders when they crowded him. Not all those bullet holes in the steamboat were the handiwork of Indians. Two attempts to kill him had been made during the trip down the river.

The shots that had been fired at him from the blackness of the decks had missed by narrow margins on both occasions. But Britt knew they would try again if the chance came. Luck had saved him twice—luck and the uncertainty of shooting in the darkness. These factors would not save him always.

The raging desire to strike back was an explosive pressure in him, for it was contrary to his nature to match stealth with stealth. He thirsted to drive this thing into the open where he could settle it as he preferred to settle all matters of violence, with his blunt-knuckled fists or his gun.

But he was forced to stand helpless, tautly aware of his danger. For he had not the faintest idea as to which of the travelers on the *Aurora* were out to kill him.

He had only one advantage. He knew why they wanted

6

to put him out of the way, and he knew there were at least two of them.

There was no doubt that these two were among the passengers who were jamming ever tighter around him, waiting for the stage plank to drop. But, scanning the faces nearest him, he was sure of nothing more. He roughly shoved men back, forcing them to give him arm space, ready to shoot at the first sign of threat.

All of these men were armed, and some bristled when Cahill shouldered them away, turning on him and ready to make an issue of it. But, after a second look, they invariably subsided.

Britt Cahill had the earmarks of a man who could take care of himself. He stood an even six feet and his brush coat hung from wide shoulders. He carried himself with the slack poise of a man who was sure of his capacity for violence. The sag of his gunbelt showed where his coat hung open. Beneath that he wore the gray flannel shirt and dark woolen breeches of a prospector.

Sandy-haired, with a rugged chin and jaw, he wore a weathered hat shading stone-gray eyes that looked back at these challengers with neither hostility nor apology. "Just give me a little room, Mister," he would say gently. "Then we'll all be happy."

There was something in his voice that convinced them he meant what he said. And so none of them thought it worth while to push the matter further. Many of them were prospectors from the Montana mines. There were plainsmen, too, in the crowd, and here and there were graying, gaunt old mountain men in buckskins—the last of a vanishing race. French *engagés* from the trading posts in gaudy shirts and sashes and blanket breeches, and soldiers on leave from the frontier forts, and frock-coated gamblers with pleated shirts sprinkled the assembly. They all gave Cahill room.

Then, with the mate pleading for the pressing mass to stand back, the plank descended. As it clanged on the levee the passengers began stampeding ashore.

Britt was among the first down the stageplank. The levee was aroar with barkers and shills from the honky-tonks and gambling houses.

"The Pink Slipper, boys!" one was bawling. "That's where

the gals prance high an' smile purty. This way, men—free tallyho to the Pink Slipper . . ."

"It's Banjo Dan's, friends!" another chanted. "Wet your whistles, an' cut a caper with the slickest little fillies in St. Louis. They're winsome an' willin'. Here's your transportation, men. This way . . ."

Other barkers joined in, proclaiming the attractions they represented. The debarking passengers were swarming joyously toward the waiting line of vehicles.

Private carriages with liveried Negro footmen stood in the background. These were from the more exclusive gambling houses, and silk-hatted shills were singling out the more prosperous-looking arrivals.

"Certainly, Sir," Britt heard one of them telling a prospect. "Pierre's offers refinement and action for your money. He does not welcome the riffraff. His establishment is famous for its cuisine and luxury. Among those who will entertain you is none other than Miss Sherry Dean, the Irish thrush. She is appearing at Pierre's for a limited engagement at great expense. Let me offer you a private carriage. You'll never regret spending an evening at Pierre's."

Britt's head lifted at the mention of that name. Sherry Dean! That brought a rush of memories—warm, exciting. And it solved one of the problems that confronted him. There was at least one person in St. Louis he could trust.

He retreated down the levee, keeping to the deep shadows of warehouses and mounded cargo. Occasionally he paused, waiting, listening for any indication that he might be followed. But no sound of stealthy pursuit came from the darkness.

Evidently he had been successful in eluding the men who sought his life. He was touched by a stubborn tinge of disappointment. He would have preferred to shoot it out with them here and now. But common sense told him it was better this way. A shooting fray might mean involvement with the law, and that would certainly lead to his identification and arrest.

He stood, considering his next move. He had no time to waste. He had come to St. Louis to attempt to find a certain person, a young woman. The men who had tried to kill him aboard the *Aurora* would now be hunting that same person, impelled by the same purpose that had brought him here.

8

He shifted the weight of the slender canvas belt poke that was strapped about his waist. It contained some one hundred and twenty ounces of raw gold, and that ten-pound burden, which had been with him continually for two weeks, was wearing on his temper.

He moved ahead again. Steamboats lined the riverfront, their stacks and pilothouses painting a ragged phalanx against the stars. Out in the stream a crack Mississippi packet, all gilt and white and as fancy as a wedding cake, was pulling in, her calliope blaring a polka. At a floating dock, another New Orleans passenger boat was making ready to shove off, her deck s crowded with gay travelers, and a banjo orchestra twanging out a lively tune on the prow.

Here and there other craft were discharging or loading, and Britt skirted these lighted areas. He paused abruptly and stood looking at a packet that was taking on cargo, with stevedores working beneath the glow of torches. The boat was newly painted in cream and tan. A sternwheeler, she bore the name *Dakota Queen* on her pilothouse. Beneath, in bright gilt letters, was the legend:

ORMSBY & JARRETT
ST. LOUIS, MO.

It was this name, Ormsby, that held Britt's gaze. Once again came memories with a rush, memories that this time brought a stab of pain and regret and the knowledge of years lost beyond recovery.

He was swept by a hopeless and intolerable yearning. The smell of the river reached inside him, earthy and muddy and wild and heart-catchingly familiar.

Once Britt Cahill had met the challenge of the Mississippi and the Missouri from the deck of his own big packet, the *Northern Star*. But the *Star* had lain rotting at the muddy bottom of the Missouri River for three years now, and he was a fugitive, skulking in the shadows along the levee where he had once walked in his young and complete confidence of the future. Now he feared to show his face among the men who had once trusted and respected the name of Cahill.

He turned at last, gazing at the city whose rooftops and building fronts loomed above the slope of the levee. He

9

could hear the carryalls clattering off through the dark, cobbled streets in the direction of a glow of lights beyond the riverfront.

He found a hiding place for his possible sack under the foundation of a warehouse, then headed in the same direction. Presently he rounded a corner and emerged on a crowded street, aglare with light and lined with gambling houses and music halls.

This was the pleasure and gambling district. A restless tide of men flowed along the sidewalks and in and out of the gaudy traps that stood cheek to cheek for half a dozen blocks.

Music blared and gravel-voiced barkers laid a steady din along the street. Hurdy-gurdies offered their tinny refrains and banjos twanged. A medicine show was in operation on a street corner, with a girl in spangles and tights kicking her heels for the edification of yelling bystanders.

The area wore gilt and rouge and bright lights, but its glitter was diamond-hard. Beneath its paint and tinsel the fandango district was brutal, merciless.

Cahill walked the length of this street, keeping his hat pulled well down over his eyes, avoiding the brightest pools of light. But he did not find what he sought.

He finally halted a passerby. "Friend," he said, "could you direct me to a place called Pierre's?"

The man eyed Cahill's rough garb dubiously. "Turn west at the corner you just passed, Mister," he said. "You'll find Pierre's up the block. But that place is high-toned. Drinks a dollar a throw, an' they don't sell anything less'n five dollar chips. They cater to the carriage trade."

"I just mislaid my carriage," Cahill said. "Thanks for the information."

He returned to the street the man had indicated, and left the blare of the fandango houses behind. Here were old brownstone mansions, relics of the days of the fur trade, whose owners had moved into newer and more fashionable districts.

Velvet curtains now veiled the windows of the majority of these houses, and discreet signs hung over the doors. Liveried doormen stood before the entrances, and the curbs of the cobblestoned street were lined with carriages.

This area looked down its nose at the noisy, hurdy-gurdy

10

district. It wore a pose of refinement and elegance. The throb of string orchestras came from the interiors and some of the carriages were unloading modishly dressed women and men in evening clothes. There were other men who, like Cahill, were not so finely clad. But they were blood brothers, with the same purpose and the same rapacity. The true key to admission here was not the way a man dressed, but the amount of money he carried.

Now Cahill heard the faint refrain of a woman singing. It came from a gambling house ahead, and his step quickened. The voice became clearer as he drew nearer. It held a husky, sensuous quality, and it carried power and volume.

Cahill knew that voice. It led him to Pierre's, and he pulled up beneath shade trees across the street from the place, watching and listening. Pierre's, in contrast to its neighbors, was housed in a big, new structure, designed for its purpose. White-painted, done in the plantation style, an open, tile-paved gallery fronted on the sidewalk, with round pillars rising through an overhead balcony.

The voice of the singer floated through the open French doors that led to the gallery. The draperies at the windows were pulled, giving a full view of the crowded gambling salon. Oil paintings hung on the walls, and chandeliers glittered. Waiters in livery moved over thick carpets, serving the players.

A stage occupied the rear of the main room, and a strikingly handsome young woman stood there singing to the accompaniment of a string orchestra.

This was Sherry Dean, the Irish thrush. She wore a low-bodiced, jade-green evening gown that did little to conceal the alluring lines of her bosom and figure. Her hair was a deep, rich, coppery red, and she had big, hazel-green eyes.

She was singing something in French. It was a love song, gay and impudent. It needed no interpretation, for Sherry Dean's mocking eyes and the inflection of her voice was sufficient.

Cahill rammed his big fists in the pockets of his coat, and began to glower. He was more than slightly shocked at the way Sherry Dean's body undulated as she sang. He was recalling the fiery, hot-tempered, impetuous girl he had known in another day—a girl who had never mentioned her own past.

11

Like everything else, Sherry Dean had changed. Her rich voice had gained in depth and held a haunting quality of a knowledge of life. She handled herself with the ease of an entertainer who had mastered all the arts of stagecraft—and all the deceptions.

But her perfection, like the place in which she was employed, was mechanical, brittle. She was not bothered by the whir of roulette wheels and the riffle of cards that continued, uninterrupted, during her number, for even the magic of her voice could not penetrate the gambling fever at some of the tables where the stakes were high.

But it was a song that was not to be finished. Her voice hesitated, then resumed, then hesitated again. Britt became aware of a stir on the gambling floor.

Men were rising, thrusting back their chairs. Voices rose in deadly fury. Sherry Dean's song broke off. The orchestra quit.

Then came a gunshot. Women started screaming and a stampede for safety began in the place. Powder smoke drove across the room, fogging the chandeliers.

CHAPTER 2

A man came backing through one of the French doors onto the open gallery directly opposite Britt's position. Middle-aged and bearded, wearing a new, poorly fitted store suit, he had the earmarks of a prospector or a trader just in from the plains. He had a gun in his hand, but seemed unsure of his ability to use it. He was shouting something in a voice thin with fright and desperation.

He kept backing in panicky retreat across the sidewalk, and then into the street, where mud puddles from past rainfall still lay in the rutted cobblestones.

Another man glided swiftly through the same door in pursuit and darted instantly to the protection of one of the pillars.

A shock of recognition hit Britt. This man was tall and handsome, with thin, crisp blond hair, and a small blond mustache. He wore a finely tailored, dark broadcloth frock coat and a black string tie against a starched white-linen shirt, and fawn-colored breeches. He also had a six-shooter in his hand, and there was nothing uncertain in his movements or purpose.

"Wait, Jarrett—wait!" the bearded man squealed frantically. "I didn't mean . . ."

But it was evident the blond man didn't mean to wait. And Britt realized that he was in the line of fire. He moved instinctively to shield himself back of the trunk of the elm tree against which he had been leaning.

As he did so he saw that there was another bystander in the same predicament. A young woman. He had vaguely noticed her a moment before the shooting had started. She had come from a walkway at the far end of the gambling house and had started to cross the street diagonally toward the sidewalk where Britt stood, picking her way past the puddles. She held in her arms an oblong cardboard box of the type in which women's gowns were carried.

She had halted in alarm a dozen feet from where Britt stood, and was between him and the antagonists, and even more directly in the path of any bullets that might come.

Then the bearded, frightened man fired at the vague gleam of white shirtfront and blond hair that showed at the gallery pillar. His bullet was wild, breaking glass in one of the windows to the right of his target.

Both guns were in action. Britt leaped toward the young woman who still stood frozen. He heard a bullet snap past both her body and his own.

He had an impression of the bearded man breaking at the waist as though he had been kicked in the stomach, and of the spurt of blood.

Britt's arms clamped around the girl, and he set his heels, hurling himself backwards, bringing her with him. A bullet slapped into the elm tree behind him as he fell. That one had missed both him and the girl only because he had yanked her off her feet in time.

His body cushioned her as they hit the cobblestones, and then he rolled over and over, taking her with him out of the line of fire.

Another bullet glanced from the paving with a wild scream, showering them with fragments of stone and hot lead.

Then the shooting ended. Britt rose to one knee above the girl. His gun had come into his hand, a thumb lifting the hammer. A cold, taut rage was in him.

The bearded man was down. He lay twenty feet away, a wet, bubbling sound coming from him. Then this agonized breathing faded away. Britt knew the man was dead.

The blond man, still partly shielded by the pillar, reloaded his gun with swift, steady hands. Then he raised the six-shooter again, took deliberate aim, and fired a final shot into the bullet-torn body of his opponent who already lay dead in the street.

"The damned fool should have known better," the blond man said. Then he slid his gun out of sight inside the breast of his frock coat, and walked back into the gambling salon, straightening his starched cuffs.

Britt got a second and better look at him as he passed through the lighted door, and now there was no doubt in his mind. A name rose into his mind. "Mead Jarrett," he murmured.

He realized now that he was still holding the girl protectively down. She was staring up at him, breathless and dazed.

Britt had noticed during that hectic moment when he had snatched her to the ground that she was a very firm and interesting armful. She was trying to push down her skirt to cover slim legs that were equally interesting. Her chip bonnet was jammed down over one eye.

Britt hastily holstered his gun, arose and lifted her to her feet. In the uncertain light her eyes were a big, excited, lively dark-brown. She had a small straight nose and good cheekbones that were just prominent enough to form soft shadows in her cheeks. Her mouth was warm, generous, with a soft underlip. She was very healthily attractive.

She straightened her bonnet on hair that was a dark chestnut shade, and blew a few loose strands aside. She said breathlessly, "Wow!"

The cardboard box that she had been carrying lay near by. It had burst open and was spilling a dress into the street. Britt hastily gathered it up, and began trying to stuff the garment back into the container.

The girl gave a little cry, and snatched it from his hand. "You'll ruin it!" she exclaimed. "It's only basted."

"Basted?" Britt marveled. "Sounds like you were cooking it—like a turkey."

"It's—it's only tacked together," she gasped. "I

14

mean . . ." She was still trying to catch her breath. She quit trying to explain and looked around wildly. She said again, "Wow!"

Her fashionable tan jacket and skirt were stained with dust and mud. Britt gazed in consternation. "I managed to ruin your dress at least," he stammered.

"Mud is better than blood," she said.

She looked at the dead man who lay in the street. "That —that was almost murder, wasn't it?" she breathed.

"He didn't have much of a chance," Britt admitted.

She now began scanning Britt. Her glance dropped to his holstered gun. She started to say something, but seemed to think better of it.

Men were pouring from all the gambling houses along the way. A circle was forming around the body of the bearded man. Britt suddenly realized his own danger. Some of the new arrivals were already moving toward him and the girl, and he knew that in the next instant he would be answering questions. He could not chance that.

He turned away suddenly. "Sorry I had to be so rough and sudden, Miss," he said.

"Wait!" the girl exclaimed. "Wait! I owe you thanks for . . ."

"The pleasure was all mine," Britt said over his shoulder, as he quickened his pace.

He reached the darkness of the tree-shaded sidewalk, and kept going until the excitement was safely behind him. He pulled up nearly a block away, and stood in darkness, looking back. He had not been followed.

Evidently the law had arrived at the scene of the shooting, for he saw the shine of brass buttons in the crowd that had formed before Pierre's gambling house.

Presently he saw the girl in the tan dress emerge from the throng. Carrying the cardboard box, she walked to a modest top-buggy which had a placid roan mare in the shafts. She unsnapped the halter strap from a hitch rail, climbed into the buggy, wheeled it around in the street, and drove away.

Britt noted approvingly that she was heading away from the fandango district. She hadn't struck him as belonging in these surroundings. Then a twinge of regret came. He was never a man to ignore feminine charm. In other circumstances he would have made sure that the girl with the lively brown eyes and soft, warm mouth would see more of him. But that was impossible.

Still, the regret lingered. Along with that was a puzzling inexplicable feeling that he had seen her somewhere in the past. But that also was impossible, he was certain. He would not be likely to forget a girl like that.

The aftermath of the killing was fading. The slain man's body was carried away in a black-curtained police wagon. The crowd drifted back into the gambling houses. The orchestras struck up again, and the modulated voices of the croupiers sounded: "Your wagers, Gentlemen. The ball is about to roll."

The street became deserted. The blond Mead Jarrett, accompanied by a big man wearing a gold badge, drove away in a police carriage. Both were smoking cigars and chatting amiably. It was evident that Mead Jarrett's trip to the police station was a mere formality.

Britt retraced his way to his former position opposite Pierre's. He ran a hand along the trunk of the elm, finding the fresh bullet scar in the bark. He remembered the firm vibrancy of the girl he had held in his arms during that moment of peril.

The red velvet stage curtain had been dropped in Pierre's, and only the orchestra was playing. Britt crossed the street and walked down an open passageway along the north end of the building. This carried him past the kitchen, and to a rear alley drive, where there was an area in which more carriages waited.

Here he found a door in the rear of the building, bearing a sign which said:

PERFORMERS' ENTRANCE

This door was open and unattended. Britt stepped in. A small stair to his right lifted to the stage level. There was action in that area, and he saw the stockinged legs of half a dozen dancing girls who seemed to be awaiting their curtain call. Another short stair led below stage. He descended, and found himself in a small, bare corridor, with dressing rooms on either hand.

Britt took a chance. He tapped on the nearest door, and called softly, "Sherry!"

16

"Yes!" He had guessed wrong. Sherry Dean's answer came from a closed door adjoining the room he had tested.

He tapped on that door. "Who is it?" Sherry Dean's rich voice demanded impatiently.

"Sherry!" Britt said again, softly.

CHAPTER 3

There was a moment of utter silence, then a swift rustle of garments. The door opened. Sherry Dean stared at him with unbelieving eyes. She was clutching a hastily donned dressing gown about her, and beneath that she seemed to be clad in little more than a chemise.

"By all the saints in heaven!" she breathed.

Then she caught his arm, pulled him into the room. After a wild glance up and down the corridor she swiftly closed the door, locked it, and stood with her back against it.

"Britt Cahill!" she whispered. "Sure, and it is your ghost that has come back to haunt me."

Then she kissed him. Tears suddenly stained the make-up on her long lashes.

"Ever kiss a ghost with whiskers before?" Britt murmured, his voice gruff with emotion.

Sherry Dean kissed him again. "Britt, you reckless divil," she choked. "Now that you mention the matter it does seem unlikely you would return wearing a stubble rough enough to bruise a girl's lips. 'Tis my opinion they would have been singed off by Satan's flames if you were a ghost."

"That's better," Britt said. "That's more like the flannel-mouthed mick I used to know."

Sherry laughed hysterically, but the tears still streamed. " 'Tis only in moments of great stress that I permit the shanty Irish in me to come to the surface. You have always had an upsetting effect on me, Britt Cahill."

She was fighting for control, without success. " 'Twas only last Sunday I burned another candle for the repose of your soul. And now you come back from the grave with your blarney and your grin to melt my heart, and you expect me to take it calmly. Britt, Britt, I had given you up for dead long months ago."

"Maybe the candles you burned helped," Britt said.

Sherry pulled back, studying him, her eyes gradually turning grave. She was taller than average and gorgeously formed. Three years had tempered the fiery impetuosity of her nature, given her poise and sophistication. But they had also deepened the loneliness that had been in her the first day Britt had met her.

The dressing room gave evidence that she had accumulated worldly possessions as well as a worldly outlook on life. The robe she clutched about her was embroidered in gold. Fine leather trunks stood by, partly filled with garments, along with hatboxes and other smaller luggage. Apparently Sherry's wardrobe was being packed in preparation for departure.

Jewel boxes glittered on the dressing table, and gowns still hung on the rack.

Sherry watched Britt's glance travel over these. "I have done well," she said, a little stir of temper and challenge in her tone.

"That depends on how you look at it," Britt said.

"I bought all this with my own money," she said ominously.

"And earned it by showing your shape in every gambling house from New Orleans to Minneapolis and from Denver to California," Britt snapped.

"Sure an' they come to hear Sherry Dean sing," she retorted, and the brogue was rich and angry. Color was rising in her beautiful throat.

"That dress you were wearing when you sang that ouioui number wasn't calculated to keep their minds on your voice," Britt said.

Sherry Dean's temper was at white heat. "I will wear what I please and live as I please. If it was to quarrel with me that you came back from the dead, Britt Cahill, I will thank you to leave by the way you came."

Britt angrily turned toward the door. With a gasp Sherry pushed him back. "You know I did not mean that," she moaned contritely. "Oh, Britt, why, oh why is it that we cannot be together for even a moment without striking sparks? We are two of a kind, Britt. Born under a dark star of violence and strife and bitterness."

She clung to him, the touch of her warm hair soft against his face. Sherry Dean—a woman of ice and fire, a woman who mocked men with her beauty and her unattainability

18

and her mystery, who sang like an angel and played poker with a devil's skill that had ruined more than one man in high-stake games—wept in his arms like a child.

Britt's arms tightened around her, soothing her. "Why don't you quit, Sherry?" he murmured. "Why do you keep driving yourself, searching, always searching for something you never can find? Who was the man who broke your heart?"

Sherry thrust him away. When she lifted her face again, her eyes were veiled, shutting him out from her inner thoughts, as she always shut out all men.

It was as though he had tried to open some forbidden door. When she spoke again, all the brogue had vanished, and she was once more a poised, cool-eyed enigma.

"Never ask me that, Britt," she said. "Now, enough of Sherry Dean and her whims and storms. Why are you in St. Louis, of all places? You may be discovered and arrested, and tried on that charge of—of . . ."

"Murder is the charge," Britt said. "We'll call a spade a spade, Sherry, as we always have with each other."

"Very well, so a spade is a spade. I know you are not guilty. You are a man who might kill in the stress of a battle, Britt, but never by stealth or for profit. But what I think would not save you. You are risking the gallows to come to St. Louis again. And you came for a purpose. I can see it in your face. And you have made a long and dangerous journey. I can see that too. There is a grimness in you. And something else I never saw there before. Something hard and relentless—something that is not good."

"I want to find a young woman," Britt said. "And at once."

Sherry stiffened a little. "Leila Ormsby?" she asked, carefully keeping any expression out of her voice.

A sudden quick pulse stirred in Britt. "Leila?" he exclaimed eagerly. "She is still here—here in St. Louis?"

"Yes. And why not? Her father is still senior member of the steamboat firm of Ormsby & Jarrett, even though they are not flying as high as they were a year or two ago."

"Jarrett?" Britt repeated. "I saw that name on a steamboat at the levee. *The Dakota Queen.* That wouldn't be Mead Jarrett, who killed a man a few minutes ago in that shooting scrape upstairs?"

Sherry nodded, watching Britt with curious intensity.

19

"You have been far away, not to know that," she marveled. " 'Tis one and the same. Mead Jarrett became Walker Ormsby's partner after your own steamboat was lost and after the fire ruined Zack Richards' company."

Britt was frowning. "But Jarrett was a pilot on Zack Richards' boats," he said.

"Circumstances," Sherry said dryly, "make strange bedfellows, and strange shipmates."

"No matter," Britt said. "I'm still wasting valuable time. Sherry, what started that gunfight? Who was the man Jarrett killed in that duel?"

"A cotton trader named Jones, who has been playing poker each night the past week, and losing big money. The dispute started when he realized, at last, that Mead Jarrett was cheating. Mead is an expert at second and bottom carding, and sleeving and palming. Jones was foolish enough to attempt to draw first. That made it self-defense for Jarrett. It was not Mead Jarrett's first experience at gunplay."

"I gathered that from the way he handled the matter," Britt commented. "He evidently has been under the gun before."

"He killed a man under similar circumstances at St. Joe last fall," Sherry nodded. "And another aboard one of his own steamboats earlier that year. Mead has also killed or wounded three or four other men here in St. Louis in matters of honor that had to do with the affections of various women. He is, in fact, this town's most famous bloodletter. He is also a very romantic figure, and women are said to swoon when he favors them with his smile."

Britt was satisfied that his narrow escape from flying bullets had been a coincidence, and had no connection with the attempts that had been made on his life aboard the *Aurora.*

"The girl I want to get in touch with is named Ann Richards," he said.

Sherry's eyes snapped wide, then narrowed. "Ann Richards?" she exclaimed. "And why would you want to see her, Britt?"

"To save her life, perhaps."

"You tell me you came to St. Louis at the risk of your own neck to save the life of the daughter of the man who ruined you?"

"Yes." Britt's voice was harsh.

20

"I wish I could believe that," Sherry said reluctantly.

"You know Ann Richards?" Britt demanded.

Sherry moved again to the door, placing herself against it as though to block any attempt at departure. "Britt," she said imploringly, "surely you would not take vengeance on a girl because of a grudge you hold against her parent?"

"Would you believe me if I told you I have ten pounds of gold in a belt around my waist that I intend to deliver to Ann Richards?" Britt asked.

"For what purpose?"

Britt's answer was blunt. "I hope it will be bait that will lead me to her father."

"It is vengeance, then, that you seek?" Sherry breathed.

"Retribution is the proper word."

"You—you've found trace of Zack Richards then? I have feared that you had been hunting him these three long years, Britt."

"You were right," Britt said. "I found him at last. Then I lost sight of him again. I spent two years trying to cut his trail. Then, by chance, I learned he was in the Montana gold camps. I went to Montana. I learned that he and a partner named Pete McLeod had showed up in Bannack once or twice to buy fresh supplies, and then had gone back into the mountains. They had not been seen for a couple of months.

"I spent all winter haunting the camps—Bannack, Florence, Elk City, half a dozen others, without finding trace of them. I began to lose hope. Then, a little more than six weeks ago I saw Zack Richards with my own eyes."

"Six weeks?" Sherry exclaimed.

Britt nodded. "He and his partner. They came into Bannack after dark. They were bearded and ragged, but they bought supplies with raw gold. That was a foolish thing to do in that camp. The Montana gold fields are infested with thieves and murderers and Bannack is the headquarters of an organized gang. I discovered presently that I wasn't the only one who was following Zack Richards and Pete McLeod that night. Three other men were keeping tab on them. I couldn't get a look at them, but there wasn't any doubt that they had picked up the scent of gold.

"But Zack Richards and McLeod gave all of us the slip. They dropped completely out of sight that same night. It was nearly a week before I picked up trace of them again.

A packer told me he had seen Zack Richards and Pete McLeod heading north through the hills. They were leading a pack string of six horses that seemed to be heavily loaded. The direction they were traveling could mean only one thing. They were on their way to Fort Benton, the head of navigation on the Missouri River. The fact they were staying off the stage trails, and that they had a big pack string, meant that they had gold and plenty of it, and didn't mean to be held up."

Britt paused, and both he and Sherry listened to a rush of feet in the corridor as the chorus number ended and the girls came hurrying downstairs to the dressing rooms.

"Go on," Sherry said tensely.

"I took the first stage to Benton," Britt said. "I was too late. I learned that Zack Richards and his partner had sold their pack string and bought a mackinaw boat, and had started down the Missouri four days before I arrived. The breakup had started only a few days before they shoved off, and heavy ice was still running, but they were taking the chance in a small boat rather than trust half a ton of gold to a steamboat purser's safe."

"Half a ton of gold?" Sherry gasped.

"Figure it up for yourself," Britt shrugged. "The packer said they had six loaded pack horses. Allow one horse for their camp outfit. The other five must have been carrying close to two hundred pounds each. And what else could it have been but gold? Zack Richards and McLeod had a fortune with them in that mackinaw. Somewhere around a quarter of a million dollars' worth of dust, is my guess."

" 'Tis enough to tempt the divil himself," Sherry breathed in awe.

"The steamboat *Aurora* was making ready to head downriver for St. Louis," Britt said. "So I took passage. It was a rough trip. For one thing, big trouble is boiling on the plains. The Sioux Nation is painting for war, and so are the Northern Cheyenne, and the Crows and the Snakes. The *Aurora* was shot up a couple of times from the brush by small war parties, but it wasn't much more than sniping.

"The *Aurora* reached Fort Buford at the Yellowstone Fork. But I learned that the mackinaw was still ahead of us. It had passed downriver two days before. Then the *Aurora* was forced to lay up at Buford for a week to repair a boiler, and it looked like Richards had out-lucked me again.

"Then Pete McLeod showed up at Fort Buford. He was alone, and on foot, and trail-worn. He bought two new rifles at the trading post and plenty of ammunition and grub, and two pack horses. He wouldn't answer questions when people tried to draw him out.

"An Army mail boat was leaving for St. Louis. I never let McLeod out of my sight, and I saw him mail a letter. The purchase of guns and grub indicated that he and Zack Richards had hit trouble somewhere down the river, and that Richards had stayed with the boat to guard the gold while McLeod made the trip back to Buford for the supplies.

"McLeod slipped away from Fort Buford before daybreak the morning after he pulled in. I gave him an hour's start, for I didn't want him to know he was being trailed. That was a mistake. It hadn't occurred to me there might be other men aboard the *Aurora* who had been trying to overtake that mackinaw also—the same ones who had picked up the smell of gold that night in Bannack. They must have talked to that same packer who spotted Richards heading for Fort Benton, and they must have been aboard the *Aurora* with me on the trip down to Fort Buford.

"And they were trailing McLeod, too, that morning, and were ahead of me. The first intimation I had of it was when I heard a man scream in agony somewhere in the brush. It was just growing daylight, and we were only a few miles out of Fort Buford.

"I worked through the brush. Three men with floursack masks over their heads had caught McLeod. They were torturing him with a heated ramrod, trying to make him talk, trying to force him to tell what had happened to that boatload of gold."

Sherry shuddered. "Ah, the poor, poor man," she breathed.

"I broke up the torture party," Britt said. "I shot over their heads. They didn't quit easy. They came up smoking. It was a pretty hot fight for a minute, but I had the advantage of surprise, and was shooting from back of a deadfall. I downed one of them, and the other two took to the brush. They didn't come back. But one of them put a bullet in Pete McLeod as a parting gesture.

"McLeod was dying when I reached him. The bullet had got him in a lung. He lasted long enough to talk a little. He carried a belt poke filled with gold, and asked me to see that half of it was delivered to a girl named Ann Richards, who lived in St. Louis. The other half was to be mine for delivering the dust. He said the girl's father was in trouble, but that she would know what to do, for he had mailed a letter from Fort Buford, written by her father, which explained the situation. Pete McLeod let slip that there was also a map with the letter. Then he died."

Britt was silent a moment. He looked at the small onyx clock on the dressing table, and began talking faster. "I buried McLeod and the outlaw I had downed, as best I could. The outlaw was a stranger to me, and there was nothing on him to identify him. I went back to Fort Buford, and left for St. Louis that same afternoon aboard the *Aurora.*

"But the two who had escaped after the torture party were aboard, too. They twice tried to kill me during the trip to St. Louis."

"To kill you?" Sherry gasped.

"They evidently want to be first to get their hands on that letter and map," Britt explained. "They must have seen McLeod mail that letter at Fort Buford, and have guessed its contents. McLeod was an uneducated man, so they'll conclude it was written by Zack Richards to some relative. It won't take them long to learn that Richards has a daughter here in St. Louis. Then they'll be calling on her, trying to get that letter and map away from her. And they'll stop at nothing. They know I was trailing Richards, and figure I'm after the gold, too. This isn't piker money, remember. They are shooting for the biggest stake of their lives."

CHAPTER 4

That had been a long speech for Britt. The recital of that scene of torture had stirred a horror in him. His lips were dry, his voice growing husky. And he was conscious of the speeding minutes.

"That's why I want to get in touch with Ann Richards

at once," he said. "I don't know who these two killers are, for I didn't get much of a look at them during that fight in the brush and, as I told you, they were masked. But they'll torture her, kill her, like they did McLeod. I've got to find her. It's for her own sake, as well as my own. She should have received that letter by this time. The army mail boat was days ahead of the *Aurora*."

"She has the letter," Sherry said.

Britt stared. "How do you know that?"

"She mentioned to me that her father and his partner were in some kind of difficulty far up the Missouri River, and that their arrival in St. Louis would be delayed. She had received letters from her father previously from the Montana camps in which he said he would be home early this spring. She is worried and at a loss as to what to do, but of course she does not know that McLeod is now dead, nor that murderers are out to find her father and the gold."

Britt said incredulously, "You seem to be well acquainted with Ann Richards."

" 'Twas none other than she who stood in this very room within the hour," Sherry said. " 'Tis a miracle your paths did not cross."

"Ann Richards—here? You mean she works at Pierre's?"

Sherry smiled a little. "Not exactly, though Pierre has tempted her with offers to wear tights and dance in his show. She has the shape for it, and the looks. And, if you ask me, she has been sorely put to it to refuse, for it is not the nature of a lovely young woman to shrink from displaying her charms. But her modesty has prevailed thus far, and she prefers to continue earning her living as a seamstress."

"Seamstress?"

Sherry nodded. "An improper word, spoken from my jealous heart," she said. "I admire Ann Richards and respect her, but it is my privilege to be resentful of her beauty. She is a challenge to me, and one difficult to overcome. I sometimes suffer by comparison when we are together. She is really not a seamstress. She owns and manages a dressmaking shop that caters only to the most expensive trade. I have been fortunate enough to prevail upon her to design my wardrobe for my forthcoming tour of the Montana camps. She has a talent for . . ."

"Wait a minute. You say Ann Richards was here just before I showed up?"

"She came with a gown she is making for me, for a fitting," Sherry nodded.

"A girl in a tan skirt and jacket—a girl with pretty dark-brown eyes?" Britt questioned.

"You *did* see her, then?"

Britt laughed helplessly. "I had her right in my arms. She and I were in the line of fire when that gunfight started. I spilled her in the dust. So that was Ann Richards?"

"Do you mean to say you never before laid eyes on her?" Sherry asked, surprised.

"Never. She was educated in the East and was away during the greater part of the time I was steamboating out of St. Louis after I came back from the war. There was no occasion for a meeting. Zack Richards and my father were never friendly. Our families had never mingled socially."

"You have already rescued her from danger in this gunfight," Sherry said slowly. "And now you intend to protect her again, but for an entirely different reason. This one is for your own purposes, Britt Cahill."

"Where can I find her?" Britt demanded. "We're wasting time."

Sherry eyed him, torn by doubt. "You will not harm her?" she whispered imploringly.

Britt only gazed at her stonily.

Sherry said contritely, "I withdraw the question. I should know you better. Ann's shop is on Willow Street, only a few minutes by carriage. Or you could wait here. She promised to finish my dress and return it well before midnight."

"If I waited it might be too late," Britt said. "She might have callers. How do I find this street, and her shop?"

"I'll call a carriage and go with you, if you will turn your back until I slip into a dress."

"I prefer to see Ann Richards alone."

Sherry sighed. "I'll call my carriage. You can trust Amos, the driver."

She left the dressing room, and was gone several minutes. When she returned she waited until sure the corridor was clear, then motioned Britt to follow. She led the way quickly from the building to the driveway at the rear.

A carriage with a Negro driver stood waiting. "Amos knows your destination," Sherry whispered.

Then she placed both hands on Britt's unshaven cheeks, peered insistently into his face in the darkness. "Do not let

26

vengeance drive you too far, Britt darlin'," she whispered entreatingly. "Ann Richards is a fine, honest girl. I know the injustice that has been done you by her father, and I can see the bitterness in you. But there still is charity and kindness in you, the same kindness that caused you to save my life that night your steamboat sank. You nearly lost your own life, but you would not give up. That is why I am still alive."

"I make no promises," Britt said, his voice gruff.

Sherry kissed him, her lips soft, forgiving. "I feel that I need none," she said. "Otherwise I would not send you to Ann Richards. Oh, Britt, will I ever see you again? Will you vanish into the blue again and never return?"

"No man would stay away from you long of his own free will, Sherry."

She smiled wanly. "You have a way with women, Britt. You are the only man I . . ."

She broke off. Then she said, "I am going aboard the steamboat *Dakota Queen* after my final show here in an hour or two, and will sail at midnight for Fort Benton. But I will cancel passage, if I can be of help to you here."

"Benton? To Fort Benton?"

"I understand they are striking it rich in the Montana mines," Sherry said levelly. "That means opportunity and profit for Sherry Dean. I play poker as well as sing, you know."

"We may be fellow passengers," Britt said.

"Provided you can force or trick Ann Richards into showing you that letter that may lead you to her father."

"Zack Richards owes me the price of the *Northern Star,* with three years' interest," Britt said, and his voice was metallic. "And he owes me other things. He tried to have me hung, and he lied to bring that about. I will drag the truth out of him if I ever get my hands on his throat."

"I will pray for you, Britt," Sherry choked. "And I will pray for Ann Richards also. The sin was not hers."

Britt turned to enter the carriage. Then he paused. "Is Leila—is she all right?" he asked abruptly. The words were almost wrenched from him.

Sherry's face was suddenly rigid in the dimness. "Leila is not yet married," she said. "That was the question you wanted to ask, wasn't it, Britt?"

She added, "But Mead Jarrett is her constant companion. It is understood that they will wed someday."

"Jarrett?" Britt was aware of a futile emptiness. Then he added, heavily, "I see."

He climbed into the carriage. "Leila is probably aboard the *Dakota Queen* tonight," Sherry said. "I understand she also is sailing for Fort Benton on this trip with her father and Mead Jarrett."

She paused, then said, her voice wire-taut, "I should not have told you that, but you would have risked danger to find her anyway. It would have been a blessing if you had forgotten something after three years, Britt."

"A man can remember happiness as well as pain," Britt said harshly.

"And can smash his heart against a stone wall," Sherry said drearily. "Let the past be buried, Britt. Forget this vengeance on Zack Richards. And forget Leila Ormsby. All this will only lead you to despair—and to your death."

Britt did not answer. Amos spoke to the team, and the carriage swung into motion. Britt looked back. Sherry still stood there, outlined against the shaft of light from the stage door—a straight and ripe and vitally alluring figure.

CHAPTER 5

A clash of emotion ran in a cross-rip through Britt's mind and through his veins as the team's hoofs rattled on the cobblestones through dark streets.

He had not intended to ask about Leila Ormsby, but her name had been drawn from him. Now, the knowledge of her nearness was a torrent through him. All the desire she had aroused in the past was back again—all the longing.

His mind raced back to the time when he had returned home from service in the Civil War to find that Leila Ormsby had grown up into amazing, enchanting, alluring beauty. He had known her almost from childhood, for she was the daughter of Walker Ormsby who operated a small steamboat on the river, but the leggy, freckled person he had remembered had been transformed by those four years into a tall, poised, cool-voiced, stunning creature. With pale, golden hair and light violet eyes that held little bright golden flecks, she was slim-ankled, slim-waisted—gorgeous, and always immaculately turned out.

Britt had courted this grown-up Leila Ormsby madly, passionately, vying with half a dozen suitors, and one night he had won from her a promise that she would marry him.

He had walked on rainbows then. He had reason, for his father had taken him into partnership in his steamboat company, and Britt had earned his license as a pilot both on the Mississippi and Missouri Rivers. He was entitled to carry the white silk gloves that were the badge of membership in that aristocracy of the rivers.

It was during this time also that his path began to cross that of Sherry Dean. The red-haired Irish beauty, with the eyes of a martyr, and the bitter cynicism of a lost soul in her voice, already was becoming a legend on the river and on the frontier.

Sherry had been a gypsy, always restlessly on the move. At times Britt would encounter her in the gay quarter in New Orleans, where she would be singing in one or the other of the more elaborate gambling houses or cafés. Then, weirdly, he would step off a packet in a rough lumber camp in the upper river, and there would be Sherry Dean singing again in some gaudy music hall. At other times he would hear that she was in California, or Santa Fe, or Colorado.

Men fell in love with Sherry, and she mocked them. Nobody knew her past. It was obvious she had opera training. She played poker with the same artistry with which she sang, and matched her skill against professional card sharps and high-play gamblers. Britt had watched her win five thousand dollars on the turn of a card, and he had seen her lose that amount also, and never had she shown either elation or dismay.

Britt had disapproved of her the first instant he had laid eyes on her. He frowned on the daring costumes she wore on the stage, and the way she flouted men's attentions. Her way of life was at odds with everything he had been taught to associate with womanly virtue.

She had seen this in him, and it had been a challenge to her. She had gone out of her way to lure him under her spell, so that she could mock him, as she had done with every other man who had fallen in love with her.

Instead she had found in Britt a temper and an independence and a restless spirit that matched her own. And

Britt had come to realize that she was truly virtuous, though it was common belief that Sherry Dean sold her body as well as her voice.

An understanding and a mutual respect had grown up between them, and it had strengthened as their wandering trails brought them together time and again.

Sherry Dean was a creature of lightning moods. Once, in a moment of vast depression, she had blurted out that she would never let any man break her heart again.

Then she had regretted even that break in her armor, and had flown into a dish-throwing temper when Britt had tried to draw out the secret of her past.

And it was during that time also that Britt's father built the steamboat, *Northern Star*. Mike Cahill, who had started on the river as a keelboat man, had been the owner of three fine packets in the New Orleans trade before the War Between the States broke out. But, like other steamboat men, his fortunes had suffered during the years of strife.

Mike Cahill had invested every cent he possessed in this new boat, which was to be the supreme achievement of his life.

He had designed the *Star,* and had overseen every plank and beam of oak and ironheart and hickory that had gone into her hull, every strip of bird's-eye maple that beautified her cabins and lounges.

She had been the creation of his dreams, and of his ambition to restore the name of Cahill to its old prestige on the river. Hulled to float on a whisper of shoal water, so flexible to the touch of the wheel that she seemed to have a mind of her own, Mike Cahill had a special purpose in mind for the *Northern Star,* when he had first laid her keel on the building ways, a purpose that he kept secret until the day of the launching.

The secret was that the *Star* was not meant for the Mississippi trade, but for the mighty, mysterious, elemental river that flowed down from the heart of the western wilderness— the Missouri River.

Mike Cahill had seen the opportunity that beckoned on the Missouri, whose dangers only the most daring steamboat men dared to challenge.

Gold was being dug in the Rocky Mountains of Montana—the Shining Mountains, the old trappers called them. It was a region almost as unknown as the surface of the moon to the rest of the world, but where there was gold, there men would go, and gamblers and outlaws and women to prey on them.

Hundreds of miles by the meandering path the untamed Missouri followed across the northern plains, the greater part of the journey passed through the heart of the hunting grounds of the mighty Sioux Nation. Here buffalo and elk and antelope held forth, and the fang of the wolf was the law of the land. Here tribesmen counted coup on a grizzly bear with the same pride they boasted of taking a human scalp.

The Missouri River run was only for a steamboat man with steel in his fibers, and a gambler's blood in his veins. Any boat that risked the Fort Benton trip was sure of freight and passengers to suffocating capacity and at the highest rates. A man could grow rich in a single season on the Missouri, and he could also go down to ruin and wreckage and bankruptcy in a day.

Mike Cahill knew the Missouri from his keelboating days, and he saw to it that Britt, after his return from service in the war, earned his papers as a pilot on that wild river. For the *Northern Star* was registered under the proud, new firm name of Cahill & Son.

And then Mike Cahill had died of a heart stroke the day the *Star* was launched. He was laid to rest beside his wife, who had passed away when Britt was a child. Britt had found himself standing in boots that rivermen said were far too big for a man of twenty-five, no matter how cocksure he might be.

Britt's biggest competitor had been the Great Western Navigation Company, of which Zack Richards was sole owner. Zack Richards, like Britt's father, was a pioneer in steamboating, his experience dating back to the great days of the fur trade and the keelboats.

Zack Richards stood six feet three, with a ram for a chin, and a mane of shaggy, matted, graying hair, and stern dark eyes that held the arrogance of a man who brooked no opposition. He owned four steamboats that he had managed to hang onto during the war. Like himself his boats were big and tough and powerful.

Britt's father and Zack Richards had clashed often in their early days on the river, and there had always been rivalry between them. When Britt found himself sole owner of the new *Northern Star* he found also that he had inherited that personal antagonism.

The *Northern Star* was faster, more graceful than any of Zack Richards' four boats. She had demonstrated her superiority on her maiden trip the first spring, beating Richards' best packet, the *White Buffalo,* by nearly sixty hours in a race to Fort Benton that had started on even terms from St. Louis.

Zack Richards had been personally in command of his boat on that trip, and had done the greater part of the piloting. Mead Jarrett, who had worked for Richards at that time, and was rated as a top helmsman on the Missouri, had served as second pilot on that voyage.

In addition, the new, graceful *Star,* with her maple wood and gleaming brass fittings, and her cream and white paint and her clean, speedy lines, had attracted a record passenger list and her freight deck had been loaded to the beams.

That defeat must have been bitter in Zack Richards' throat. He had shoved off from Fort Benton for the return trip to St. Louis three days ahead of the *Northern Star.* But Britt's craft, carrying another capacity load of freight and passengers, again had proved not only her speed but the superiority of her design as well. For, with midsummer at hand, the Missouri was shoaling rapidly. Where Richards was forced to capstan and pole his *White Buffalo* off many mudbanks, the *Northern Star* escaped from the plains into the lower Missouri without delay.

The two boats pulled into Independence on even terms before starting the last leg of the trip to St. Louis.

Sherry Dean had come aboard Britt's steamboat at Independence. She had walked up the gangplank that day three years ago as casually as she had always stepped in and out of his life. On that occasion she had just arrived by stage from the Colorado gold camps.

She was bound for St. Louis, and Britt had turned his own captain's cabin over to her. Sherry had been asleep in her berth at midnight when the *Northern Star,* her first round trip to Fort Benton never to be completed, was rammed and sunk.

Britt had been at the wheel when the *Star* met her doom. The *Star* and Zack Richards' steamboat had pulled out of Independence before sundown on even terms, but the *Star* had forged some two miles ahead during the evening.

They were not racing, for it had already been demonstrated, even to the satisfaction of Zack Richards, that it was useless to attempt to match the *Star's* speed.

An hour before midnight, fog began to drift over the river. It was tricky piloting, with the boat running in clear starlight at times, then plunging unexpectedly into blinding mist that limited vision to only a few yards beyond the prow.

Britt had rung down to quarter speed. He had a deckhand stationed at the roof bell, and its solemn tolling carried for miles in the night silence. He had been tense and uneasy at the wheel, facing the open night and the drifting fog while he spelled out the channel.

The river was widening and deepening here, preparing for its junction with the Mississippi, and the fog became more patchy, offering open stretches where Britt could orient his position before pushing into the next ghostly wall of mist.

He had listened for the bell of the *White Buffalo*, but, not hearing it, concluded that Zack Richards' boat must have also slowed and was still far astern.

He had been wrong. The *Star* pushed from a wall of fog into another stretch of open starlight, and from directly abeam, the *White Buffalo*, running at full ahead, came bearing down on a collision course.

Britt had hit the whistle treadle and the *Star's* mighty voice lifted a bellow of warning. He had rung for full ahead, and the *Star's* wheel had lifted her with a surge.

Britt expected Richards' boat to shut down and reverse and swing to port, a maneuver that would have averted the disaster.

Instead, the *White Buffalo* veered to starboard and drove her prow into the *Star* amidships.

Zack Richards' boat was damaged but stayed afloat. But the *Northern Star,* her bottom ripped out, capsized and sank in deep water in mid-channel in less than a minute.

More than a hundred human beings went down with the *Star* to their deaths in that midnight collision. Survivors managed to make it to shore or were picked up by the *White Buffalo.*

Britt saved Sherry Dean's life. She was trapped in her cabin by a jammed door, and was going down with the boat, when Britt freed the door, swam into the water-filled cabin in which she was drowning and carried her clear.

The current swept them far downstream. They were

picked up by a Negro catfisherman who came out from his shanty in a flatboat. Sherry apparently was dead, but Britt worked over her in the starlight aboard the flatboat, forcing water from her lungs, and using artificial respiration, refusing to concede that there was no hope.

The fisherman had prayed, his eyes rolling whitely in awe, for Britt was an ashen-faced, tooth-bared madman—a demon from the river with death and vengeance in his face. Britt had cursed Zack Richards, and had fought to save a woman's life. And Sherry Dean, her soaked silk nightgown clinging to her body, had been like an Aphrodite, plucked from the river.

As he worked Britt had vowed that he would kill Zack Richards on sight. For there had been no question in his mind but that the *White Buffalo* had deliberately rammed and sunk his packet.

The fisherman had taken them to his shack on shore and the man and his wife had chanted prayers and fingered voodoo charms while Britt fanned the tiny spark of life in Sherry and fought for hours to nurse it into strength. At last, by sheer will, he brought Sherry back from the brink of death.

It was nightfall, two days later, when Britt finally stepped ashore on the levee at St. Louis. He had left Sherry with the fisherman's wife, for she was still too weak to be moved.

Zack Richards' damaged steamboat had brought the other survivors of the *Northern Star* to St. Louis the previous day. Both Britt and Sherry had been listed among the drowned. When Britt, gaunt, grim, unshaven and still in the wrinkled captain's uniform that he had been wearing on the night of the disaster, appeared on the levee, rivermen gazed uneasily at the gray, granite set of his face.

Britt seemed to have aged a dozen years in those two days. "Where's Zack Richards?" he had asked, his voice as thin as the cutting edge of a knife.

Nobody would answer that, for they had seen the vengeance in Britt's eyes. Someone had the presence of mind to summon Leila Ormsby in the belief that she could reason with Britt. Leila came, accompanied by her father.

"Zack Richards says it was an accident," Walker Ormsby had told Britt.

"Who was piloting the *White Buffalo*?" Britt had asked, his voice implacable.

Walker Ormsby had hesitated. "Richards, I believe," he had finally murmured reluctantly.

Leila had pleaded with Britt. "Don't do anything rash," she had said. "You can never prove it wasn't an accident."

"No use trying to buck Zack Richards, my boy," her father had nodded. "He's rich, powerful. He has gotten away with this sort of thing before. He won't stand for any real competition on the Missouri River."

Britt, the vengeance still in his eyes, had left them, and the darkness of St. Louis had swallowed him. He began searching the town, seeking Zack Richards. But Richards was not to be found.

It was midnight when the great fire broke out. It started in the office of Zack Richards' Great Western Navigation Company on the riverfront. A high wind was blowing and the flames raced through Richards' warehouses, and to the docks and boatyards where all four of his steamboats, including the damaged *White Buffalo,* were moored.

The wind carried the fire onward down the levee to other boats and warehouses. More than forty steamboats were destroyed and half of the riverfront was leveled before the flames were brought under control twenty-four hours later.

Worse yet, the body of one of Zack Richards' night watchmen was found in the ashes of his office after the flames had burned out. The watchman, who was an old-time riverman named Jim Finn, had not been killed by the fire. There was a bullet in his heart. He had been shot in the back before the fire charred his body.

And the safe in the debris of Zack Richards' office was found open and looted. There had been nearly a hundred thousand dollars in the safe and the greater part of it was gold that prospectors had placed in Richards' care for safekeeping.

That made it murder and robbery. Even before that discovery, an ugly, volcanic fury was rising in the city. Men had been too busy battling the fire to have time for vengeance, but Britt Cahill's name had been in the mind of every riverman. The catfisherman who had brought Britt to St. Louis had told of Britt's maddened threat to kill Zack Richards on sight.

Now they believed Britt had started that fire to get even with Zack Richards for the sinking of the *Northern Star,* and that the fire was only to cover the murder and robbery he had committed.

Then new word spread that Zack Richards himself had seen Britt fleeing from the vicinity of the boatyards just as the fire broke out. The volcano burst. A mob formed.

Britt had actually been in the vicinity of Zack Richards' establishment earlier in the night, hunting the owner. But, seeing the office dark, he had searched elsewhere.

He had helped fight the fire. He had worked in heat and smoke for twenty-four hours. Like a thousand other men he was black with grime, his face blistered, his hair and eyebrows singed short.

He had been aware from the first of the mob spirit that was growing against him. Grimy as he was, he was unrecognized by the men working with him in the turmoil of the fire, but he had heard what they were saying.

Now the word that Zack Richards had seen him fleeing from the burning boatyards raced along the fire-gutted riverfront where the smoke still rose from a mile of destroyed steamboats.

Britt listened to screaming shouts: "Hang the dirty killer. Lynch the son . . . Find him an' string him up."

Britt knew he would likely be torn limb from limb if he was identified. There was only one person he felt he could turn to in his need, and that was the girl he loved. He made his way to Walker Ormsby's home, where he found Leila and her father.

Walker Ormsby confirmed the story that Zack Richards had gone to the police with a sworn accusation that he had sighted Britt at the scene of the start of the fire.

"You say you are innocent," Walker Ormsby had said dubiously, "but I'm afraid that won't help you if the mob gets its hands on you. Out of consideration for my daughter I'll do my best to help you escape from St. Louis."

Walker Ormsby had made it plain he believed Britt was guilty. But he spirited Britt out of the city in a wagon that same night and furnished him with a flatboat in which Britt, never traveling in daylight, put hundreds of miles between him and St. Louis.

After that Britt drifted to the plains. Under the name of Bill Clay he worked at various jobs, swamping for freighters, wrangling horses for stage companies, even doing a turn as section hand on the new Union Pacific Railroad out of Council Bluffs.

He had avoided direct contact with rivermen for fear of recognition, but whenever he deemed it reasonably safe, he lingered around bars at riverfront ports.

For he had only one purpose in life. That was to learn Zack Richards' whereabouts. After a year, his patience was rewarded. One night, standing well in the background, he heard steamboat men in a saloon at Omaha reminisce about the big St. Louis fire and that had reminded one of them that Zack Richards had gone to the Montana gold camps in the hope of making a strike to recoup his lost fortune.

Britt had started for the Montana diggings the next day. Now he was back in St. Louis, with the gallows awaiting him if he made a wrong move.

The deep voice of Amos, the carriage driver, aroused him from these long and bitter memories.

"Dis am Missy Richards' dress shop, Suh," Amos was saying. "Looks like she's workin' late. They's a light in de sewin' room."

CHAPTER 6

The carriage had halted before a white-painted cottage on a side street just off the substantial business district. This area, once entirely residential, was now being given over to trade and small shops.

The cottage had a green-trimmed veranda, and on the little strip of flower-bordered lawn stood a small sign:

ANN RICHARDS
GOWNS AND MILLINERY

Britt alighted, handed Amos a coin. "I won't need you any longer, Amos," he said. "Go back to Pierre's."

As the carriage pulled away he inspected Ann Richards' establishment. The front rooms of the house had been converted into a sales shop, with millinery and dresses on display on wax models and in showcases. A single china lamp burned there.

A door led to a rear room. It was partly open, and lights

glowed there. He saw the shadows of movement and heard the whir of a sewing machine.

The street, tree-shaded, was otherwise dark and deserted, with only a few night lights burning in some of the other small shops.

Britt moved up the short brick walk to the porch of the cottage and mounted the steps on tiptoe. He deliberately silhouetted himself against the lighted glass in the upper half of the door, then stepped swiftly aside, crouching down, peering at the dark street.

Nothing happened. If the two who had tried to kill him aboard the *Aurora* were hunting Ann Richards, they evidently had not located her as yet.

Britt found the key of the doorbell and twisted it. The brassy vibration echoed in the shop. The hum of the sewing machine stopped. Then a young woman came hurrying from the workroom.

She was the same person Britt had snatched from the path of bullets in front of Pierre's gambling house. Ann Richards had changed to a simple white shirtwaist and a pleated dark skirt. She was slim-waisted, but above and below that were the firm and interesting curves Britt had been conscious of during that moment he had held her in his arms.

Her chestnut hair was piled high on her head and caught with a shell comb at the back. She had a pencil thrust in her hair and carried a scissors in her hand. She wore the abstracted, impatient look of a woman who had been interrupted at some important domestic problem. Britt saw now that it was the way she carried herself that gave the straight lines of the skirt a certain swing of style.

She opened the door, which had not been locked, and looked at Britt inquiringly. "Yes?" she asked.

Britt now understood that puzzling sensation of having met in the past. She was Zack Richards' daughter, and while he could not put his finger on any exact physical resemblance to her father there was an unmistakable family heritage—her frank, direct way of speaking, above all, that told of her paternity.

His mind was eased on one point. She had never laid eyes on him before tonight. There was no recognition in her gaze. And she was of the same blood and bone as Zack Richards. That steeled him in his purpose.

"You should keep your door bolted, Miss Richards," he

said. "Most anybody could walk in on you at this hour of night."

Ann Richards gasped, "What . . . ?"

She peered closer. And now she did recognize him, but only in connection with the shooting at Pierre's. "Why, you're the man who . . ." she began, surprised.

"Yeah," Britt said. He was aware that he stood outlined again against the light. Abruptly he stepped through the door, almost pushing her aside, and closed the door behind him, then moved away from it so that his back was to the wall.

"Stand over here where we can't be seen so easily from the street," he said.

Ann Richards backed away from him quickly. He saw apprehension in her, but her annoyance was greater.

"I'm sure I am very appreciative of your help on that occasion," she said stiffly. "But I believe I tried to thank you at the time. Is there anything else I can do for you?"

She continued moving away from him until she stood in the door of the workshop. Britt could see the corner of a flat-topped, walnut desk just inside that door, and he guessed that there was a gun in a drawer there.

"We could talk more freely in the back room," he said.

"We'll talk here," Ann Richards answered indignantly.

"I went to a lot of trouble finding you," Britt said.

"I'm sure you did," she said acidly. "But it would have been better if you had waited until tomorrow. If it is money you need, come back then and I will see what I can do for you."

"Money?" Britt said, forcing a hurt into his tone. "Do you think I'd ask for money for a thing like that?"

"You had better go," she said scathingly. "You may have saved my life tonight, but seem to want to presume on my obligation to you. Are you drunk?"

Britt had learned what he wanted to know. Ann Richards wasn't easily panicked. She had courage and likely she would use a gun if it became necessary. That meant he must be very careful in each step he took if he was to succeed in hoodwinking her.

"Seems like you got the wrong slant on me, Miss," he said complainingly, using the diction of an uneducated man. "I didn't know who you was when we had that little excitement

39

at Pierre's. If you'd mentioned yore name I'd have been saved time an' trouble."

"What are you talking about?" Ann Richards demanded.

"I've got a jag of gold in a belt around my middle thet belongs to you," Britt said.

"Gold? What do you mean?"

"A man named Pete McLeod gave it to me just before he died, askin' thet I deliver it to you."

"Pete McLeod! Dead?" Her face was suddenly ashen.

Britt nodded. "I'm sure sorry to have to fetch the news, Miss. Was he related to you? I don't know whether I ought to tell you how he died. It wasn't purty. But it was mysterious. I didn't savvy what it was all 'bout."

Ann Richards left the doorway and now moved nearer. "Go on!" she exclaimed, her voice shaking. "What happened? Where—how did Mr. McLeod die?"

"It was a long ways from here," Britt said. "More'n two weeks ago. I was on a huntin' trip in the brush along the Missouri River a little ways below Fort Buford that mornin'. Buford is near the mouth o' the Yellowstone an' . . ."

"I know where it is," she interrupted fiercely. "I know the Missouri. My father used to steamboat to Fort Benton."

"I heard some strange sounds in the brush," Britt said. "Sounds that made me weak in the stomach. A man was screamin' in pain. I figgered it was the Sioux that had got some poor devil, an' I worked through the thickets. But it wasn't Injuns. It was white men. They was torturin' this fellow who turned out to be Pete McLeod."

"Torture?" she gasped.

"Burnin' him with a hot ramrod," Britt said. "They seemed to be tryin' to make him tell somethin'."

Ann Richards breathed faintly, "Oh, no!"

"There was three men doin' the torturin'," Britt said. "They wore masks. I hollered for 'em to put up their hands, but they started shootin'. I killed one an' the others skedaddled into the brush. One of 'em put a bullet in Pete McLeod."

"Who—who were they?"

"It was just breakin' daylight, an' I couldn't see well enough to make 'em out," Britt said. "But the one I killed had the earmarks of bein' one of a bunch of outlaws that are ridin' high in the Montana gold camps."

"And Mr. McLeod . . . ?"

Britt shook his head. "He was dyin' when I got to his side.

He had this belt of gold an' asked me to see that it was delivered to Miss Ann Richards of St. Louis. He also asked me to send word to Ann Richards as to what had happened to him, an' to warn her thet these men was tryin' to find her father an' thet her father would need help. He mentioned he had just mailed a letter to you at Buford, an' thet you'd understand what it was all about."

Ann Richards stood horrified. But she wasn't giving in to tears or hysteria. There was a sturdy courage in her.

"It happened I was headin' fer St. Louis aboard the steamboat *Aurora*," Britt said. "So I fetched the gold with me. The *Aurora* docked early this evenin'.'"

Britt loosened the belt of dust and offered it to her. Ann Richards took it with stiff hands, but its weight was unexpected, and she let it slip to the floor with a thud. She did not even look down at it.

"McLeod sorta promised me half of that dust if'n I fetched it to you," Britt said hesitantly, for he wanted to convince Ann Richards that he had become involved in this affair only by chance.

"Of course," she said, her voice high-pitched. "And you shall have it. I'm very grateful."

"I sorta figgered I earned it," Britt explained awkwardly. "Bein' as how they tried to kill me on the *Aurora*."

"Tried to kill you? Who?"

"The same ones thet tortured McLeod, I reckon. I was shot at twice durin' the trip down from Buford. Somebody aboard the *Aurora* didn't want me to reach St. Louis alive. An' thet means they didn't want me to deliver McLeod's message to you."

Ann Richards stared. Then the significance of that hit her. Her eyes widened. "That means they're—they're . . ." she whispered.

Britt nodded. "They're here in St. Louis this minute."

Now she understood why Britt was avoiding showing himself at the windows.

"Come!" she said and led him into the rear room.

This was the workshop, cluttered with sewing machines and dress forms and cutting tables and shelves that held bolts of cloth and boxes of lace and ribbon and cases of thread. The curtains were drawn. There was another door at the rear, which was closed.

"You will be safer here," she said.

41

"An' you also," Britt commented.

"You mean . . . ?"

"It seems they was tryin' to torture McLeod into tellin' where they could find your father. An' I gather that this letter that McLeod mailed tells where your Dad kin be found. If these two are in St. Louis thet means they're followin' thet letter. An' if they tortured a man they likely wouldn't stop at torturin' a girl to find out what they wanted. They already tried to murder me, figgerin' I knew too much about 'em."

"Did McLeod say anything more about my father?" she asked.

"Nothin', except thet your Dad seemed to be in some kind of a fix. Didn't the letter explain it, or haven't you received it?"

"Yes." Ann Richards was off guard. Her eyes turned involuntarily toward the big desk. "It was this way. My father and Mr. McLeod had started from Fort Benton for St. Louis in a mackinaw boat. But they were attacked by Indians. They managed to stand off the Indians and escape downriver after dark. But Dad had been badly wounded. And to add to their troubles, the boat was caught in an ice jam and smashed. It sank in—in a certain place. Mr. McLeod got Dad ashore and took care of him. A bullet had broken Dad's leg. He was unable to travel, but after a few days he had strengthened enough so that it was safe for McLeod to leave him and make the trip to Fort Buford to buy supplies. They had lost nearly all their food when the boat sank. And now . . ."

"I see," Britt said. "Your father's up there in the Sioux country with a busted leg an' nobody to help him."

Ann Richards moved nervously about the room. "I've got to go there, of course," she said. "But—but . . ." Her voice almost broke. "Dad is probably dead by this time."

"If he was well enough for McLeod to leave him, even if it was only to be for a few days, likely he could make out," Britt said reassuringly. "He had a gun, no doubt. There's plenty of game in that country."

"And Indians, too," she almost sobbed.

"Zack Richards likely will know how to keep out of the way of the Sioux," Britt said.

"You—you know my father?"

"Everybody's heard of Zack Richards," Britt explained hastily. "McLeod told me you were his daughter."

Ann Richards tried to organize her thoughts. "I haven't much time," she said nervously. "I happen to know that a steamboat, the *Dakota Queen,* is leaving at midnight for Fort Benton. I must arrange for accommodations."

"You mean you aim to go up there an' search for your father personally?" Britt protested.

"Of course," she said, almost indignantly.

"That's a wild country and mighty dangerous."

"But I know just where to find Dad. . . ." she began.

She broke off. For the first time she really seemed to see Britt. Up to now he had been just a rough-clad stranger who had brought news that had shocked all thought of caution or suspicion out of her mind. She moved so that she had a view of him from head to foot, and she studied him with a sudden, searching intentness. Ann Richards, Britt surmised, was beginning to fear she might have told too much.

He endured that inspection without change of expression. He had already learned what he wanted to know. He was remembering the way she had glanced at the desk when she had mentioned receiving the letter. Beyond a doubt the letter and the map that Zack Richards had sent her, marking the exact location of the sunken mackinaw boat, was in that desk.

It was all clear enough. Zack Richards, knowing the dangers he and McLeod faced, had drawn that map for his daughter, so that she would have a chance of finding the gold in case he and his partner did not survive.

Now that information which would lead Britt to the gold and—far more important—to Zack Richards himself, was within arm's reach in this room.

If Ann Richards found anything during her scrutiny of Britt to alarm her she kept it hidden. But she plainly drew into herself, shielding from him all her emotions.

"It seems I'm doubly in your debt," she said. "You saved me there at Pierre's tonight, and now this. And I don't even know your name."

"Clay," Britt said. "Bill Clay."

She repeated the name thoughtfully. "Bill Clay. In other words a common man. Humble and honest."

"Maybe not so humble," Britt said.

Again her eyes traveled over him, marking his size and the way he stood. She noted the small scars on his strong jaws and on his knuckles, for Britt had seen his share of rough-and-tumble fighting on steamboats and other places.

"No," she remarked musingly, "you are not a humble man." Her glance rested on his holster briefly, and Britt guessed that she was remembering that moment when he had crouched above her in front of Pierre's with the six-shooter poised and ready to strike back at any danger.

"You say you were hunting in the brush when you found these men torturing Mr. McLeod?" she asked. "What were you hunting?"

"Elk," Britt said. "Maybe a fat doe if I come across one that looked like it would make good meat. I'd had a steady run of smoked sidemeat and salt pork aboard the *Aurora*. I was hungry for a nice thin elksteak or some venison."

"Wasn't it dangerous to leave the Fort alone? From what we hear in St. Louis the Indians are growing ugly up on the plains. They say a big war is starting."

"I wasn't likely to bump into Injuns thet close to the Fort," Britt pointed out.

She debated that a moment in her mind. "You mentioned that the man you killed had the earmarks of being a member of an outlaw gang in the Montana camps. Then you had been to Montana also?"

"I prospected there for a year," Britt said easily. "But my luck don't seem to run to gold. I gave up an' was on my way out."

"Were you acquainted with my father in Montana?"

"No," Britt said.

"And so you went to the trouble of looking me up and delivering Pete McLeod's message," she observed, "and bringing the gold to me, a total stranger."

Britt knew she was quizzing him in an attempt to make certain he was what he pretended to be. She was now carefully keeping her gaze away from the desk.

Britt feigned resentment. "Don't forget thet I was promised half o' that bunch of dust," he reminded her in an injured tone.

He had struck the right note. Ann Richards' expression changed a little. He sensed that some of her half-formed suspicions had faded.

But she had another question. "It was very fortunate for

44

me that you happened to be there at Pierre's tonight," she remarked. "A lucky coincidence."

"I have a friend at Pierre's," Britt said. "I was goin' there to ask this friend to help me find you."

Ann Richards drew a kerchief from her sleeve. Before Britt realized her intention she moved near and rubbed it across his mouth. She held the kerchief to the lamplight.

"And you kissed this friend also, it seems," she said lightly. "There is grease paint and rouge on your lips, Mr. Clay. And a smudge of powder on your shoulder. Is she a dancing girl at Pierre's?"

Britt scrubbed his mouth with the back of his hand. He was genuinely embarrassed and flushing. "Reminds me of bein' caught in the jam jar when I was a kid," he said.

Ann Richards chuckled. It was a pleasant sound, musical, frank. "I won't pry," she said, "though I'm mad with curiosity. I know all the girls there. I make most of the costumes for the entertainers. That was why I was there tonight."

She became serious again. "I'm forgetting your reward, Mr. Clay."

She went into the showroom and returned with the belt of gold and placed it in his hand. "It's all yours," she said.

"But . . . !" Britt began.

"It's all too little for risking your life for a person you never before laid eyes on," she said. "I want to thank you again for . . ."

Britt had abruptly lifted a warning hand, silencing her. She had heard it also, the faint creak of a board on the porch.

They stood taut. The board protested slightly again, the sound faint and slow as though someone was shifting his weight with painstaking care.

Then silence. But someone was out there!

CHAPTER 7

Britt pointed to the sewing machine. "Act like you're working," he murmured, his voice a mere sigh. "Move around. Make it seem like you're alone. If it's who I think it is they don't know I'm here, or they wouldn't make their play now."

Ann Richards hesitated, panic rising in her. Then Britt saw the way her small chin firmed. Resolutely, she seated herself at the machine, spun the wheel and began working the treadle. The hum of the machine arose.

Britt grudgingly gave her credit for possessing real nerve. She was obviously frightened. The color had gone, even from her slim hands. But her fingers were steady.

Britt made sure his own shadow did not fall across the path of the door. He edged an inch at a time to the desk, and got behind it. The desk was big enough to conceal him if he crouched down.

A long minute passed, and another. Five minutes. Then Britt knew the front door was opening, for a draft of air came through the room, stirring scraps of cloth on the cutting table. Ann Richards gave him a quick glance of dismay. She was blaming herself for forgetting to lock that outer door. But Britt had forgotten that detail also.

She kept the treadle going. Britt had his six-shooter in his hand. He crouched, his ears straining against the hum of the sewing machine.

He sensed, rather than heard, the outer door being closed with the utmost caution.

There was more than one intruder in the showroom. He sensed that also.

Then came fast movement. A man with a blue bandanna handkerchief tied over the lower part of his face charged into the workshop.

Britt huddled out of sight below the desk. Ann Richards was still partly in his line of vision. She turned from the machine and started to rise with a scream.

Her outcry was cut off as the masked man grabbed her, clapping a hand across her mouth, pulling her against him in a grip that squeezed the air from her lungs.

Britt did not move. There were at least two of them and he had to locate all his opponents before making his play.

Ann Richards struggled frantically, still trying to cry out. "Take it easy, sister, an' you won't be hurt," her captor panted.

A second figure now came partly into Britt's line of vision and gave his partner help. Britt chanced a glimpse. The one who had first seized Ann Richards was thick-shouldered, with a leathery, wrinkled neck and greasy hair curling over his coat collar.

The second arrival was smaller, with bulging, watery eyes showing above his neckerchief mask. Both wore grimy brush coats and corduroy breeches and boots that were typical of the mining camps. Britt remembered having seen the pop-eyed man aboard the *Aurora*. He knew these two were the ones who had tried to kill him during the steamboat journey.

The pop-eyed one seized up a length of cloth from a table and began forming a gag. "It'd be easier if you talked, girlie," he said viciously. "All we want is a certain letter that was sent to you from Fort Buford. Give it to us an' you won't be hurt."

Ann Richards fought with tigerish fury, twisting and kicking at her captors with a violence that sent her skirt swirling above very shapely knees.

"Slap her one!" the heavy man panted. "Damn her, she's bustin' my shins."

The pop-eyed one lifted a grimy hand to deliver a blow at Ann Richards' face.

Britt came from cover then, swinging his gun. The seven-inch muzzle of the .45 chopped the raised arm aside. The force of the blow whirled the pop-eyed man aside and he fell on his haunches.

The bigger man gave a grunt of consternation. With his left arm still clamped around the girl, he swung her before him as a shield. A short-muzzled gun appeared in his right hand. But the girl was still kicking and fighting. That upset his aim. The bullet missed Britt and thudded into the wall.

Britt did not dare fire for fear of hitting the girl. He dived ahead bodily, ramming his shoulder into both of them, hurling them backwards against the cutting table. The table went over, and all three of them fell with it.

Britt rolled, realizing that the pop-eyed one was his danger now. This opponent was crouching in the door to the showroom, trying to steady his gun on Britt.

Britt fired twice as he rolled. He was in a tangle, with the legs of Ann Richards and the heavy man flailing and kicking around him, and he was shooting more to shake the man's aim than in the hope of scoring a hit. He was successful, for the pop-eyed man's gun exploded, but it was a wild shot.

Ann Richards was trying to scream now, but the sound was only a choked gasp. The heavy man surged to his feet, lifting her with him, and tried to bring his gun to bear on

Britt again. The girl swung around, bracing her slippers against shelves that held bolts of cloth. She thrust with all her might.

That sent her captor staggering, and both of them fell sprawling. The shelves toppled also, spilling their contents into the room that was becoming a shambles.

Then Britt got his chance at the heavy man. Ann Richards' violence had partly torn away the clamping arm that gripped her waist. Now she fought entirely free.

For a moment there was an opportunity for a clear shot. Britt's gun roared and the bullet tore into the man's chest and through his heart—killing him.

Britt whirled even as this opponent was falling. He was expecting to take a bullet from the pop-eyed one.

But the doorway was vacant. The man apparently had seen enough and had fled. Britt heard the pound of desperately running feet on the porch, and then on the sidewalk.

Britt lurched to his feet, tripped over some object, leaped to his feet again and raced through the showroom and to the porch. The faint sound of the man's flight came echoing from the shadows of the tree-lined street. Britt ran a hundred feet along the sidewalk, his gun poised.

Then he pulled up, realizing it was futile. He could no longer hear the footsteps. His quarry must have escaped between buildings. Britt had no idea in which direction the man had gone.

A police whistle was shrilling somewhere, the sound rising and falling. The gunfire had been heard by a patrolman.

Britt became aware of his own situation. Above all, he could not risk falling into the hands of the authorities. He raced back to the dress shop. Ann Richards had got to her feet and was staring dazedly at the sprawled dead man who lay among the wreckage of her shop. The room was fogged with powder smoke. Her waist was ripped from her shoulders, hanging by a fragment, and her camisole was torn. She was still gasping for breath.

Britt thrust his six-shooter into her hand. "Take this," he panted. "The police are coming. Tell them you shot this man in self-defense with this gun. Tell them you were here alone and that they evidently intended to rob or harm you."

She took the gun mechanically. "But . . . !"

"I had some trouble with the police the last time I was in St. Louis," Britt said hurriedly. "Do you understand?"

She nodded numbly, still too confused to think clearly or to protest.

Britt glanced toward the desk, thinking regretfully of the letter from Zack Richards. It was so near and yet so far. Given a minute or two to search the desk he was sure he would find it. But there was no time.

He raced to the rear door and unbolted it. It opened on a small garden, and beyond that was a white-painted picket fence.

"Hide that letter in a safe place," he said tersely to the girl. "One of those men is still alive. Remember that. And he may try again."

"Wait!" she protested. "I'll . . ."

But Britt shook his head. He ran through the garden, leaped the picket fence and found himself in the darkness of an unpaved alley. He heard more police whistles and running feet in the street. Heavy shoes pounded the sidewalk and mounted the porch of Ann Richards' shop.

Britt made his way down the alley to the next street, peered until sure his path was clear, crossed and continued onward through back areas.

He headed for the levee, more by instinct than plan. Soon the smell of the river and the tang of cotton and tar and steamboat smoke strengthened and he felt safer and on more familiar ground.

He came out on the levee presently and paused in the black shadow of a warehouse while he considered his next step.

There was no activity around the moored steamboats near by but a distance south of him the stacks and pilothouse of the *Dakota Queen* showed in the glow of the torches as she continued to load for departure at midnight for the Missouri River and Fort Benton.

Britt gazed at the *Dakota Queen* for a long time. His pulse began to hammer queerly, and a tightening came into his throat. He knew now the instinctive urge that had drawn him to this place. Leila Ormsby! Sherry Dean had told him that Leila was sailing for Fort Benton, and that she probably would be found already aboard her father's boat.

He acknowledged now that Leila had never been entirely

out of his mind since he had stepped ashore from the *Aurora*. It had been a slow, smothered fire within him. And now, the realization that Leila was probably so near fanned the fire to eager life.

He moved toward the *Dakota Queen,* drawn by this longing and desire. He knew he was risking everything—his chance of finding Zack Richards, his very life, by approaching that activity, for there were rivermen there with eyes to see and minds that might remember him.

But he could not resist. He paused again just beyond the reach of the torchlights, in the shelter of stacks of baled buffalo hides that gave forth their wild, rank odor.

The *Dakota Queen* was moored abeam of the levee with deckhands and roustabouts handling cargo over forward and aft stageplanks. All the staterooms on the cabin decks were lighted and, with departure time little more than two hours away, passengers were beginning to go aboard.

Two fuel scows were moored close against the *Queen,* one directly at her prow, with its wide, blunt prow against the levee. The second barge lay directly against the steamboat on the outstream starboard beam. The scows were empty and deserted now, waiting a towboat to pull them away. The *Dakota Queen* was fueled and taking on the last cargo for the departure.

Then a door opened in the texas. Lamplight streamed out.

A young woman stepped from this door, which was to one of the staterooms in the texas that were usually reserved for the captain and pilot and special guests.

It was Leila Ormsby. She was a slim, alluring figure in the door, with the light touching the pale golden hue of her hair. She moved out on the deck, away from the lamplight, walked aft on some errand, then returned and entered the stateroom. Britt could see her shadow moving about. She evidently was unpacking her luggage for the long trip up the Missouri.

Reason implored Britt to give up this attempt to see her. But she was a magnet he could not resist. Now that he had seen her at long range he wanted to be close to her, to hear her voice, to ask her if she really believed that he was a murderer.

CHAPTER 8

Britt awaited his chance, then boarded the near fuel barge, wriggling over its coaming, and dropping into the darkness of its flat bottom amid an underfooting of dust and splinters and wood bark.

Moving to the stern he made sure he was unobserved, then vaulted to the coaming and leaped the six-foot space to the lip of the out-river barge, and dropped into its bottom.

This brought him to the starboard side of the *Dakota Queen*. The decks towered above him and seemed deserted, for the main activity was forward and on the levee side of the boat.

The bull rails—the removable barriers that enclosed the cargo deck—were up. These offered footholds and Britt climbed easily to the passenger deck. He slid over the rail to the promenade. A line of stateroom doors opened off this walkway. Some of them seemed to be already occupied. A man came from one, smoking a stogie. He said, "Howdy," and passed on by in the uncertain light without really looking at Britt.

Britt moved aft to the steep, narrow companionway that mounted to the boat's roof. Ascending he stepped out on the open sweep of the hurricane deck. The pilothouse and stacks loomed bulkily above the squattier shape of the texas.

Britt moved forward and reached the shadow of the texas. The door of Leila's stateroom still stood open, with the lamplight laying a yellow slash across the deck and off into the darkness where it finally lost itself in the Mississippi's surface with a flash of sullen, watery reflection.

There were three other staterooms in the texas. Except for Leila's quarters, light glowed only in the forward cabin. This was customarily occupied by the captain, and Britt guessed that Walker Ormsby was in this room.

He moved to the open door of Leila's cabin. She stood before a trunk, lifting a gown, and arranging it on a hanger. She had been gracefully beautiful when he had last laid eyes on her—when he had last kissed her. Now she was a poised young woman. She was still slim-throated, slender-waisted, but three years had filled and firmed her curves. The dark-hued dress she wore complimented the delicate tint of her pale skin and pale hair.

She stood admiring the gown, and also critically appraising it. She turned to a mirror, holding the garment against her while she studied the effect, and she was frowning a little, seeking some flaw.

Britt remembered that it had always been this way with Leila. She had always been meticulous of her appearance and critical of her garb and coiffure to the point of torture. She abhorred disorder, both in her own appearance and in others.

Britt spoke. "Leila."

She turned. She stood motionless for a long time, staring. She did nothing until she had made certain that this was really Britt Cahill and that he was really alive. She did not scream or cry out. Britt had known she would not. Leila had always abhorred scenes. She was always in firm command of her emotions.

She said, "Britt Cahill!" But, if she was outwardly in control of herself, there was no calmness in her voice. Strained, utter disbelief was evident in the way she spoke his name. And he wondered if he had not detected dismay and a trace of anger also.

She then swiftly made sure the gown was hung carefully and neatly before doing anything more. Then she faced him. But she made no move to come to him. She said again, "Britt! Surely, it can't be you?"

Britt stepped into the cabin, moved away from the open door. Leila watched this and understood. She hesitated, debating it in her mind, then crossed the small space with her straight, poised stride, and closed the door.

"I saw you on deck as I stood on the levee, Leila," Britt said. "I had to speak to you."

He saw the way her glance traveled over him, marking his rough garb. Her gaze was disapproving of his appearance.

Britt moved closer to her and she did not retreat from him. She merely stood watching him. Her eyes held little yellowish-golden highlights that he remembered were a sign of excitement within her. Those violet eyes, strikingly light in hue and set at almost an Oriental angle above her cheekbones, were her only weakness. They often betrayed the trend of her thoughts.

Britt took her in his arms almost roughly and kissed her. She did not resist. But her lips were cool, unresponsive.

"You need a shave, Britt," she said.

Britt let his hands fall away from her. "I've had several shaves lately," he said. "Close ones, Leila."

"The police?" Her question was direct, almost brutal. "Are they hunting you? Do they know you're in St. Louis? You have been in a gunfight, Britt. I smell powder smoke on you."

"Not the police," Britt said. "At least not yet."

"You shouldn't be here," Leila remarked, keeping her voice to the same murmur he was using. "You know that. Why did you risk coming to St. Louis?"

"Perhaps to see you, Leila."

She appraised him for a long moment. "Possibly. You always were a reckless, impulsive man, Britt. But there must be other reasons."

"Do you believe I killed that watchman that night and robbed Zack Richards' safe and started that fire?" Britt asked abruptly.

Leila walked to her trunk, thoughtfully brought out another garment, a silk nightgown, which she straightened, brushing out the folds with slender fingers. She hung the garment in the clothes cubby and finally looked at him directly.

"I don't know," she said.

A cold and empty and helpless terror formed in Britt. "I've found trace of Zack Richards," he said tiredly. "I've been hunting him ever since that night."

"Zack Richards? Why would you be hunting him?"

"To make him pay for the *Northern Star*," Britt said. "To force him to admit that he lied when he said he saw me running away from his warehouses just as the fire started."

"But . . ." Leila began, a startled look momentarily on her face. Then she halted and asked, "You mean Zack Richards lied about that?"

Britt was silent for a time. He turned suddenly toward the door to leave. "You were right, Leila," he said heavily. "I shouldn't have come here. It wasn't fair to you. Three years is too long."

She barred his path. "Wait! You don't understand, Britt. Everyone said you were guilty."

"And you believed them?"

"I don't know what to believe. I thought you were dead, Britt. Three years and never a word from you. What was I to think in all that time?"

Her nearness 'was overpowering. "You're not to blame, Leila," Britt said, his voice suddenly blurred. "I know that."

He was thinking of what Sherry Dean had told him about Leila and Mead Jarrett.

Leila clung to his arm. "Do you really believe you could compel Zack Richards to clear you of this murder charge?" she asked.

Britt said nothing, looking at her. Leila pulled back a little, staring at him, almost frightened. She was seeing the' grimness in the set of his mouth and eyes. She was seeing that the pliability by which she had once been able to sway him to her whims with a smile or a tear were gone. Time had tempered him until he was now steel, unyielding and unbreakable.

"Britt," she whispered, a little shudder in her voice, "you have the look of a wolf in your eyes. You scare me."

"I've run with wolves," Britt said.

There was a silence. "Where is Zack Richards?" she finally asked. "Is—is he here—in St. Louis?"

"He's up in the Sioux country, either dead or alive, alone with a sunken mackinaw boat that had a cargo of gold."

"Gold?"

Britt tersely told her the story, making it as brief as possible. He omitted any mention of Sherry Dean, saying he had learned of Ann Richards' whereabouts merely by chance.

A wild excitement grew in Leila's violet eyes as she listened. When he finished, she drew a deep breath.

"How much gold did you say?" she asked tensely.

"Five packloads," Britt said. "It could be worth up to a quarter of a million."

"A quarter of a million dollars!" Leila's voice held almost a sensuous quality. A sudden pulse was driving color up from her throat. The ivory whiteness of her skin was enhanced by a new, rich warmth. The little golden flecks deepened in her eyes. Britt had never seen her lovelier.

"You—you would be rich!" she breathed.

"I only want enough to build me another steamboat," Britt shrugged.

"You mean you would only take part of the gold?" Britt

wondered if he only imagined that he heard swift anger and impatient scorn in her tone.

"That and Zack Richards' confession that he lied about what he saw that night of the fire," he said.

He frowned. "I never understood why he lied. What good did it do to pin that crime on me? He was ruined by it, I understand. He even had to sell his home to make good on the gold that miners had left in his safekeeping. And the fire wiped out his steamboat business. He was left bankrupt. What was his purpose in trying to have me hung for something I didn't do?"

"He hated you, Britt," Leila said quickly. "You humiliated him in that race to Fort Benton, remember. That's the answer."

"That seems to be it," Britt said. "But I never would have picked Zack Richards as the kind to hit below the belt—until the night he sank the *Northern Star*. I had him judged as proud and tough, but I figured he would fight fair."

"What are you going to do next, Britt?"

"Follow Ann Richards wherever she goes. She said she would try to engage passage on the *Dakota Queen* tonight. If she is aboard when this boat pulls out, then I intend to be aboard also."

Suddenly Leila slid her arms around his neck. She pressed her lips fiercely against his. "That gold should be yours," she whispered. "All of it, Britt. Every ounce of it. Why, even that wouldn't begin to pay for what Zack Richards has done to you. Think of the steamboats it would buy. You could be a millionaire in a few years. Think of what it would do for you—for us."

She drew herself tight against him, and Britt's arms held her.

"I'll help you," she told him, her lips close to his ear.

"Then you don't believe that I killed that watchman and robbed Zack Richards' safe?" Britt murmured, a vast thankfulness in his voice.

"I know now how sinful it was to even let you think I had a doubt in my mind," Leila said. "But I was angry at you, Britt. Angry because of all those silent years. After all, I waited too. Three years was as long for me as it was for you. And you never even bothered to write to me."

"A man in hell doesn't write to angels," Britt said. "I

didn't want to hold you to promises that could never be kept. I wanted you to forget me."

"But I never did. You know that, don't you?"

Britt kissed her again, fiercely, hungrily. Leila pushed him away at last and reluctantly. The golden flecks were bright and dancing in her eyes. "You had better go," she sighed. "Please. I—I can't trust you."

She turned to the door, opened it and peered out. "All clear," she whispered and pushed Britt out of the cabin.

"Or perhaps it was myself I couldn't trust, Britt," she murmured.

Then she closed the door before he could speak.

CHAPTER 9

The deck was black and lonely and brushed by a dank breeze off the river. From below came the steady grind of winches and the rattle of handtrucks and the thud of cargo arriving aboard as the stevedores worked. Voices drifted up from the cabin deck where the clerk was showing new arrivals to their quarters. Stokers were busy and a crimson light played over the river like sheet lightning as fire doors were opened and closed in the boiler room.

The riding lights of a small steamboat were visible out in the river. The craft was approaching the *Dakota Queen* at slow speed. Her safety valve popped, splitting the night with the deafening roar of steam. Then her whistle grunted twice, and the slip valve closed, ending the din.

Britt saw now that this was a towboat evidently arriving to pick up the empty fuel barges. He had no time to lose if he meant to make his way back to the levee by the same route by which he had boarded the *Dakota Queen* unseen. And he wanted to return to the vicinity of Ann Richards' dress shop to keep watch on her.

He hurried to the rear companionway. Footsteps were clumping on the promenade below, and he paused. He heard a deep voice speak. "Here 'tis, you worthless cotton-picker. Numbah 208. Thet's Miss Sherry Dean's cabin. An' mind you, set thet trunk down with care. Miss Dean'd skin me alive if you scratched thet piece o' baggage."

Britt recognized the voice as that of Amos, the coachman

56

Sherry had employed to drive him to Ann Richards' shop earlier in the evening.

A scornful exchange of remarks followed. Then luggage thumped on a floor. Presently the footsteps and the voices faded forward.

Britt descended cautiously. The promenade, lighted by lamps fore and aft, was momentarily vacant. He swung over the rail, lowered himself and dropped into the safer blackness of the empty barge bottom. The towboat was still a hundred yards out in the river, nosing toward the levee to pick up the forward barge.

Above him, on the passenger deck, a man stood flattened against the forward wall of the lounge. This man had rounded into view of the promenade just as Britt had slid over the rail to make his descent into the barge. He had got a brief glimpse of Britt—and had instantly shrunk back out of sight.

This man was the handsome, blond partner of Leila's father—Mead Jarrett.

Jarrett now turned, raced up the forward companionway to the deserted hurricane deck where he would have the advantage of darkness. Crouching, he moved to the rail so that his head would not be skylined. Peering down, he followed Britt's movements in the shadows of the barge.

Jarrett wore a dark top hat and a black topcoat over his fashionable garb. He had just come aboard, ready to take up his duties as business partner of Walker Ormsby on this trip to Fort Benton, and also to act as first pilot.

Jarrett's hand slid inside his coat and emerged gripping a black-muzzled six-shooter that he carried in a shoulder holster. It was the same gun with which he had killed a man at Pierre's in a gambling dispute little more than two hours earlier. And that same gun had killed others.

Now, Mead Jarrett meant for it to kill again. He lifted the gun and its muzzle swung in a slow arc as it followed Britt's course below.

But Britt was a vague shadow in the black maw of the barge bottom. Jarrett saw that his quarry meant to vault to the inshore barge, and he held his fire waiting for the moment when he would be more certain of his target.

There was an icy impersonality in the slow shift of the gun's sights, and this same wicked, implacable coldness was reflected in Jarrett's pale blue eyes. His purpose now brought his thin skin tautly drawn over his jaws and cheekbones, revealing the sharp and rapacious structure of his face. At this moment Mead Jarrett was neither suave nor handsome. He was a killer who meant to slay without a qualm.

Then Britt vaulted to the coaming of the barge and poised to leap to the inshore craft.

It was an easy shot now. Jarrett, the muzzle of the gun steadied on the rail, laid a bead between Britt's shoulders and began squeezing the trigger.

As he did so, the safety valve on the nearby towboat tripped again, and escaping steam erupted with a deafening screech once more.

Jarrett's gun exploded, the report feeble amid the blast of steam. Jarrett, startled, ripped out an oath. His nerves were quivering. He brought the sights of the gun down instantly for a second shot, for he felt that the unexpected interruption had shaken his aim.

But there was no need to fire again. Britt's body was falling. He had started his leap as Jarrett fired. But he did not make it to the inshore barge. His body jerked in mid-air as the bullet struck with the impact of a hammer blow. He turned, twisting in shocked agony. He tried feebly to grab at the coaming of the barge, but failed.

Then he plunged between the barges into the black Mississippi River.

Jarrett remained crouched for a moment at the rail. Finally he turned, peering around, running his tongue over his thin, dry lips. The burst of steam from the towboat ended as abruptly as it had started, as pressure equalized. The fireroom glow from the *Dakota Queen* flickered again on the river. The smaller sounds of activity aboard the steamboat took over again.

There was no sign the shot had attracted attention. Jarrett walked aft, shoving his hand into the breast of his coat, his fingers still clutching the gun. He descended to the passenger promenade, made his way to the rear where he was overlooking the stern of the barge that was moored alongside. He stood, his elbows on the rail, as though lost in his own thoughts while he contemplated the river.

He was, instead, scanning the black swirl of water astern of the barge where the current worked. A small, dark object appeared momentarily, then was drawn beneath the surface again as it drifted away. Jarrett decided it was the hat that Britt Cahill had been wearing.

Nothing more came to the surface. The towboat fussily worked its way into position and finally succeeded in taking the two barges in control. It swung away into the stream, heading off downriver with its charges.

The *Dakota Queen* lay clean and clear now for her midnight departure. The river ran smoothly beneath Jarrett's position—as silent as death itself.

Gig Harney, the chief clerk, came by, recognized Jarrett, and said, "Mead, I've stared at that damned river, too, night an' day the most of my life, an' never found what I was lookin' for. It don't never answer your questions. But it knows. It knows."

"This time," Jarrett said, "it gave me the answer, Gig. The right one."

He strolled forward and entered the lounge. He joined the drinkers at the bar and called for bourbon and mineral water. His right hand came from the breast of his coat. This time it bore nothing more deadly than a cigar. His slender, almost feminine hands were deft and without a quiver as he lit the cigar at the bar candle.

CHAPTER 10

After the door had closed on Britt, Leila Ormsby stood motionless in her cabin, thinking. The high color ran deeper in her throat, pulsing in a changing tide in her slim face. The golden flecks played feverishly in her eyes.

She spoke aloud in a husky, longing murmur, "A quarter of a million!"

The very sound of it drove a shivery ecstasy through her. She was breathing faster. She clasped her arms about herself, tight against her bosom, as she would a passionate lover, as though seeking to hold forever this thrilling mood.

Her hot glance traveled around the cabin. It was well appointed as such quarters go. There was a bedstead in golden oak instead of the customary fixed double berth, and it was fitted with good linen and eiderdown and a sateen coverlet. She had a dressing table with a mirror and two brocaded chairs and the floor was warmed with a thick carpet.

Still, her pale eyes held disdain for these accommodations. This same unhappiness extended to the wardrobe she had been unpacking. She was remembering that only a year ago she had her own personal maid to take care of such menial tasks, and her wardrobe had almost measured up to even her standards of adornment.

A year ago she would have scorned the thought of subjecting herself to the boring discomforts of a steamboat journey to Fort Benton. A year ago she had been on her way east to spend the summer at a fashionable resort where she had lived in the refined luxury that was worthy of the daughter of a successful man.

That had been the fulfillment of her ambitions. From her viewpoint, that period had marked her real birth, the beginning of the life for which she had really been meant. Everything that had taken place before that time had been only something that had happened to a person she wanted to forget.

Fearfully her thoughts went back to what her life had been before that opulent interlude. Her mouth turned bitter and rebellious as she remembered. As far back into childhood as she could recall, her father had operated a shabby, small steamboat that picked up what business it could at isolated, poverty-stricken landings along the upper Mississippi, where bigger boats did not deign to stop.

That had been a humble existence, adequate enough in that it furnished a solid, modest livelihood, but it had been crushing to Leila's pride. Walker Ormsby, a pompous, heavy-stomached, hard-drinking man, had always talked of the killing he would some day make in the river trade, but he had lived, in fact, only on the crumbs that were dropped by more energetic and imaginative men like Zack Richards and Mike Cahill.

Walker Ormsby had hated these more successful men, even while he toadied them for what favors they could throw his way. In addition, he had been harassed by a daughter who wanted silk and satin and sable and diamonds instead of the middle-class existence his income afforded.

And Leila had envied and hated people like Zack Richards and his daughter, also. Then Britt Cahill had come back from the war, and she had seen to it that he was given every opportunity of falling in love with her.

She had promised to marry Britt the day he escorted her through the proud and gleaming new steamboat of which he had become sole owner after the death of his father. That had been on the eve of the *Northern Star's* maiden trip to Fort Benton—the trip from which the boat never returned—the trip that made Britt a fugitive.

But the ill wind that had sent Britt's steamboat to the bottom of the river, and the fire that had ruined Zack Richards, seemed to change the fortunes of Leila's father for the better.

With a bewildering rush, prosperity came to Walker Ormsby. He had, to Leila's surprise, formed a partnership with Mead Jarrett. For Jarrett, who had been one of Zack Richards' best Missouri River pilots, had already gained a reputation as a romantic, dashing figure and a dangerous man in a gunfight. It had seemed incongruous to her that a man like Jarrett would associate himself with her bombastic threadbare father.

At first she had flattered herself with the belief that she was the magnet that had drawn Mead Jarrett into this partnership. Now she was no longer too sure of that. She was not sure of anything in regard to Jarrett.

However, whatever the reason, the partnership seemed to be the golden key to the success that Walker Ormsby had always talked about. Mead Jarrett, from somewhere, apparently had command of considerable financial backing.

The new firm of Ormsby & Jarrett had sold the small craft that Walker Ormsby operated and had bought a big Mississippi River packet, which they shifted to the Missouri River trade.

With Zack Richards and his Great Western Navigation Company ruined by the fire, and with Britt's steamboat gone, the upper Missouri River run to Fort Benton was a bonanza.

In a single season the new firm netted profit enough to take over control of three more packets. Walker Ormsby bought a fashionable home in the best district of St. Louis for Leila, along with carriages and blooded horses. He began strutting in the company of bankers and wealthy merchants who were only too anxious to advance money and credit to this expanding firm.

Mead Jarrett became a fashion plate. Leila, like Cinderella, found herself suddenly wearing the magic slipper. She had her diamonds and her sables and had servants at her command, and a retinue of suitors always at her heels whenever Mead Jarrett was away.

But the wheel of fortune soon turned again. The Missouri River could make a man wealthy in a season, but it could also destroy him overnight, just as Zack Richards and Britt Cahill had been destroyed.

Two of the packets Ormsby & Jarrett had acquired were lost within a day of each other in the upper river, snags and sawyers ripping out their bottoms. A third boat was destroyed by fire when some drunken deckhand overturned an oil lamp as the craft lay tied up at the wharves at Independence.

Ormsby & Jarrett had borrowed to the limit during their rapid ascent. They still owed to the banks the biggest part of the price of the three lost packets.

The fine mansion had gone under the auctioneer's hammer along with the carriages and the stable of horses, and along with Leila's diamonds and sables.

Mead Jarrett had gone back to the gambling tables in an attempt to retrieve their fortunes, but luck had run against him there also and he wore no rubies in his cravat now, no emerald cuff links. But, with his gambler's acceptance of circumstances, he was far less affected than Leila or her father by their descent from the heights.

Walker Ormsby had lost all of his expansive self-importance. He had grown flabby almost overnight and began drinking harder than ever.

Leila had moved back into a middle-class home with her father and returned to a hateful middle-class existence. The wardrobe she had salvaged from the debacle was last year's styles, and that was as damaging to her pride as the fact that her list of admirers had also vanished.

Still, not everything had been lost, as Mead Jarrett had pointed out. The partnership had at least saved control of the *Dakota Queen* out of the disaster, even though one banker held a sizable claim against even that. And the Missouri River trade was still there, rich and beckoning.

Big profits had seemed certain again, provided the sawyers and the rock chains were merciful.

Even a week ago the *Dakota Queen* had been booked to utmost capacity for this first trip of the season to Fort Benton, with men clamoring for more deck and cargo space, and offering double the fare if they could be accommodated.

"Give us a season like the one we had that first summer, and we'll be back in clover by fall, with the bankers falling over each other to ask favors," Mead Jarrett had said with his thin smile.

He had patted Leila in a place no man other than Jarrett would dare place a hand. "You'll wear diamonds again, my dear," he had said. "I'll hang them on you with my own hands."

"See to it that it is me you hang them on, and not some other woman you take a passing fancy to," Leila had said, wise and bitter in the knowledge of past neglect.

Then, three days previously, an Army mailboat, the first craft of the season to arrive from the upper Missouri, had docked at St. Louis on the heels of the last run of ice from winter's breakup. It brought news from the Dakota country.

The Sioux! The powerful red nation of the upper plains was riding. The Northern Cheyenne and the Crows and the Snakes were painted for war, too. Even the Blackfeet, decimated by smallpox, had come to bay, realizing that it was now a battle to death to save their hunting grounds from the ever rising tidal wave of immigration that was sweeping upon their strongholds.

The Army was warning that anyone who traveled the plains did so at his own risk.

Jarrett had done his best to counteract the alarm that swept the westbound travelers. He had scoffed loudly at the story in every gambling house and bank and brokerage in town, saying that the Army, as usual, was making a mountain out of a molehill.

But the more timid passengers began canceling passage. Shippers hesitated on delivering cargo commitments and some consignments that had already been stowed aboard had been withdrawn.

Then Jarrett, without Leila's knowledge, had spread the word that Walker Ormsby's daughter was making the trip to Fort Benton on the *Dakota Queen*. And when he learned that Sherry Dean, the gorgeous music-hall singer, was also to be a passenger, he had made capital of that fact also.

"Would Walker Ormsby expose young women and his own daughter, in particular, to any real danger?" he had asked derisively. "Apparently the female of the species has more sand and common sense than the male."

Leila had been furious, but helpless, when she heard what

was going on. She had not been consulted, and this trip to a frontier outpost had been farthest from her plans. But, as Jarrett had sardonically pointed out, she did not dare refuse. To do so would be disastrous. He and her father stood to lose even the *Dakota Queen* unless this first trip was a financial success.

Leila could understand that talk of money. Angrily, she had this stateroom fitted with what comfort she could hurriedly arrange and had resigned herself to months of ordeal on a crowded, odorous steamboat. She was making this sacrifice for the sake of future luxury.

Jarrett had kissed her with his careless, mocking sureness. "And I'll also buy you a sealskin coat and teams of pacers," he told her.

The word that Leila and Sherry Dean were to be passengers had its effect. Cancellations stopped, but only for a day or two.

Then the *Aurora,* which had brought Britt Cahill to St. Louis, had arrived only a few hours ago with its bullet holes and arrow jutting from the pilothouse. The owner of the *Aurora* had let it be known that he, personally, was not risking another trip to Benton, this year at least, and was diverting his packet to the safer Mississippi.

In the past few hours more than two-thirds of all passenger reservations on the *Dakota Queen* had been canceled. The majority of the remaining travelers had paid fare only to Independence or to Council Bluffs, which was the last stop before the jump-off across the plains. At Council Bluffs they would make up their minds whether to chance the remainder of the trip. The *Dakota Queen* now might run nearly empty beyond Council Bluffs, and that meant a profitless venture.

Leila murmured again in that yearning tone, "A quarter of a million."

The thrashing of a paddlewheel sounded on the river near by, and then the safety valve on the neighboring craft tripped so abruptly that the unexpected din almost caused her to scream. She had not realized how taut her nerves had become during those moments while she had been standing there looking at that blank door through which Britt Cahill had gone.

Mingling with the roar of escaping steam came a faint, sharper impact. The thought crossed her mind that it

64

sounded like a gunshot. Then she forgot it, for her thoughts were racing along, fixed on her own plans.

The hiss of steam ceased. Leila suddenly made her decision. She presently opened the door and stepped on deck. A towboat was nearly alongside, maneuvering to pick up the fuel barges.

Leila walked to her father's cabin and tapped on the door, her knuckles tight and peremptory.

"Who is it?" her father's voice sounded irritably.

She found the door unlocked and stepped in. Walker Ormsby sat at a table, a whiskey bottle within reach. His pouchy jowls sagged over the collar of his captain's coat. Purple-nosed, with thinning, coarse, graying hair, he had taken off his stomacher, and his soft bulk seemed to overflow the chair. His eyes were muddy with self-pity and sullen with drink.

Gazing at him, Leila's only emotion was contempt and impatience. Seeing this expression in her face, her father sat up straighter, an uneasiness stirring him, as though he sensed that this interview was to be unpleasant.

"What is it, Leila?" he demanded.

Leila took the bottle and placed it out of reach. "Quit drinking for a moment," she said coldly. "I believe you are still sober enough to understand what I am going to tell you."

"Dammit, Leila," Walker Ormsby exploded in a rage that he knew was futile, "why do you have to be so much like your mother? Cold and heartless. Hard as a diamond. Domineering. Why . . . ?"

Leila had heard all this many times before. "Try to understand this," she interrupted. "I talked to a certain man a while ago. His name is—Britt Cahill!"

She coolly watched the effect of this announcement. For a moment or two it did not register. Walker Ormsby's fogged mind was slow to respond.

"Britt—Britt Cahill!" he repeated.

Then he struggled to his feet, his clouded eyes brightening with consternation. "Did—did you say—Britt Cahill?" he whispered hoarsely, fear suddenly in his face.

Leila nodded, cynical amusement twisting her lips.

"You're lying!" her father said, almost imploringly. "Cahill's dead. He must be dead. He must be."

"Why would I lie, Father?" she asked.

"Where—when . . . ?"

"Within the last few minutes," Leila said. "In my cabin. We had quite a long conversation. A very interesting talk."

Walker Ormsby studied his daughter suspiciously and finally decided she was telling the truth. He looked longingly toward the bottle, running a putty-hued tongue over loose, dry lips that were the same lifeless hue. "Here—here aboard the Dakota Queen?" he muttered.

Some inner desperation became stronger than his fear. He turned, lurched toward the door.

Leila stepped in his path. "Where are you going?"

"To the police. He's wanted for murder, remember. He killed a man in cold blood."

"Did he?"

Walker Ormsby had started to push her aside, but he found her slim body strong and unyielding. And now, this question halted him. He stood staring into his daughter's mocking eyes. His hand fell away from her.

"Of course he did," he said uncertainly.

"Sit down, Father," Leila said. "Britt Cahill is no longer aboard anyway. He left the boat."

"What was he doing here?"

"He came to see me, of course. He was—is in love with me, as you must recall."

"Are you trying to say that Cahill still thinks—still thinks you . . ."

"He's in love with me," Leila snapped. "He will again ask me to marry him, if he can find Zack Richards and clear himself of that murder charge."

Ormsby sank back into the chair. "Zack Richards?" he mumbled. "Where is . . . ?"

"Britt Cahill hasn't found Zack Richards yet," Leila said. "But he will sooner or later. Britt is a determined man."

She watched a small flame of relief spring to life in her father's eyes.

"It would be rather embarrassing to—to someone—if Britt and Zack Richards ever met and compared notes, wouldn't it, Father?" she asked softly.

Their gaze met. Walker Ormsby tried to show anger and defiance, but it wouldn't work. He couldn't offer a challenge against the cold certainty and cynicism in the pale violet eyes that looked back at him.

Leila spoke again. "On the night of the murder and robbery someone went to the authorities and stated that he had seen Britt Cahill skulking away from Zack Richards' office just as the fire broke out. That was enough to put Britt's neck in a noose if the lynch mob had caught him. But you talked him into escaping, and helped him flee from St. Louis. That, of course, was taken as final proof that he was guilty."

A silence came. "Britt Cahill believes Zack Richards was the man whose testimony would cost him his life at the end of a rope," Leila went on.

Again there was a silence. "Actually you were the one who went to the authorities with the statement that you had seen Britt at the scene of the crime," she said softly. "You are the eyewitness against him, aren't you, Father? You are the man whose testimony can hang him."

CHAPTER 11

Walker Ormsby's loose lips moved several times before any sound came. "It—it was my duty!" he croaked. "What else could I do? I could not protect a murderer—even a man who was to marry my daughter. I did it for your sake, my dear."

Leila's icy smile remained unchanged. "Of course," she said. "That is a commendable attitude, Father. Then there will be nothing to fear if Britt Cahill confronts Zack Richards. Britt intends to choke the truth out of Richards, force him to confess that he lied. But, naturally, if Zack Richards never made such an accusation, then there will be nothing for him to confess. Britt Cahill will probably learn who the man is who really has the power to hang him."

Walker Ormsby's fists knotted on the desk until his knuckles showed a sickly, yellow hue. "You she-devil!" he said thickly. "What is it you want from me this time? More money? More fine clothes?"

"Perhaps," Leila said, and the fever was in her voice and in her eyes again. "Britt Cahill told me a story about half a ton of gold. It lies in a sunken mackinaw boat at the bottom of the Missouri River somewhere below the Yellowstone Fork . . ."

Again their eyes met. "Britt told me how that gold might be found," Leila went on. "Ann Richards knows where it is."

"Ann Richards? Zack Richards' daughter? Why, she is here in St. Louis, a dressmaker."

Leila nodded. She picked up the whiskey bottle, sloshed a tumbler nearly full and handed it to her father. "Take this and listen," she commanded. "Listen closely."

At that moment the door opened back of her. She paused, turning. Mead Jarrett stepped into the cabin. He still wore his topcoat, but was bareheaded. His crisp, blond hair clung close and dry to his head. A little sardonic smile lay on his thin lips but there was no humor in his ice-pale eyes.

"I hope I'm not intruding," he said with velvet politeness. "You two seem to have had your heads together for some time. Is it a secret that can't be trusted to your father's business partner and your own devoted slave, Leila?"

"How long have you been out there eavesdropping, Mead?" Leila asked calmly.

"Several minutes," Jarrett smiled. "But I heard only enough to whet my curiosity. I fancied that I heard Britt Cahill's name mentioned. Don't tell me that he has turned up alive?"

"He's alive," Leila said. "As a matter of fact I'm glad you came, Mead, even though I resent your continual pussyfooting and spying on me. It saves repeating the story to you later. I was just about to tell Father a rather strange tale about half a ton of gold that we might be able to find during this trip to Fort Benton."

"Half a ton?" Jarrett murmured slowly. "Now you really do interest me, Leila."

"That would make the trip profitable after all," Leila said evenly. "In fact it would set Ormsby & Jarrett & Ormsby up in business very nicely."

"Ormsby & Jarrett & Ormsby?" Jarrett questioned.

"Yes," Leila smiled. "I'm entering the firm as a new full partner. I'm the Ormsby of the third part."

She waited, watching their expressions with amusement. "Agreed?" she asked.

Jarrett chuckled. "I would say that the contribution of that much gold to the company would entitle you to a membership in the firm. I trust you are not letting your imagination run away with you, my dear. Just where and how are you to produce this fortune?"

"First," Leila murmured, "make sure there's nobody else emulating your example as an eavesdropper, my darling."

Jarrett complied with that suggestion, leaving to make sure the deck was vacant. When he returned, Leila motioned him to a chair. Then she bent close and related the story Britt had told her.

As she talked Mead Jarrett drew from a pocket a deck of cards, and his slender, delicate fingers began automatically toying with them, riffling them in sharp staccato bursts, spreading them in flower-like fans that bloomed and vanished as swiftly as they appeared, cutting, recutting them with eye-baffling speed. This was a pastime that Jarrett invariably turned to when he had a problem to consider.

Jarrett was incredulous at first as he listened. Finally he began to believe. An excitement grew in him, sending color into his thin face. The cards moved faster in his hands.

Walker Ormsby watched their expressions and edged away from them a trifle. He swallowed hard at times. He had heard of the gunfight at Pierre's in which Jarrett had killed a man. He was remembering other duels and other men Jarrett had shot down in similar disputes.

Walker Ormsby had never taken a life, not because he did not have the desire at times, nor because of any compunction. It was only that he had lacked the moral fiber. He did not even carry a gun. The thought of physical violence always made him ill.

Leila's voice died and Jarrett sat chewing on an unlighted cigar while he thought it over.

Walker Ormsby said shakily, "Forget the gold. Forget Zack Richards and Britt Cahill. We'll only get into trouble mixing into this thing."

Neither Leila nor Jarrett answered. They ignored him, as they always had ignored him in matters of decision.

Leila waited, watching Jarrett. "Apparently Ann Richards and this map or information that her father sent her, is the key to all this," Jarrett finally murmured. "Let us hope she does not change her mind about engaging passage with us. She might be a very profitable fare and . . ."

Steps sounded on the deck. A hand tapped the door. Leila hesitated, then opened it. Gig Harney, the balding, big-toothed, first clerk stood there. And a few steps back of him stood a young woman.

"This here young lady," Harney said a trifle breathlessly,

"allows as how she wants to buy passage as fur as Fort Buford."

Mead Jarrett came to his feet. His glance met Leila's for an instant in mutual elation. "Why, it's Miss Richards!" he exclaimed, and was every inch the polished gentleman. "This *is* a surprise—a very, very pleasant one!"

"Good evening, Mead," Ann Richards said impersonally. "And Leila. And Captain Ormsby."

She had known Jarrett when he was a pilot on her father's boats. And her acquaintance with Leila and Walker Ormsby dated back to her girlhood.

"Why, Ann!" Leila cried out. "Do you actually mean you're traveling with us? To Fort Buford, of all places!"

"I expect to meet Dad there," Ann explained briefly. "I hope you can find space for me."

"Of course," Jarrett said. He turned to Harney. "See to it that Miss Richards is made comfortable in our very best accommodations."

Ann Richards moved into the lamplight. A straw bonnet, bearing a wisp of lace and a gay feather, was perched pertly on her chestnut hair. A fawn-colored, short jacket with muttonleg sleeves fitted snugly at her supple waist and flared at the hips. Below that was a pearl-gray skirt with a small train which she held clear of the deck with a wrist loop. She carried a reticule that matched her hat, and wore slippers of alligator leather.

Leila was forcing a bright smile, but her eyes roved jealously over Ann Richards' costume. The slippers, hat and reticule were surely from Fifth Avenue, she reflected. The jacket and skirt bore the stamp of Ann's own design and make. They were certainly far ahead of any fashion Leila had seen in St. Louis.

She resented Ann's figure and the way she gave a swing of alluring style to everything she wore. Leila, no matter how she tried, always seemed to fall just a little short of this chic effect.

"It will be just heavenly to have a person of my own sex aboard," Leila gushed. "We will have so much to talk about."

"Thank you, Leila," Ann said. "I'll have the clerk bring my luggage aboard."

She was smiling a little, inwardly, as she turned to follow Gig Harney below. Leila had gone out of her way to be seen with Ann Richards in the days when Ann's father was a successful and important steamboat operator, but when Zack Richards went bankrupt, Leila made it plain that they were no longer equals. After Ann had gone into dressmaking as a means of livelihood, Leila' had patronized her shop. Patronized was the exact word, for she had treated Ann as a menial, below her own station in life.

Now, this new attitude of Leila's amused Ann, but it also puzzled her somewhat. It evidently indicated Leila's acceptance of her father's more precarious financial state. But Ann had known the violet-eyed girl a long time, and had learned that whenever Leila went out of her way to be especially nice, she had some purpose in mind or some favor to ask that would be to her own benefit. On the other hand, Ann decided in the frankness of her own heart, she was probably being unjust to Leila, and Leila was genuinely happy to have her aboard.

Mead Jarrett was offering his arm. "Allow me, Ann," he was saying grandly.

Ann did not accept his assistance as she gathered her skirt to descend the companionway. "That's your shooting arm, Mead," she said mildly. "Surely, you wouldn't want to be impeded if you were called upon to engage in a little more bloodletting."

Jarrett looked at her swiftly with his chill eyes. "You haven't changed, Ann," he commented. "You still have a whiplash for a tongue. You are referring, I imagine, to a little matter of honor in which I was engaged this evening?"

"It happened that I had a very close view of this matter of honor," Ann said. "Front row center in fact. I almost stopped some of your bullets, Mead. I was in the street in front of Pierre's at the time of the affair. A perfect stranger snatched me out of the path of your gunplay."

"What in the world were you doing at Pierre's after dark?" Jarrett asked.

"I was there on business. I was making a gown for Sherry Dean."

"If you had such a close view of the shooting, then you must have seen that it was entirely self-defense on my part," Jarrett smiled.

"How did it start, Mead?" Ann asked coolly. "Did that poor man catch you palming cards or using a sleeve set?"

Jarrett laughed. "The last time I tried to kiss you, Ann, was when you were raking me over the coals for having to shoot to defend myself. That was at Independence, I believe, when I was working as a pilot on one of your father's boats. I remember how I bled. You had sharp fingernails, Ann, when you were nineteen."

"They're sharper at twenty-four, Mead," Ann said.

They had reached the passenger deck, where Gig Harney was waiting. Ann turned her back on Jarrett and began instructing Harney as to where to find her baggage.

Leila had followed them. Now she spoke sardonically at Jarrett's elbow. "Your charm," she murmured, "seems to have been spattered with a very ripe tomato, Mead. So you tried to kiss Ann Richards when she was nineteen, and you'd like to try again. Perhaps you have forgotten that you are supposed to marry me—when you get around to it."

Jarrett did not answer. He was still smiling a little as his gaze appreciatively followed Ann Richards' trim figure.

Gig Harney led Ann to a stateroom on the larboard deck. It contained the usual double berth, a commode and a cubby for hanging a wardrobe, a chest of drawers and a stiff-backed, cane-bottomed chair.

"Seems like you gals has got more sand in your craws than men," the clerk observed gloomily. "Sherry Dean, thet red-headed gamblin' hall singer, is also travelin' to Benton on this trip. Her baggage come aboard a while ago. Looks like she don't intend to cancel out in spite o' all this talk about Injuns waitin' to lift our sculps up on the plains. But there ain't many that's buyin' passage west of Council Bluffs. Lots of 'em has got their wind up, an' won't go any further unless things look better by that time."

A cabin boy brought Ann's luggage. After she was alone she began to shake a little. The reaction of the hectic events of the past few hours began to hit her now.

First there had been that narrow escape from wild bullets at Pierre's. Even that seemed inconsequential in contrast to that second desperate gunfight that had left her shop a wreck, with a dead man lying in his own blood amid the tumbled dress forms and spilled shelves and tables.

She stood there, thinking of Bill Clay and his abrupt departure ahead of the authorities, and his request that she withhold any mention of his part in the battle.

She had complied. When the police arrived she had told them that the two intruders had surprised her while she was working in the shop, and that during her struggle to free herself from the grasp of one, she had managed to snatch up a gun that she kept handy, and had begun firing frenziedly. When it was over she had found one man dead and the other gone.

The police had searched the street with lanterns and had found something else. They had discovered a trail of blood. Following it, they came upon a second dead man in an alley two blocks away. It was the pop-eyed ruffian. He had not escaped after all. Ann realized that one of Bill Clay's bullets had struck the man, and he had been dying as he ran away into the darkness.

The authorities had gazed with awe at the heavy .45, the tip of its muzzle filmed with the gray fog of burned powder, that Ann handed them. They had no reason to doubt her word. They knew she was Zack Richards' daughter, and they told her admiringly that she was a chip off the old block.

They had finally left, taking the dead man with them. Ann was supposed to appear in the morning at the hearing that would be held. But they did not know that by that time she would be bound up the Missouri River.

The police had even given her back the gun, with the gallant observation that she likely would prefer to keep it handy in view of the fact that she knew how to use it so well.

Ann still had the gun. She drew it now from a bag. She gazed at it, shuddered a little, then thrust it beneath a pillow on the lower berth.

Bill Clay had forgotten the belt of gold when he had hurriedly left her shop. She had packed the belt in her trunk to keep it safe for him. But she wondered if she would ever see him again. She reflected on the mystery of him. She had already decided that Bill Clay was not his real name. But he had mentioned that he had had trouble with the authorities in the past, and that could explain why he wanted to hide his real identity in St. Louis.

But there were other puzzling details. He had used the slurred diction of an uneducated man, but she remembered that, after the excitement of the gunfight, he had forgotten and lapsed into the crisp, authoritative tone of a man who had been well schooled.

Her hand went to the bosom of her dress, where she was carrying for safekeeping the letter and the map from her father that had arrived on the mailboat.

The pop-eyed ruffian and his companion had died trying to obtain possession of that key to the sunken boatload of gold. She need not fear them now. But—she was wondering about Bill Clay's real motives.

One thing was certain. Bill Clay knew she had received the letter that Pete McLeod had mailed before he died. She uneasily felt that she had made a mistake in admitting even that much to him, for she wondered if his appearance in her life had been entirely coincidental after all.

The *Dakota Queen's* whistle burst hoarsely into life, its vibration jarring the deck beneath her feet. It rose and fell in a wailing warning. The roof bell began tolling steadily. The signal that departure time was at hand.

Ann stepped on deck. A cabin boy was ushering a new arrival to a stateroom just a few doors from her own. He was a tall, long-legged, dark-haired man who seemed to be in his late twenties. He wore a dark tweed business suit with a thin gold watch chain across the vest front, and a flat-topped bowler hat, which was just coming into fashion. Ann's trained eye noted that the material in his garb was the very best, and that its extremely conservative and yet casual fashion must be the handiwork of some expert tailor.

He bowed to Ann, lifting his hat, and said, "Good evening," in a cultured voice. He had dark, intense eyes, a sensitive mouth and a good, high forehead.

"This am it, Doctah Howe," the cabin boy said with the respect he accorded only to gentlemen, as he led the way into the stateroom.

Ann waited until she could speak to the cabin boy alone. "Has Miss Sherry Dean come aboard?" she asked.

"Yes, Ma'am," the boy said enthusiastically. "Yes, indeedy! Missy Dean done joined the boat a little while ago. She's in 208. Thet's on the stahbo'rd deck, Ma'am."

Ann returned to her cabin, satisfied. She felt that she had at least one ally aboard, one person she could go to for advice and help if need be.

74

CHAPTER 12

Britt was caught in the constricting grip of a fearful nightmare. He was living over again that terrible moment three years in the past, when the *Northern Star* had gone down beneath him.

He was under water, trying to drag Sherry Dean from her submerged cabin. But, in the weird nature of such hallucinations, Sherry Dean had Ann Richards' face and she was trying to fight him off. She was staring at him with accusing eyes and pointing a finger at him and saying, "You're not Bill Clay. You're the man who hates my father. Liar! Liar! Liar!"

And all the time the wild current of the river was dragging at him, too, seeking to wrest him away from her and pull him to the surface. And there on the surface was a man with a gun waiting to shoot him when he appeared, a man with the face of a frog and big pop eyes that were glittering with murderous anticipation.

Britt was trying to plead his case with this girl, who was both Sherry Dean and Ann Richards. And all the time the current was dragging him farther from her and toward the gun that awaited him. Each time he tried to speak, no words would come, for he was choking—suffocating—drowning.

But Ann Richards seemed able to keep saying in that accusing, grieving voice, "Liar! Liar!"

Ann Richards' voice and her face faded. And now the sensation of drowning became a reality. He was under water and a steady, relentless weight was pulling at him.

Even through the daze of his nightmare he had been swimming instinctively, and now he lifted his head and found air to pull into his lungs. His face was on the surface.

He seemed to be caught in the tentacles of some monster. He fought this new horror frenziedly, the panic of the nightmare still upon him.

Slowly realization returned. The actuality was almost as horrifying as the hallucination had been. He seemed to be in a black cavern, and in freezing water.

Then he remembered. He had been leaping from the

prow of one barge to the stern of the other. There had been that blast of steam from the escape valve of the towboat, and amid that a bullet had hit him.

He knew it had been a bullet, for his eyes had registered the spurting flame of the gunflash from the upper deck of the *Dakota Queen,* and his ears had heard the thud of the shot.

He had toppled into the river between the two barges. He now realized that the slimy tentacles that he was fighting in terror were only the branches of some dead tree limb that had wedged against the barge's prow. The cavern was only the overhang of the barge's blunt prow which loomed above him.

The current had carried him into this trapped driftwood, and that had saved his life by preventing him from being sucked beneath the flat hull of the barge. The weight that he had struggled against in his nightmare was the ceaseless push of the Mississippi's current, which held both his body and the driftwood pinned against the downslope of the craft's prow.

His left arm was numb. He wondered if it was broken. Agony began to push through him. He tasted his own blood in the muddy water.

The frog-faced man, who had fled from Ann Richards' shop, must have followed him to the levee, and had fired that shot. That seemed the only reasonable explanation.

That rationalized everything and the nightmare aspect of his predicament seemed less fantastic.

But it was still fearful enough. He had the impression that he had been in the river for hours, but he now became aware of the slap of the towboat's paddlewheels near by and the normal sounds of activity from the *Dakota Queen.* Reason told him that probably no more than a minute or two had passed since the bullet had struck him.

The stabbing agony was in his left side. There seemed to be no sensation at all in his left arm.

His mind was entirely clear now and the will to live was back again. He appraised his situation. The shot had come from the hurricane deck of the *Dakota Queen.* He was certain of that. The chances were that his assailant was still up there somewhere, peering to make sure he did not come to the surface alive.

The barge was moored tight against the *Dakota Queen's*

guard, that two-foot projection of the deck which overhung the slope of the hull.

Britt worked his way free of the stiff branches of the drifter and pulled himself along the water-slimed face of the barge. The current helped pin him there and it also fought to drag him beneath the keel.

He stroked with his right arm, and finally clawed and swam beneath the protection of the steamboat's guard. He now let himself drift along the length of the boat until he reached the paddlewheel. He clung there for a long time, hiding beneath a broad, uplifted bucket plank.

Pain now began in his left arm and the numbness was fading. He found that he could use that arm a little and decided that it was not broken at least.

The towboat loomed almost alongside. Mooring lines were being cast free, and presently the towboat ground past, pushing the barge clear.

Britt knew that his wound was taking toll. He became aware of a creeping inertia, a desire to resign himself and sink to rest in the river. He realized that he had to take a chance on his assailant's patience while he still had the strength to pull himself from the river.

He forced himself to climb the spidery, slippery framework of the paddlewheel, fighting nausea and racking pain. He was an easy target now for any enemy who might be peering down from the decks of the boat above him. But no shot came. No head appeared there.

He finally reached the paddlebeam and clung to it for a time until the world stopped spinning. At last he worked his way inboard. He had to find refuge and help at once. He remembered the cabin into which Sherry Dean's baggage had been carried. He recalled the number—208.

He climbed the bull rails until his eyes reached deck level. Waiting until the promenade was clear, he dragged himself up and over the rail and got his feet on the deck.

He was staggering drunkenly. With his last strength, he made his way along the line of cabin doors until he found the number he sought.

He tried the door. Someone had been careless. It was unlocked. He reeled inside an instant before more arrivals appeared from forward on the promenade. He closed the door. An oil lamp burned in a wall bracket. There was the usual double berth, fitted with draw curtains, a chair and a commode on which stood a white china basin and ewer. A spray of hothouse roses and a sweating bucket bearing iced champagne waited on the locker beneath the single small window. A card was pinned to the roses, on which a message had been written.

Vaguely Britt read the words "Happy voyage, Sherry, for both of us." The greeting was penned on an engraved calling card carrying Mead Jarrett's name.

A sizable wardrobe trunk stood near a wall, along with a mound of hatboxes and other luggage. The curtains of the berths had not been drawn, and the lower bed was made up.

Britt attempted to appraise his injury. Blood was draining steadily from his left arm and side, mingling with the river water that dripped from his clothes. He tried to pull off his soaked jacket and that effort sent nausea through him again, leaving him gagging, his head swimming.

He waited, with set teeth, until he could go on, then managed to remove the jacket and his shirt. In the mirror above the commode he saw an ugly gash along his ribs and another wound in his left arm. He discovered that the bullet was lodged in the muscles of his left forearm.

He tried to form a tourniquet for his arm, using the sleeve of his shirt, but the room was spinning and his fingers seemed wooden and without strength. He was reaching his limit and knew it.

Then he became aware of heavy footsteps on the deck, along with the decisive, crisp tap of high heels. Voices sounded at the door.

He reeled toward the nearest hiding place, which was the wardrobe trunk, and dropped into concealment back of it an instant before Gig Harney opened the door to usher Sherry Dean into her quarters.

"Here 'tis, Miss Dean," Britt heard Harney say. "The bucket of champagne an' the flowers are for you. Mead Jarrett's compliments."

Sherry's voice rose scathingly. "Champagne is it, from that scut?"

The high heels rattled vigorously in the room and then on the deck. Gig Harney uttered a wounded croak of protest. Then there was a splash in the river alongside.

"Now, it's champagne for the catfish," Sherry sputtered as she came walking angrily back into the room. "And your oily-fingered Mead Jarrett will meet the same reception if he appears in my door."

Then the door closed and Britt heard Gig Harney retreating down the deck. There was silence for a moment.

Sherry stood in the lamplit cabin. She was gazing at fresh water stains that were soaking into the uncarpeted floor, and seeing the crimson tinge of blood in those marks. Then she saw the blood-stained shirt and canvas jacket that lay in a corner. These things had not been visible to Gig Harney who had not entered the stateroom.

Sherry had come directly by carriage from Pierre's after making her final stage appearance. Her high-heeled, black velvet slippers were only inches from one of those blood and water stains. She had tied a dark scarf over her titian hair to protect the coiffure from the night dampness, and had thrown a heavy walking coat over her shoulders. Beneath the coat she wore a black, bare-shouldered evening gown that was as revealing as the green dress that had aroused Britt's criticism earlier in the evening.

Then the coat dropped to the floor and she came with a rush to peer down at Britt where he lay huddled back of the trunk.

"Britt!" she gasped. "Britt!"

She dropped to her knees beside him, her fingers quivering as they fearfully touched his face. He stirred and his eyes opened sluggishly. "Sherry, I . . ." he began apologetically.

That was the last he remembered for a time.

Sherry moved swiftly, certainly, but without panic. The sight of blood and bullet wounds was no novelty to her. She had witnessed more than one gunfight in gambling houses where she had entertained. First, she made sure the door was bolted and the curtain was drawn at the single window. Then she pulled off the evening gown—not because she did not want it soiled, but because it was an impediment.

Clad only in a thin black silk petticoat, she moved the trunk with lithe strength in order to gain room in which to work. She found scissors in a bag and delved into other luggage, scattering the contents recklessly until she found garments that would serve as bandages. With these she began staunching the flow of blood from Britt's arm and the long, ugly gash in his side.

The whistle bellowed and the roof bell began tolling as Sherry worked. The tempo of activity reached a climax

79

below decks. Presently the mate's voice sounded, "Stand by to cast off."

That command penetrated the haze of pain that fogged Britt's mind. He floated back to consciousness. Sherry was bending over him, looking down at him with big, worried green eyes.

"Sorry I had to inflict myself on you, Sherry," Britt mumbled. "Someone put a slug in me."

"Don't talk, darlin'," she cautioned. "There's time enough for that later."

She was still working on his injuries. Britt's mind cleared. He discovered that he still lay on the cabin floor, but he was swathed in blankets that had been removed from the berth.

Then he became aware that he was stripped to the skin. He stared up at Sherry. "You . . . ?" he murmured, appalled. "My clothes . . . !"

Sherry said tartly, " 'Twas not a time to be standing on false modesty. Otherwise I would not be in my scanties with a man present. But I am safe enough for the time at least. You are as weak as a kitten, praise the saints."

She sobered. "You have a bullet in your arm. That, I cannot cope with. It needs the attention and skill of a doctor. I will . . ."

The *Dakota Queen's* whistle blasted again, drowning out her voice.

The mate's long-drawn shout arose as the whistle died away. "Br—eak up—break up!"

Winches began to grind, swinging the stageplanks aboard. The footsteps of hurrying deckhands clattered below.

"Too late!" Sherry groaned.

The mate's voice arose again. "All gone, Sir."

That was the all clear signal. The engine bell sounded below. A tremor ran through the vessel. The paddlewheel was turning, the bucket planks taking their first bite at the river. The *Dakota Queen* suddenly was alive, moving.

Sherry said desperately, "It is possible there may be a medical man among the passengers. If not, I will have them return to the levee so that we can summon one."

As she spoke she rushed to search in the big trunk. She brought out a dark, conservative dress which she began hastily pulling over her head.

"Stop it!" Britt said. "Wait, Sherry! You know that's impossible. I want nobody to know I'm aboard this boat. I . . ."

The effort of speaking thinned his voice, and the words ended in a gust of agony.

" 'Tis a chance that must be taken," Sherry said. "You will die. I could not remove the bullet. It needs a trained hand, one who knows how to tend the arteries and check the loss of blood and sew the muscles."

She straightened the dress with a twist of her supple body and smoothed its lines into place as she raced to the door and unlocked it. Stepping out she found a cabin boy in sight forward, and beckoned him. She closed the door so that he could not see what was in her stateroom.

"I have had the bad luck to be made miserable by a very severe headache," she said in her winning, pathetic Irish brogue. "Sure, an' would you be good enough to tell me if there is a doctor aboard?"

"Yassah, yassah, Mis' Dean," the boy chattered. "They suah is a doctah travelin' with us. I brung his baggage aboard my own self. Doctah Philip DeWitt Howe, accordin' to the way he signed the book. He's quartered on de larboard deck. I'll shoah fetch him."

" 'Tis a name that should belong only to a crusty old moth-eaten professor," Sherry commented. "No doubt he wears a beard and carries a cane and is near-sighted. At any rate I hope he is not the quack I suspect he will turn out to be with such a grand name. Summon him at once. And hurry!"

The boy hastened away. Sherry stepped back into the stateroom and closed the door. "You may be playing in luck," she told Britt. "But then they do say the divil takes care of his own. There seems to be a medical man aboard."

"I need a gun," Britt said from taut, ashen lips. "I lost mine tonight."

Sherry studied him somberly. She shook her head. "I have a gun in my handbag," she said. "But this is not the time for such things. I will keep it in my possession. You should pray that you do not lose your life, or at least your arm. A gun is not what you need at this moment."

She bent over Britt again with water, lifted his head on her arm so that he could cool his dry, hot lips.

Presently a hand tapped the door. Sherry moved the trunk again so that Britt was hidden, then opened the door a mere slit. She looked out at the man who stood there.

"I am Doctor Howe," the arrival said. "The cabin boy told me a physician was needed here."

CHAPTER 13

Sherry stared, taken aback. She straightened, her nose going up a trifle, as though she found something antagonistic in that statement.

Dr. Philip DeWitt Howe was neither ancient nor motheaten. Sherry's gaze traveled over his tall, lank length, marking the conservative cut of his business suit, and the style of the bowler hat, which he had removed in her presence. In his other hand he carried a medical bag. The bowl of a meerschaum pipe was hung in the corner of a coat pocket. He had a cultured voice with a very definite Boston accent. Sherry's nose lifted still higher.

"An Easterner!" she commented challengingly. "A tourist?" Her own voice had lost all trace of brogue.

Philip DeWitt Howe blinked, disconcerted. He was looking at Sherry in amazement, not expecting to be confronted by such a comely, coppery-haired, beautiful woman.

"Not exactly a tourist," he said uncomfortably. "I am traveling west, expecting to engage in practice in Montana."

"A Harvard man by the way you speak," Sherry said bitingly.

"I studied there, too," he said. "You don't seem to approve. Perhaps we're both wasting our time, Miss?"

Sherry opened the door just enough to admit him. "Come in, Dr. Philip DeWitt Howe," she said with icy politeness.

The tall young doctor hesitated, then stepped in. Sherry swiftly closed the door and bolted it.

Philip Howe now saw Britt. Startled, he glanced at Sherry. A frown began to pinch at his fine forehead. His dark eyes were puzzled, and a little annoyed. "I understood that it was a lady with a headache," he said.

"This is—is a friend of mine," Sherry said tersely. "He is badly injured and needs attention."

Phil Howe's gaze traveled over the stateroom. He looked at Sherry's opened baggage and the feminine garb that had been spilled about in her hurried search for material for bandages. He saw the wet, blood-smeared clothes that she had removed from Britt.

He walked to Britt, bent over him, then knelt for closer examination. He opened the temporary bandages that Sherry had placed.

Britt said nothing, watching this stranger, measuring him. He saw the frown deepen on Howe's face.

"A gunshot wound," Phil Howe said slowly.

"That's right," Britt murmured.

He endured Phil Howe's closer, disturbed expression. Britt's bristle of sandy whiskers was now matted with dried blood, and his hair was a wild tangle. He knew he was a tough, hard-looking figure.

Phil Howe, without a word, pulled off his coat, rolled up the starched sleeves of his white shirt. He spilled water into the basin, placed it handy, and drew a roll of bandage material from his medical bag.

"Please hold the lamp near so that I can see better," he said to Sherry.

She knelt with the lamp in her hand and Howe made a closer examination. Britt set his teeth against any sign of protest as the doctor's fingers probed.

"Considerable hemorrhage and shock," Howe finally muttered. "It is possible a rib may be fractured, though I doubt it. The bullet is lodged against the ulna in the left arm. Evidently it glanced along a rib, then struck in the arm. It must be removed at once, of course."

He straightened and looked around. "I can't operate here, naturally. I'll call the clerk and have him arrange a table and plenty of lamps somewhere. . . ."

"I prefer to keep the clerk out of this," Britt interrupted, each word an effort. "And everyone else except yourself and Miss Dean."

The frown returned to Phil Howe's brow. He turned and eyed Sherry questioningly.

She let her eyes drop in confusion. "It is this way," she murmured. "My friend had come aboard to bid me bon voyage. He presented me with a gun, urging me to carry it for protection. But I became confused while he was instructing me in the operation of the thing, and it discharged, the bullet striking him. You can see that this situation might be misunderstood. It is very embarrassing."

"I see," Howe commented. "Yes, I understand your viewpoint." His gaze traveled around the cabin again and lingered for a moment on Britt's clothes in the corner.

Britt saw distaste form in Phil Howe's dark eyes. That aroused him and he pushed himself up on an elbow. "Miss Dean is trying to make you believe she shot me in some kind of a lover's quarrel, Doctor," he said haltingly. "If that were really the truth, she would have said so without trying to act like a bad little girl who was afraid of being caught in a scandal. The real truth is that I was shot by a man I didn't even see. I know why he shot me, but that is another story. I fell in the river, but managed to drag myself aboard. I took refuge in Miss Dean's stateroom. It happens that Sherry is the kind of a person who stands by her friends. I took advantage of that knowledge and imposed on her for help."

"I see," Howe said again, a trifle helplessly.

"If you say that once more I will blow a boiler, Doctor Philip De Witt Howe," Sherry exploded. "A fine doctor you are, letting him lie there suffering while he protects my reputation."

Phil Howe gazed at her, a strange, wondering expression on his fine face. "So you're Sherry Dean," he muttered. "I've heard of you."

"I am flattered," Sherry said, her voice strained. "And what have you heard, may I ask?"

"No matter," Howe said.

Abruptly he made his decision. "Clear the bunk down to only a sheet, Miss Dean," he said tersely. "I will try to make out there."

Britt sank back. Phil Howe, no doubt, had decided that he had a wounded fugitive from justice as a patient, but he had overcome his scruples for the moment at least.

Britt pushed Howe and Sherry away when they came to lift him. "I climbed aboard this boat on my own power," he said. "I can make it across the room to the berth. I'm no baby. Turn your back, Sherry. You may have pulled the clothes off me, but there's a third party present now, and that makes a difference."

In spite of Howe's remonstrances, he walked to the bunk

unassisted, and pulled a sheet over him. "Carve away, Doc," he said with an effort.

A needle jabbed into his arm. "Hypodermic of morphia," Howe said. "Now just lie back and don't think of anything. Just relax."

Britt felt himself drifting off into a lethargy. Through that coma he vaguely knew that Phil Howe was working on his wounds. He heard the dark-eyed man speak to Sherry at times, asking for some surgical instrument or help, and the voice seemed to come from an interminable distance.

Pain stirred, but its impact was also dulled. At times the hallucinations returned. Ann Richards again walked through them with that betrayed look in her clear brown eyes. Then, it would be Sherry's hazel-green eyes and red hair that he saw, and Sherry was also warning him sadly against this trail of vengeance that he was following. And Leila's pale hair and inviting lips moved before him.

He aroused at times to full knowledge of pain and ordeal, and with the fear that he had been babbling names he had not wanted to utter. He tried to steel himself against such revelations, tried to fight off the effect of the morphia which robbed him of his will.

Phil Howe worked with precision, using probe and scalpel. Presently the bullet dropped from forceps into the china basin.

"Bone seems to be intact," Howe muttered with professional satisfaction. "This man has tremendous stamina. He's all muscle, and as supple as a cat. A very healthy specimen. That bullet had the force of a sledge when it hit him. The shock, alone, would have stopped the heart of a weaker person. Now, he's over the worst of it. You'll be surprised at the speed of his recovery. He'll be on his feet in a day or two, and in a week or ten days he'll be almost as good as new. He'll have to carry that arm in a sling for a while, of course."

Sherry said, "He had something to live for. Hatred is often a driving incentive for a human being to stay alive."

She was smoothing back Britt's hair as she spoke, soothing his forehead with her cool hand. He had been mumbling Ann Richards' name as well as her own. And he had spoken Zack Richards' name also.

She was watching Phil Howe closely. But if he had taken

85

any notice of those names, or of any of Britt's mutterings, he gave no sign.

Afterwards Britt drifted back to full consciousness again. Phil Howe sat in the chair, his pipe in his hand, watching him. Sherry was moving about, straightening up the cabin.

Britt made an effort to speak, and failed. Howe arose and stood over him. "You were fortunate, in addition to having a tough constitution," he said. "You're in for considerable pain and some fever tonight, my friend, but you should feel much better tomorrow."

Howe closed his medical bag, rolled down his sleeves and drew on his coat.

Sherry spoke, "You will report this matter to the captain, I assume."

"That is my duty," Howe said evenly.

"We must never forget our duty, must we?" Sherry said icily.

Howe reddened. "Miss Dean," he said rigidly. "You seem to have taken a dislike to me from the first instant you laid eyes on me. Just how, may I ask, have I managed to displease you so completely?"

"Why, Doctor," Sherry said with sugary sweetness, "you have been nothing but the perfect gentleman. Every inch of you—from your well-bred voice down to the tips of your fine, bench-made shoes."

Phil Howe looked down at himself, puzzled. "So that's it," he muttered. "You consider me conceited. A snob, in other words."

"Perish the thought," Sherry said. Suddenly, amazingly, she seemed near to tears. The brogue came back into her voice. " 'Tis only grateful I should be that so grand a gentleman would condescend to tolerate the likes of a notorious person such as Sherry Dean."

Phil Howe stood stricken and bewildered. He looked appealingly at Britt, as though for help. But Britt was gazing at Sherry, a startled, dawning discovery in his eyes.

Then Howe became angry. "Apparently," he exploded, "what the notorious Sherry Dean needs is a good, sound spanking. You've gone out of your way to patronize me and scorn me, and to ascribe thoughts to me that you can know nothing about. That's exactly it, a damned good spanking would be a lesson to you. You're vain and spoiled, and—and—you're the most beautiful creature I've ever seen."

He turned to stalk from the cabin. "Wait a moment, Doctor," Britt said. "This may help you in deciding whether to go to the captain. I was shot in the back, as I told you. It was the third attempt to bushwhack me lately. He will try again—if he learns I'm alive."

Phil Howe halted, looking at Britt grimly.

Britt said, "The point is, Howe, that I don't even know who this fellow is. That gives him a certain advantage over me. Otherwise it would be a matter I could settle easily."

"In other words I might be letting you in for another bullet in the back if I revealed the fact that you are aboard," Phil Howe said slowly. "That puts a rather heavy responsibility on me."

He gazed thoughtfully at Britt, considering. Suddenly he seemed to make his decision. He spoke to Sherry, his tone very brisk and professional. "I have left a laudanum pill on the commode, in case your friend becomes too restless. If necessary, call me. I am in cabin 203 on the opposite deck. In any event I will be back before breakfast to see how he is doing. Give him what water he needs during the night, and nothing more."

He opened the door, made sure no one was passing by. He said, "Good night, Miss Dean," and walked out, closing the door carefully behind him.

Sherry moved to her trunk and began making a show of arranging her wardrobe.

Britt said, "He won't talk."

"Apparently," Sherry said, her voice strained, "he found you more to his preference than he did Sherry Dean. He even seemed to respect you, even though he suspects that you are a lawless person, and perhaps a fugitive from justice."

"Where did you and Philip DeWitt Howe meet in the past?" Britt asked evenly.

Sherry whirled, staring, and there was almost terror momentarily in her face. "Sure, I never laid eyes on him before this moment," she burst out.

"Then it was someone just like him, wasn't it?" Britt said. "Someone he reminded you of. Someone with that aristocratic voice and way of handling himself. A gentleman, to the manner born."

The tears that had been just below the surface brimmed over in Sherry's eyes, staining her cheeks. "Don't!" she choked. "Please, Britt!"

"Who was he?" Britt went on relentlessly. "Who are you, Sherry? Don't let this thing fester inside of you any longer. No man is worth it."

She came with a rush, almost like a little girl, throwing herself beside the berth, burying her face in the sheet at Britt's side. With his uninjured arm he drew her closer.

"I turned a knife in an old wound, didn't I, Sherry?" he murmured contritely. "In your heart. Forget it. Don't talk about it if it hurts that much."

Sherry was torn by sobs for a long time. Finally she gained control of her voice. "Maybe you are right, Britt," she whispered. "Maybe it is better to talk—to someone."

She was silent a moment, staring at nothing. "There was an Irish girl named Mollie O'Toole," she finally said. "In Boston, she lived, with her father Patrick O'Toole, who was a ditch-digger, and with her mother, who took in washing to help provide for the children. Shanty Irish, they were, the O'Tooles, like the other shanty Irish in paddy town. But Mollie O'Toole had been gifted by God with a voice. She sang in the choir, and her father and mother, with the help of the priest, poor as they were, saw to it that she was given the chance to train for a singing career under very fine teachers.

"But along the way, Mollie O'Toole met a young and handsome and cultured gentleman. He was many cuts above the O'Tooles in the social scale, far, far above them. He had been born with a gold spoon in his mouth, and he was everything that Mollie O'Toole from paddy town had dreamed about when she dreamed about having a sweetheart. He was her knight on a white charger. And he said that he loved her as much as she loved him."

She was looking at Britt now, but not seeing him. She was seeing the past. Her mouth was a bitter slash in her pale face. Her voice was lifeless, as though she was reciting a story of the dead.

"They were to be married," she went on. "Mollie O'Toole stood waiting at the altar in her fine satin wedding gown which her father had sacrificed to provide and which her mother had made with her own hands. All of her friends were there in the church—all her friends from paddy town, and all her kinfolk. But there was hardly a handful on the groom's side of the church. And he, himself, did not appear to claim Mollie O'Toole as his bride. She waited, with the shame growing upon her, and he never came to fulfill the promise of love he had made to her. His father and mother had finally prevailed on him not to marry so far beneath his station in life. He obeyed his parents, and he let Mollie O'Toole wait there at the altar."

Sherry's voice began to break. "Mollie O'Toole never saw him again," she went on. "Never heard from him. Within a month he married another girl, a girl of breeding and refinement on his own social scale. And Mollie O'Toole's father and mother died within the year. Their pride was broken."

She quit talking. "How old was Mollie O'Toole?" Britt asked after a long silence.

"Just seventeen." Sherry's head now lay on his shoulder. She was cold, limp, exhausted. Mollie O'Toole, who was now Sherry Dean, the flaming, exotic, mysterious enchantress of the wild frontier, huddled against him, finding solace at last in sharing the secret of her past with someone.

Britt thought of the times Sherry Dean had ruined rapacious men with cold precision in poker games, and of the broken hearts she had left in her wake. He knew the reason now for this ironic vengeance that she was taking on men who attempted to match their skill at cards or at love with her.

"Strange," he murmured, voicing his thoughts, "that you would trust me enough to tell me this. And also that you would help me—against your own conscience."

She said nothing for a time. Then, with that quick impulsiveness that was her characteristic, she lifted her head, and kissed him. "At least you are a man who would keep a promise," she said. "A promise to wed, or . . ." Her eyes darkened, became almost a somber gray. ". . . Or a promise to kill."

She arose to her feet with that flowing grace that also set her apart from other women, and stood looking down broodingly at him. "Ann Richards is aboard this boat," she said slowly. "I saw her name on the passenger list when I signed."

Britt's head lifted. He drew a sigh of satisfaction. "That," he said fervently, "is the first good news I've had in a long time."

He sank back, the pain racing through him. Sherry tipped a water glass to his lips. "Do not ruin the innocent to gain your vengeance, Britt," she murmured tiredly. " 'Tis a method that exacts its own great price. Too great a price. Vengeance is bitter, and its reward is loneliness. Mollie O'Toole has learned that lesson."

She remained at Britt's side long after he had drifted into restless sleep. The *Dakota Queen* was on full wheel in mid-channel now, steaming upriver, her wheel taking its full and deep bite at the water. Soon the boat would be pushing its prow into the mouth of the great and wild and hostile Missouri.

The steady thrust of the engine was a powerful pulse, beating through the vessel. Sherry could feel that pulse moving in the deck beneath her feet. Britt, even in his stupor, was aware of it and responding to it. He muttered thickly, "Full ahead! Full ahead!"

Far, far ahead lay the plains where the Sioux and the Cheyenne waited. And somewhere in that hostile country was half a ton of gold, and perhaps a man who would kill or be killed, but never could be broken. Zack Richards.

Sherry shuddered a little, gazing at Britt's strong jaw and brows, seeing the purpose and the resolution that was almost an elemental force in him. She remembered that Zack Richards was like that, too.

Her lips moved in a prayer that she had learned as a child. She bent over, and her lips brushed Britt's forehead lightly again. He stirred, moaned, and muttered, "Leila— Leila . . ."

Then he fell into a deeper lethargy, and his breathing became harsh and feverish.

The whistle lifted mournfully overhead. The *Dakota Queen* was steaming steadily through a starlit darkness. The lights of St. Louis were already far astern.

CHAPTER 14

Britt opened his eyes. After a time the dullness cleared from his mind. Sunlight came through the small window. Its band moved across the small stateroom, touched the berth and was cut off as the boat swung, following the channel.

Sherry lay asleep on the hard cover of the locker beneath the window, wrapped in a quilt. His gaze seemed to arouse her, for her eyes opened. She sat up. "Good morning!" she said, her voice mellow with a woman's first awakening.

She came to him, gave him water. Britt drank thirstily. She felt his forehead. "You are better," she said. "You are not as feverish."

"If I'm better now I must have been in a hell of a shape last night," Britt said, his voice a mere croak. "My legs weigh a ton. I've got rocks pounding in my head."

He managed to lift his head enough to gaze around the stateroom. "Where are my pants?" he asked anxiously.

Sherry laughed. "In the river. They were beyond repair. I threw them overboard."

"Hell's fire!" Britt gasped, horrified. "What . . . ?"

"Be quiet!" Sherry commanded. "Sure, an' you are not dreaming that you can rise up from your bed and be fit as a fiddle so soon? I'll find pants for you when the proper time comes, my lad."

Britt had to accept that. His mind turned sluggishly to other matters. "Has anyone . . . ?" he asked, and then let the question remain unfinished.

Sherry shook her head. "No one has come to inquire about you. Evidently Philip DeWitt Howe overcame his principles and has not reported the presence of a wounded stowaway to the captain—at least not yet."

At that moment a knock came on the door. Britt glanced swiftly at Sherry. She hesitated. Then, as though it was against her better judgment, she lifted a gun from beneath the quilt on the locker and handed it to him. It was a pearl-handled .38, a beautiful gun but precisely balanced. A deadly gun. He understood that she had kept it close at hand during the night.

He murmured, "Thanks!"

Sherry called, "Who is it?"

She had hoped that it would be Phil Howe, keeping his promise to visit his patient at first rising. She feared it might be the captain coming to take a stowaway into custody.

Instead, it was a girl's clear voice that answered. "It's Ann Richards, Sherry. I came to say good morning."

Sherry drew a long, deep sigh of relief. She swiftly drew

the curtains on the lower berth so that Britt's presence was concealed.

He heard her open the door and exclaim, "A banshee it is I'm seeing. It can't be you in the flesh, Ann darlin', aboard this steamboat."

Ann Richards' laugh came. It was a pleasant, honest sound, musical and pleasing. Britt suddenly resented Ann Richards and her fresh, healthy, vital frankness.

"I made a sudden decision late last night to take passage for Fort Buford," Ann Richards was explaining. "I even brought along the dress I was supposed to finish and deliver to you before sailing last night. I still haven't finished it, but I will before we reach Buford."

"Let us stroll the deck while we talk," Sherry said. "It will be more pleasant. I have not yet had time to tidy up my quarters, and I am ashamed to let you see the disorder."

Britt sank back as he heard the door close. The faint sound of their voices faded as they moved forward.

It was evident there was a mutual liking and respect between Ann Richards and Sherry. They met as equals rather than as seamstress and patroness.

Britt lay there, thinking. It was all too clear to him the conflict that must be in Sherry's mind. She was caught between her obligation to him on the one hand, and her innate natural loyalty to the friendship she held with Ann Richards on the other.

Sherry was gone for some time. She did not look directly at Britt when she re-entered the stateroom, but busied herself arranging her wardrobe. Britt could see that her thoughts were far from this task. The conflict was plainly mirrored in her eyes.

"Dr. Howe will be here shortly," she said. "I had a word with him on deck. And I'm having the steward serve my meals here. You and I will share them. I am still pleading an indisposition."

Presently Philip Howe knocked on the door. He entered with professional briskness and said very formally, "Good morning, Miss Dean. How is the patient?"

"How do you do, Doctor," Sherry said, with equal formality.

Howe was carefully impersonal as he examined Britt and questioned Sherry about the patient's condition during the night. Finally he said, "Very good. Extremely satisfactory, my friend."

"You can call me Clay," Britt said. "Bill Clay."

Howe made no comment. He produced an object from a vest pocket. "Here is the bullet that hit you," he said, handing Britt a flattened pellet.

Britt inspected it. "A .45," he shrugged. "That's a very popular caliber. Thousands of 'em being carried."

"You take it casually," Howe remarked. "Apparently being shot is no novelty to you. I noticed two other old scars on your body. They looked like bullet wounds too."

"Yeah," Britt said. "I picked one up at Shiloh and the other near Vicksburg. Confederate sharpshooters. And you . . . ?"

Phil Howe shrugged. "Fighting was not included in my education," he said, and there was a regret in his voice. "I served in field hospitals."

"You may have to take a postgraduate course if this boat bumps into any Sioux war parties up ahead," Britt observed.

"So I understand," Howe commented. He finished redressing Britt's injuries. Sherry furnished a silk scarf with which he arranged a sling for the wounded arm.

He made ready to leave. He said to Sherry in his cultured voice, "Would you honor me by permitting me to escort you to supper this evening, Miss Dean?"

Sherry's expression did not change. "I am sorry, Doctor," she said. "I am taking all my meals here."

Phil Howe's tall body stiffened a little under that rebuff. He glanced at Britt. "I see," he said. "You are a fortunate man, Clay, to have so devoted a—a friend."

Then he left the cabin. Britt watched Sherry, but her face was inscrutable. "At least he has not gone to the captain," she said.

"I'll remove myself from your hands at first chance," Britt told her. "Then your conscience will be clear. I know how you feel about Ann Richards."

Sherry turned on him, a small fury blazing in her eyes. "Conscience!" she burst out, and laughed mockingly. "The notorious Sherry Dean has no conscience. She is the kind who entertains gentlemen in her cabin."

"The notorious Sherry Dean is a fraud," Britt said. "She is really a soft-hearted Irish girl who has tried to be bitter and hard. And what she really wants is to sing in a choir again. To be Mollie O'Toole once more."

"And to be patronized and treated as a plaything by the likes of such men as Philip DeWitt Howe from the upper-crust of Boston," Sherry said, her face now white.

"I pulled you from a sunken steamboat once," Britt said. "Any man would have done the same, Sherry. You know that. You owe nothing to me. You are free to tell Ann Richards who I really am. She will learn soon enough, anyway, that I am Britt Cahill. I can't stay hidden forever on this steamboat. Mead Jarrett will know me on sight. And there is Captain Ormsby. I can't expect them to keep it a secret—especially Jarrett. He and I never were exactly friendly."

"And Leila," Sherry said.

Britt's expression did not change. "We were talking about Ann Richards," he said.

Sherry smiled wryly. "Sure, and it seems that Ann Richards is in the same fix with me. The man she knows as Bill Clay saved her life, too. Not once, but twice. She told me about your first meeting at Pierre's. And then about the shooting in her dress shop in which Bill Clay fought against odds and killed two men in order to protect her from possible torture and death."

Britt stared. "Two men? Did she say two men? But one got away!"

"The one who ran also had a bullet in him," Sherry said. "Your skill with a gun seems to be better than even you know, Britt. The police, with their bull's-eye lanterns, found a trail of blood in the street. They followed it and came upon the body of the second man, dead, some distance from Ann Richards' shop."

"The one with pop eyes?" Britt asked unbelievingly.

"That is exactly the expression Ann used in describing him," Sherry nodded.

The significance of this suddenly hit Britt hard. He sat up, oblivious of the wrench of pain from his wounds.

"But that's impossible," he said. "He's the one—he must have been the one . . ." He broke off, staring at Sherry grimly. "Then who was it who shot me from the deck of this boat last night?" he asked.

"Apparently there must have been a third member of

this outlaw party," Sherry said. "One you did not see during the fight at the dress shop."

That seemed the only reasonable explanation. Britt sat frowning. That meant nothing was solved for him. If there was a third man, then he was aboard the *Dakota Queen*, no doubt, and in possession of the knowledge of Ann Richards' mission up the Missouri. Britt realized that he, as well as Ann Richards, was still in danger every instant.

CHAPTER 15

Ann Richards sat alone at a small table in the dining room, awaiting her breakfast order. The green hills of the state of Missouri were sliding slowly past, and the steady drive of the engine below came soothingly.

She was able now to take full stock of her situation. The past twelve hours had been a blurred and violent sequence that had uprooted her from the routine of her life. She should, she reflected, be trembling with apprehension. Instead, she was aware of an excitement within her that amounted almost to an exhilaration.

Deep within her something reckless and elemental and gratifying responded to the amazing things that had happened to her. It was good to be on her way to attempt to find her father—to meet this responsibility personally. It was good to be on the river again, with a steamboat alive beneath her. She had almost grown up on steamboats.

She smiled a little as she pictured what a shock it would be to the ladies who had patronized her shop when the news got about that Ann Richards had killed two robbers and had then mysteriously dropped out of sight, abandoning her business without explanation.

It would be a much greater scandal, she told herself, if these same people could know that she had deluded the police with the version she had given them of the shooting, and that she now carried a loaded derringer in her purse for her own defense, and had Bill Clay's .45 under her pillow in her stateroom, and that she believed she might have to use both those weapons before this was ended.

Her heart failed for a moment, as she was struck by the

realization of her feminine inadequacy. Alone, she admitted that she would have little hope of finding her father. She would have to enlist help at Fort Buford—experienced plainsmen or rivermen who knew the country. And she could see that this might offer difficulties if there was real Indian trouble on the plains.

That brought her thoughts back to the wide-shouldered, deeply tanned, blunt-jawed man who had called himself Bill Clay, who had entered her life in moments marked by gunplay and death, then had vanished again without explanation.

Indeed, he had never been entirely out of her mind since that hectic battle in her shop. She particularly remembered Bill Clay's stone-gray eyes. From the first instant when he had appeared at her shop she had a curious, instinctive sensation that his eyes held a fixed and hostile warning for her. Those eyes had said, almost as though he had spoken aloud, "Beware of me."

Her own eyes were thoughtful as she considered this. She had hardly slept at all during the night, lying in her berth, thinking and planning. Still, the excitement had overborne her lack of rest, and the shadows that lay beneath her eyes only brought out the clear, amber hue of their depths.

She wore a summery, striped full skirt that was a modification of the passing crinolined styles, a becoming cinnamon-hued jacket and a small chip bonnet with a spray of artificial daisies. It amused her remotely to realize that the habit of three years of earning her living as a dress designer remained with her and she had arrayed herself as carefully as though she was to meet possible future customers.

She knew she was winning glances from the male passengers. There was no other feminine diner in the room, and she was content to enjoy this monopoly for the moment. She was femininely pleased that she did not have to compete for attention with the gorgeous, titian-haired Sherry Dean, who had sidestepped a suggestion that they breakfast together.

A quirk of puzzlement formed above her nose as she thought of her meeting with Sherry earlier. Sherry had strolled the deck with her, and had listened to her excited, whispered story of the shooting at her shop. But Sherry had changed the subject each time Ann had started to explain

96

why she had made this sudden decision to take passage on the *Dakota Queen*.

Sherry's attitude worried and hurt Ann. It was as though she was suddenly being held at a distance by a friend whose help she had counted on.

Mead Jarrett strolled by on the promenade deck. He evidently had just come off duty in the pilothouse, for he wore the white gloves and black silk shirt that were the emblems of that aristocracy of the river. He bowed to Ann through the intervening glass window. Annoyed, she expected him to enter and insist on joining her, but he continued on by, strolling aft.

She toyed with the meal the mess boy set before her, a solid riverboat fare of fruit and steak and eggs and hot cornbread and cracklings, and small, crisp-fried catfish and a variety of preserves and strong coffee.

Leila Ormsby came into the dining lounge, followed by her father in his captain's brass buttons and blues.

Leila uttered a little squeal of delight and rushed to Ann's table. "Ann, dear! Having breakfast alone! How awful! You should have let me know. I took it for granted that you would rest late this morning after a midnight sailing."

"Good morning, Leila," Ann said, "and Captain Ormsby. Won't you join me?"

"An honor," Walker Ormsby said, as he seated his daughter, "even though it is usually the captain's privilege to confer the honor."

"Of course," Ann said. This little conceit was in keeping with Walker Ormsby's love of protocol and self-importance. He looked as if he had not slept well either, and palpably had drunk too much recently. The pouches beneath his eyes were marked with blotches of purple. His hands were very unsteady.

Leila, in contrast, seemed fresh and rested and immaculately turned out. She wore a flowered morning dress, full-skirted, tight-bodiced. This gave her a fullness of bosom and hip that was not entirely genuine, as Ann happened to know, having designed dresses for her in the past. Leila's pale golden hair was held in a snood, every strand perfectly disciplined and molded in place.

"Just a small portion of steak, rare, and the fruit," Leila told the mess boy. "And coffee. Lots of coffee."

She beamed on Ann and squeezed her arm. "It's so marvelous, having you with us," she said. "I do hope you rested well."

"Well enough," Ann smiled. She tried to match Leila's bright manner, but found that something inside of her drew away from the golden-haired girl. She wondered at this change in Leila. This was not the Leila she had known in the past. She was going too far out of her way to be enthusiastically friendly.

Ann told herself that her nerves must be playing her false, and that she was imagining all this. Surely, everyone could not be posing. First she had thought there was a warning and a danger for her in Bill Clay's eyes, even though he had saved her life. Then she had tried to find an insincerity in Sherry Dean. And now she was searching beneath Leila's manner, hunting for some inner motive for her effusive friendliness.

And Walker Ormsby's apparent lack of ease was due, no doubt, to his overindulgence. The man could hardly hold his coffee cup steady as he lifted it to his heavy lips. And he drank the contents to the bottom, scalding though it must have been. He barked at the boy for an immediate refill.

She was growing supersensitive, Ann told herself. She forced herself to meet Leila's warmth in the spirit in which it surely must be offered.

"And so you intend to meet your father at Fort Buford?" Leila was saying. "How nice. But I will surely miss you after you leave. I am going through to Benton."

"Is it true there is Indian trouble on the plains?" Ann asked. "I heard some of the passengers talking. They seemed to think . . ."

"Bosh!" Walker Ormsby exploded, slamming his cup on the table. "Utter nonsense! The Army is always yelling wolf. It's a piece of hokum to worm more money out of Congress. In any event Indians wouldn't have the sand to jump a steamboat, you can bet your bottom dollar on that."

"But I heard that they shot up the *Aurora*," Ann said.

"Some young bucks full of firewater," Ormsby snorted. "Fired a few shots and arrows from the brush, then ran like rabbits. Indian war! Poppycock!"

"Don't get your pressure up, Father," Leila smiled. "Ann knows there's no real danger. Otherwise she wouldn't be here, would you, dear?"

"At least I have a very healthy desire to retain all my hair," Ann shrugged.

"Let's forget about Indians," Leila laughed. "Finish your breakfast, Ann, and we'll go up to my cabin and gossip about clothes and people. It's nice on the hurricane deck, and this Missouri country is beautiful. Let's enjoy it while we can. I dread the monotony of the plains that we're facing later on."

Ann complied, with some inner reluctance, for she was not in the mood to match small talk with Leila. But she could not refuse without appearing rude. So she presently went above with the golden-haired girl and spent upwards of an hour in a patient attempt to interest herself in Leila's conversation.

She felt a trifle guilty when she at last seized a chance to excuse herself, for Leila was obviously doing her best to be gracious.

Returning to her stateroom she removed her bonnet and jacket and turned to the task of completing the unpacking of her luggage. She found that her thoughts had swung back to the mystery of Bill Clay as she busied herself with this homely duty.

Presently she became aware of an increasing sense of uneasiness—of something wrong. Then she placed its source.

The garments that remained in the partly unpacked trunk were not exactly right. She straightened suddenly, moving a step back from the trunk, frightened. Her alarmed glance sped around the room. She rushed to the clothes cubby, pulled the curtain and gazed at the dresses and other articles that she had hung there during the partial unpacking of the previous night. She turned to her smaller luggage.

Everything seemed to be in order, and yet not exactly as she had left them. She hurried to kneel beside the trunk and delve through its remaining contents to the very bottom. There she had hidden the belt of. gold that Bill Clay had brought to her shop and which he had forgotten when he left ahead of the police.

The heavy poke belt was still in place, but not precisely as she had left it. But now she was sure! Her trunk had been emptied, then repacked during her absence!

Every item she possessed had been searched thoroughly, even the garments in the cubby and her small luggage. She was positive of that now. Only her own sense of orderliness would have detected it, for the hands that had gone through her effects had been deft and neat, as careful as a woman's hands.

Ann again came to her feet. She was breathing fast now. She was thinking that, except for Leila Ormsby, the only other woman aboard the *Dakota Queen* was Sherry Dean. The intruder, of course, could not have been Leila, for she and Ann had been together for almost the past two hours at breakfast and on the upper deck.

There was no question in Ann's mind as to the purpose of this search of her belongings. Her hand went to the bosom of her dress where she carried the letter and the map that her father had sent her.

Her first impulse was to destroy the map, for its possession, she saw clearly now, was a source of deadly danger to her. And it offered the same threat to her father if it fell into the wrong hands, provided he was still alive. For whoever was after that fortune in gold would not want to leave Zack Richards alive to hunt them down in the future.

But reason prevailed in time. The penciled map that her father had drawn contained intricate directions, mentioning landmarks such as trees and ridges and river banks, and with distances and bearing points estimated in feet. There were general directions as to the location of the sunken boat that were easy to keep in mind, but she did not trust herself to memorize the intricate details.

She thought of taking the map to Walker Ormsby and asking him to lock it in the purser's safe. She even started for the door with that in mind.

Then she hesitated, reluctant to part with that paper, which—far more valuable than the gold to her—was the key to finding her father and possibly saving his life if he still survived.

Womanlike, she decided its present hiding place was the safest, there against her breast.

CHAPTER 16

Britt paced Sherry's stateroom. Darkness was coming again, and the *Dakota Queen* drove steadily northward on the long climb out of the timbered shores of Missouri. The boat was due at Council Bluffs at midmorning the following day. Beyond that lay the plains.

St. Joseph was astern. There the *Queen* had lost more passengers, because that border town seethed with talk of Indian war to the west. Only some fifty passengers remained aboard, and the majority of these were merely putting off their final decision until they reached Council Bluffs.

Britt had learned all this from Sherry, for he had not yet ventured from the cabin in daylight, although he had been on his feet since the first day of the trip.

As Phil Howe had predicted, his recovery was swift. He still carried his left arm in a sling, but even that would not be needed much longer. The injury along his ribs was healing cleanly and gave only an occasional twinge to remind him that the bullet had missed his heart by only a few inches.

Howe had gone ashore at Independence, and had bought clothes for him and a hat that he had not yet worn. He chafed at his confinement, driven by a caged impatience. He was waiting only for full darkness so that he could escape from the stateroom and breathe clean air on deck. Even so he would have to be careful, for it was too early to risk being identified. That dim shoreline that marched past was still the state of Missouri, and that meant he was still within reach of Missouri law.

However, he had no intention of remaining hidden for the duration of the journey. He had stayed this long only because of the determined insistence of both Howe, who was professionally concerned with his recovery from his wounds, and Sherry, who knew that he was risking the gallows if he was to land in the hands of the law in Missouri.

On the other hand it would be impossible to stay out of sight much longer, for the cabin boys and the clerk were certain to become suspicious of Sherry's continued pretense at an indisposition as an excuse for having all her meals served in her cabin, and would guess that she was harboring a stowaway.

Once they journeyed beyond Council Bluffs he would not only be beyond Missouri jurisdiction but would be moving farther away from any real authority. The only law beyond Council Bluffs was the power a man carried in his own

101

gun holster. And he had his own gun again. Sherry had handed him a new Colt .45 only that morning, exchanging it for the pearl-handled weapon she had first given him.

"You're the kind that feels naked without a holster gun on your hip," she had said dryly.

Britt guessed that she had induced Phil Howe to buy the gun along with his new clothes. He understood that Sherry had armed him with a weapon that he preferred only because of the danger that hung over him, the mystery as to who had tried to kill him that night from the top deck.

Sherry had not mentioned Ann Richards since that first morning. She evidently had not accepted Britt's invitation to tell Zack Richards' daughter that Bill Clay and Britt Cahill were one and the same, and that Britt Cahill was bent on vengeance on her father and was using her as a dupe to help him in that vengeance.

Instead, Sherry had reverted to the brittle-voiced, flamboyant siren of the riverboats and music halls. She was particularly flippant whenever Phil Howe came to dress Britt's wounds. She treated Howe with rigid decorum, matching his well-bred manners with a mocking pose as a grand lady.

Britt had seen the puzzlement and hurt in Howe's eyes as he winced beneath the form of torture that Sherry inflicted. And he had also seen a raging fury and resentment beneath the young doctor's poise.

"You're asking for it, you Irish hellcat," Britt had told Sherry only this same evening after Howe had left the stateroom, smarting again from her barbs.

"Asking for what, pray tell?" Sherry had asked loftily.

"For that spanking that Howe said you needed."

Sherry's brittle mask had slipped, and she was Mollie O'Toole again, for a betraying moment. "A spanking, is it?" she bristled. " 'Twould be beneath the dignity of Doctor Philip DeWitt Howe to engage in violence with the likes of me. And 'tis myself that would scratch out his aristocratic eyes if he demeaned himself by laying a hand on me."

"Don't push your luck too far," Britt had warned her. "That silver spoon in Howe's mouth has developed a pretty stubborn jaw, if you ask me. He probably has never laid a hand on a lady in his life, but there might come a time. Then you likely will find a pretty tough character beneath that polished shell he lives in."

102

"This is an aimless discussion," Sherry had said. "Turn your back. 1 am dressing for the evening."

She had presently said, "I am now respectable."

Britt had eyed the result with scowling disapproval. Sherry had donned the revealing black evening dress that she had worn for her last appearance at Pierre's the night she had come aboard. Her bare shoulders were perfection in pale ivory against the midnight hue of the clinging lines of the dress. Her slippers were adorned with sequins and brilliants, and had three-inch French heels. A bandeau of black velvet around her hair carried a diamond ornament.

"Is anything wrong?" she asked blandly. "Is my chemise showing?"

"It would if you had one on," Britt commented. "Everything else does."

"Why, darlin'," Sherry had beamed. "That is exactly the compliment I hoped for. I am going to the lounge for the evening. I may be late. Mr. Mead Jarrett has asked me if I would favor the passengers by singing tonight."

"What are you trying to prove by rigging yourself up like a fancy-woman?" Britt had snapped.

Sherry had drawn a scarf of sheer silk over her bare shoulders, picked up the train of her dress. "There is nothing to prove, darling," she had said. "I am concealing nothing—as you just pointed out." Then she had left the stateroom.

Now, Britt heard the piano strike up in the lounge. Sherry's rich voice joined in. She was singing the great, sentimental ballad of the Civil War, which had been the favorite of both the blue and the gray in the bivouacs.

> "A hundred months have passed, Lorena,
> Since last I held thy hand in mine. . . ."

Sherry's voice had the depth and power of an organ, carrying across the gathering darkness of the river to the wildness of the forested shores.

Britt stood there, thinking of Leila Ormsby. Always during these days aboard he had been aware that she was near, within reach. Now the longing to see her again was overpowering, as insistent as the throbbing yearning in Sherry's song.

Leila, he reflected, might be in the lounge where the passengers were gathered, but there was a possibility that she would still be above in her stateroom on the texas, alone.

Driven by his impatience he opened the door before making sure the promenade was clear, and stepped out.

That was a mistake. As he emerged he nearly collided with a person who was strolling by on the deck. Britt started a word of apology. Then he went silent.

It was Ann Richards. She also stood peering at him in the dim light from the deck lamps. She had a light scarf over her hair, and tied loosely beneath her chin, and wore a trim, dark dress.

"Bill—Bill Clay!" she breathed incredulously.

Her eyes moved to the open stateroom door, looked into the interior, where some of Sherry's belongings—feminine and completely damning—were in sight.

Her glance swung back to Britt and he saw a rush of shamed color in her cheeks. "Oh!" she said confusedly.

Britt, moving deliberately, closed the door. He stood waiting Ann Richards' next words. He knew what she was thinking.

"I—I can't believe it!" she stammered.

"Just what can't you believe?" Britt asked tersely.

"Why—why, that you are here, aboard this boat." She tried to be matter-of-fact, but even in the vague light he saw the embarrassed color growing deeper.

"I came aboard at St. Louis," Britt said stonily.

"I see."

Britt suddenly wanted to shake her. His anger, he realized, was childish. What did Ann Richards' opinion of him matter now or in the future? She was only a means to an end. Yet the impatience boiled in him along with the desire to set her right about at least one matter.

"No, you don't see," he snapped. "You think I've been living in sin with Sherry Dean."

She stepped back a pace, amazed by his vehemence. Then she bridled, her chin firming. It was very apparent that Ann Richards also possessed a temper. "I recall now that you had been kissed by an old friend at Pierre's before you came to my shop that evening," she said. "But I hardly imagined it was Miss Dean."

"Look . . . !" Britt exploded.

"You owe me no explanations," she interrupted him. "It is a subject that doesn't interest me in the least. But you can understand that I am curious about you, Mr. Clay. After all, you saved my life. Then you vanished. Now you have bobbed up again, and I have the chance to express my appreciation. Incidentally, I have a gun that belongs to you. Also a belt filled with gold. Come with me to my quarters and I will give them to you."

"Later," Britt said. "That can wait."

Ann Richards now discovered that his left arm was in a sling. "You've been hurt!" she exclaimed.

Britt nodded. "That same night. That bullet came a little closer. It knocked the ambition out of me for a few days. Sherry Dean was kind enough to take care of me until I got back on my feet."

"I see," she said again, her voice very neutral.

Again Britt fought the impulse to shake her. "Oh, hell!" he groaned. "Why is it that a woman is always ready to believe the worst about another woman?"

"I have already told you that your private affairs are none of my concern," she said stiffly.

"But there's another matter that does concern you," Britt said grimly. "Apparently there must have been a third man in on that affair at your shop that night. Sherry Dean has told me that they found the frog-eyed man dead later. But this other one must have followed me and he tried again to put me out of the way."

The temper faded out of her. The realization of what this meant began to dawn on her. "Oh!" she gasped again.

"At least you are able to figure out some things straight," Britt said sardonically. "I can figure, too. It seems as though this outfit aims to find your father, and to find him they've got to get their hands on that letter McLeod mailed at Fort Buford. If one of them is still alive he probably is aboard this boat. He would be here because he knows you are going upriver to try to find your father. He'll learn eventually that I'm still alive. But I'm not the only one he'll be hunting. If you'll stand for a pretty bad pun, Miss Richards, you and I are in the same boat."

Ann Richards shivered and instinctively moved closer to Britt, glancing fearfully up and down the deck.

"Who . . . ?" she whispered.

"That is what I would like to know," Britt shrugged. "There are nearly seventy men aboard this steamboat, counting the crew, and it could be any one of them. And maybe there's more than one. There's no way of knowing."

She became aware she was pressing so close to Britt that her shoulder was touching his arm. She drew abruptly away. Britt suddenly found himself acutely conscious of that contact. The red glow of an opened firebox flickered over the river, and in that reflection her hair was the hue of dark, molten copper. Deep worry lay on her face which was heart-shaped in the frame made by the knotted scarf. Trouble pulled at the corners of her mouth, a mouth that could be warm and soft with a woman's promise. He remembered again the firmness of her figure during that moment when he had protected her from the bullets at Pierre's. He recalled the litheness of her movements and the perfection of her legs during that fearful battle with the masked men in the dress shop. She was gorgeous. And she had iron in her fibers, like her father. Like Zack Richards.

That last thought came jarringly, bringing him back to the purpose that was responsible for his presence here. The red glow was cut off abruptly and they were again in semidarkness.

She spoke after a moment of thoughtful silence. "I imagine you have guessed there is something more at stake than my father's life, at least as far as these other persons are concerned. It would hardly be reasonable for men to attempt torture and murder and robbery unless there was something worth while—gold, for instance."

Britt saw where this was leading. He had to admire her courage. He answered with equal bluntness, knowing there was no use being otherwise. "I guessed as much," he said.

"Perhaps you knew about it from the very first, Mr. Clay," she remarked.

She put just a little emphasis on the way she uttered that name.

Then she said levelly, "Good night. Thank you for the information—and the warning. I will be on my guard."

She turned and walked forward. Britt watched her until she had moved out of sight on her way to her own state-room on the opposite deck.

Sherry Dean's singing had ended. The riffle of cards and the click of poker chips drifted from the lounge. The engine bell jangled faintly below as the pilot rang down to steerage-way while he puzzled out some dark stretch of channel. Soon the boat steadied and resumed her full drive ahead.

Britt stood for a time, thinking. Ann Richards, he realized, was suspicious of him and his motives. She had guessed that Bill Clay was not his real name, and she had as much as told him that his continual appearance in her affairs was more than mere coincidence. She was almost sure that he was interested in finding her father's gold. But she did not yet know that it was vengeance on her father that he really wanted. She did not yet know that he was Britt Cahill.

Presently he remembered the purpose that had brought him into the open deck. Leila.

He walked forward until he could see into the lounge. Several poker tables were in operation. Sherry sat at one, a champagne glass at hand, a stack of blue chips before her. It was a five-handed game. One of the players had the earmarks of a professional riverboat gambler. Two seemed to be well-to-do traders or merchants. The fourth man was Mead Jarrett, nattily garbed in gray waistcoat and breeches and a ruffled shirt with a flowery stock. Leila was not in the lounge.

Jarrett won a pot. He smiled and leaned close to Sherry, saying something in her ear. Sherry smiled back at him—the frozen, mechanical smile of a gambler.

Britt stood scowling, driven by the same urge to shake some sense into Sherry that he had held toward Ann Richards a few minutes earlier.

He turned away, knowing that Sherry would only fierily resent any interference. He moved aft and ascended the narrow companionway to the hurricane deck. It was deserted, and he walked forward to the texas.

Light showed in Leila's cabin. He tapped softly and heard her sure step come quickly to the door. It opened hurriedly, impatiently. Leila was becomingly dressed. The impatience that had brought her so swiftly to the door was burning in her face. There was a harsh and demanding rage in her eyes and in the taut set of her lips.

Leila had been waiting for more than an hour, expecting Mead Jarrett to come and escort her to the lounge for the evening. She had taken pains to look her best, and had paced the cabin, listening to the piano and Sherry's singing, while a shrewish, gnawing fury had built up inside her—the fury of a neglected woman.

All this was in her face in that first moment as she stood in the lighted doorway, gazing at him. Then recognition came. Her expression changed. For an instant her features were blank, inscrutable, as though walling him off from her emotions. Britt had an uneasy and sinking thought that the surprise was not pleasant to her.

Then a smile rushed to the surface. "Britt!" she cried out. "Britt! How in the world . . . ? What are you doing aboard this steamboat?"

She suddenly moved close to him and kissed him on the mouth. Then she drew him inside the cabin and closed the door.

"Britt! I can't believe it!"

Now she saw that his arm was in a sling. She uttered a little exclamation.

"Someone took a shot at me as I was leaving the boat that night in St. Louis after I had talked to you," Britt explained.

"How terrible!"

"The slug glanced off a rib and got me in the arm," Britt said. "The force of it knocked me into the river. I managed to crawl aboard later. I stowed away in the stateroom of a friend."

Leila was staring at him strangely, and Britt wondered if he was imagining startled speculation in her eyes. "Who shot you?" she asked quickly. "Did you see him?"

"No," Britt said. "The bullet came from this top deck as I was making my way ashore through the fuel barges that were moored alongside. Someone must have trailed me to the boat after that gunfight at Ann Richards' shop."

It seemed to Britt that Leila's thoughts were working on some other problem. And he fancied that she must have found an answer, for something that was almost like an amazed comprehension was in her eyes.

Then that was gone and she was only sympathetic. "You should have let me know, you poor dear," she said.

"I was in good hands and it was better to stay out of sight," Britt said. "You understand why."

"Who is this friend who helped you?" Leila asked.

"It doesn't matter."

"Tell me," she insisted eagerly. "I'm just dying of curiosity. And i'm offended, too, that you would turn to anyone but me for help, Britt."

"I'm here now," Britt smiled.

Leila squeezed his arm. "Of course. I'll forgive you this

time, my dear." Then she added significantly, "Do you know that Ann Richards is also a passenger?"

"I know," Britt said.

Leila pouted a little. "That is why you are aboard, isn't it?" She took the roughness off that with a little, chiding laugh. "I had hoped it might be another reason."

"You are one of the reasons, Leila," Britt said.

Leila laughed delightedly, hugged him swiftly. "It is a happy coincidence, for me at least, that both I and Ann Richards are on the same steamboat."

She became serious. "She is bound for Fort Buford to find her father, just as you had predicted."

Britt hesitated, not wanting to put the next question, "Leila, did you mention to anyone what I told you that night in St. Louis?"

Leila drew back, offended. "You should know me better than that. Did you think I would go to Ann Richards and tell her about you? I detest her."

Leila made that final statement with a vehemence that jarred Britt a little. Suddenly he regretted that he had come here. He had a sense of futility, of having found only a shadow when he had wanted a full substance. There was an elusiveness in Leila. He could not help remembering the way she had looked in that first instant in the door. Now, although he felt disloyal to her, it seemed to him that this bright and warm affection she was showing him was entirely on the surface, and that there were reservations and knowledge that she was carefully keeping hidden from him.

"I had better go," he said abruptly. "I don't want to be seen until we are well clear of Omaha. After that it doesn't matter."

Leila's lips brushed his cheek again as he moved to the door. She said, "Until next time, dear."

Britt's step was weary as he made his way below. He carried with him a dissatisfaction and an inexplicable uneasiness. Leila, he was certain, had known more about many matters than she cared to reveal.

And Leila, in her cabin, waited only long enough to make sure Britt had gone below. Then she hurried to the captain's cabin where her father was finishing off his nightly bottle of whiskey.

She carefully closed the door. "You may be interested in

knowing, Father dear," she murmured, "that Britt Cahill is aboard."

She watched Walker Ormsby's jowls suddenly turn the color of putty. "Cahill—alive!" he croaked. There was almost despair in his voice.

Leila's thin, long face took on a bloodless rigidity, and she was suddenly unattractive. In her expression there was none of the fear that showed in her father, but only an icy acceptance of a situation.

"I guessed right," she said, and she was voicing her thoughts more than she was speaking to her father. "I've wondered ever since we left St. Louis why you and Mead did not seem to be worried about Britt Cahill's whereabouts. Both of you have been acting like the cat that swallowed the canary."

Her eyes met her father's. She added in a murmur that was no more than a chill sigh, ". . . but now I know."

Walker Ormsby could not meet his daughter's eyes. "Does —does Cahill . . . ?" he began hollowly.

Leila shook her head. "No. He thinks he was shot by some person who doesn't even exist."

She went on with bitter relish, "At least this will spoil Mead's evening with that poker-playing Irish bitch. Some day I am going to claw out Sherry Dean's eyes. Then she won't be so fascinating to Mead."

She stood for a moment, measuring her father, seeing his uncertainty and weakness. There was a curl of contempt on her lips. She was thinking of the gunshot she had heard that night amid the escape of steam from the towboat's safety valve. She knew now that shot had been fired at Britt. She knew also who had fired it and why it had been fired.

She turned suddenly and left the cabin without another glance at her parent. Between them now was a new and damning secret—a knowledge of attempted murder—a knowledge that murder would be attempted again when Mead Jarrett learned that his other effort had failed.

CHAPTER 17

Ann Richards, after she left Britt, walked past the lounge, crossed the foredeck, and turned down the larboard promenade toward her stateroom. She saw the scene at the poker table where Sherry Dean in the revealing black gown sat like a vivid flame, matching her skill against Mead Jarrett and three other men.

Ann was shocked. She had designed that daring gown, but it had been intended only for professional use on the stage. This new brazen display on Sherry's part only confirmed the belief in Ann's mind that she knew the identity of the person who had ransacked her stateroom in search of the map.

She had originally been drawn to Sherry during their association as patron and dressmaker. It had seemed to her that there was a warm and deep honesty of character in the enigmatic Irish songstress, a basic integrity. And she had sensed there was loneliness and heartbreak in Sherry's life.

Now Ann distrusted her. Bill Clay, she was convinced, was after the fortune in gold that belonged to her father, and Sherry, apparently, was in league with him. Again Ann was gripped by a freezing knowledge of her own inadequacy against the forces that were arrayed against her. There was Bill Clay on the one hand to contend with, and then there was this mysterious third party who was trying to remove him from the competition.

She found herself fervently hoping that she was wrong about them. It seemed to her, forlornly, that if this Bill Clay and his level eyes, and Sherry Dean with her open-hearted manner, could not be trusted, then there was no one in the world who could be counted on.

A lone man stood leaning on the rail not far from the door of her cabin, puffing on a pipe and gazing off at the dim line of the shore. He was the young Boston doctor, Philip Howe, who had been introduced to her at the captain's table in the dining room.

Phil Howe turned, hearing her step, "Oh, Miss Richards," he said in his pleasing voice. "A beautiful evening."

Ann paused beside him, aware of her need for companionship and a man's strength. She also gazed for a time at the black river, watching the flashing ripples where the current broke in the torn wake of the boat, held by the same mood that seemed to weigh upon the tall doctor.

"What is it, Doctor, that brings you aboard the *Dakota Queen?*" she asked presently.

"Restlessness, the urge to see new country, the need for a beginner in medicine to establish himself where the field is

111

not crowded," Phil Howe shrugged. "But why I am aboard this boat in particular I don't know. Shouldn't I be?"

"I didn't mean to put it that way," Ann said.

"Something in the way you said it gave me the impression that you wish you were not here. Is it the Indians?"

Ann said wearily, "Indians I can understand. I know why they would try to torture and kill me if they got their hands on me."

Phil Howe eyed her wonderingly. "Now that's a strange statement. Are there others who would do those things to you?"

Ann hadn't meant to turn the conversation into such channels. "I'm having the vapors, Doctor. Don't pay any attention to me. Good night. I believe I will turn in."

"Hold on," he said, his hand halting her. He turned her to the light so that he could see her face more clearly. "A thought like that is nothing to take to your berth with you, Miss Richards. Imagination can be a terrible companion. As a doctor I prescribe staying up a while longer until these vapors are dissipated. A stroll might be the right antidote—for both of us."

He added slowly, "I have my moods, too."

He offered his arm. Ann accepted it almost gladly. "That stateroom is the last place I wanted to go right now, at least," she admitted.

Howe rapped the ashes from his pipe and they walked forward. As they passed the lounge where the poker tables were visible through the windows, she felt his arm tighten beneath her fingers. Sherry Dean was sitting facing them, and her eyes had lifted, seeing them. For a moment Ann saw Sherry's glance lock with Phil Howe's. Then Sherry turned away, saying something gay to Mead Jarrett.

They moved on to the forward rail, and Howe seemed to be lost in his own thoughts as they paused for a time, gazing at the river, a black, oily sheet that came sliding endlessly out of the darkness to meet the prow and be torn apart.

"Should we go above?" Phil finally asked. "I like the top deck at night. It's so free and wholesome. Nothing but the wind and the stars."

Ann took his arm again and they ascended the forward companionway. Their heads reached deck level, and they halted abruptly. They had arrived in time to see the man they knew as Bill Clay being kissed by Leila Ormsby in the

112

door of her cabin. Then Bill Clay entered the cabin and the door closed.

For the second time that evening Ann felt shamed color rise into her face, and Bill Clay was again the cause. She saw that Phil Howe's sensitive face was suddenly white and hard and angry.

Ann said, "I don't feel up to facing this wholesomeness you spoke about after all, Doctor. There seems to be more than the wind and the stars up here. I believe I will turn in now."

"Nor I," the doctor said, his voice taut.

He escorted her back to her stateroom. "You were right," he said. "Torture is not entirely the prerogative of the Indians. There are other forms of crucifying the spirit. Good night, Miss Richards."

Ann said, "Good night." She paused a moment in the door of her stateroom, watching him walk away. She realized that Sherry Dean and Bill Clay, somehow, had been responsible for his original somber mood, and that the scene on the top deck had plunged him into a new and deeper depression.

She saw him turn into the door that led to the bar at the rear of the lounge. Then she closed and bolted her own door. She made sure the curtains were tightly drawn at the single window. Next she got out the six-shooter that Bill Clay had given her and made sure of its action before placing it again beneath the pillow on her berth.

As she prepared for bed she envied Phil Howe's masculine privilege of seeking forgetfulness at the bar.

But the whiskey that Howe drank in steady, thirsty gulps was wasted. It had no effect on his mood. He gave it up at last, and returned to his own cabin, which was a few doors from the one occupied by Ann Richards.

He paused in stride as he entered, looking at the man who was sitting in the one splint-bottomed chair, awaiting him. It was Britt.

"You left the door unlocked, Doc," Britt said. "I would like to move in with you for a day or two if you don't mind."

Phil closed the door. He moved across the room, a blaze in his dark eyes, lifted a hand and slapped Britt across the cheek with a stinging palm.

Britt came to his feet, his fists knotted. He took a long, predatory stride, his face granite-hard as he measured the doctor with a fighter's ruthless purpose.

113

Then he halted abruptly, staying the swing of his fist. "Maybe I'll take that, Howe," he said slowly. "Maybe you think I really had it coming."

"I'm armed," Phil said. "And so are you."

Britt studied the tall doctor, seeing the blind fury in his dark eyes. "Have you ever drawn a gun in anger on a man, Howe?" he asked curiously.

"Nor in contempt of a man," Phil said, his voice obviously near the breaking point. "This will be the first time."

Britt carefully placed his hands in plain sight on the back of the chair. The sting of Phil's blow burned on his cheek in a crimson stain. He fought back the driving urge for retaliation and shook his head.

"I'll take that, too," he said. "Because you're wrong. Some day you'll know that, and ask Sherry Dean's forgiveness."

Bitter conflict raged in Phil. Britt met his gaze steadily.

"Who are you?" Phil asked hoarsely at last. "What are you to Sherry Dean—and to Leila Ormsby?"

Britt's glance thinned. He said nothing. He turned suddenly, moving toward the door.

"Where are you going?" Phil demanded.

"Not back to Sherry Dean's cabin," Britt said. "That was only a matter of necessity. Sherry couldn't refuse to shelter a wounded man. You can believe that or not, as you choose. But now I'm able to take care of myself."

The conflict still worked harshly in Phil. He made a helpless gesture. "The hell of it is that I really want to believe you," he said wryly. Then he spread his hands in defeat and pointed to the double bunk. "The upper berth is yours, Clay."

He added reflectively, "Perhaps it is because, as a doctor, I feel responsible for you. Perhaps it is because you are a mystery and a challenge to me, Clay. You are a fugitive from the law. I have guessed that much. You are aboard this boat for some desperate purpose. I've seen that in you, and I've seen it in Sherry Dean's eyes. She opposes that purpose, yet she is afraid for you at the same time. You are the kind beautiful women fall in love with—and would sell their souls to protect. There is a capacity for great violence and death in you. And compassion too. You could have killed me just now. I know that. I would have been no match for you at gunplay. You spared me."

114

He shrugged again and said, ". . . And perhaps it is because I want to believe I am wrong about Miss Dean."

CHAPTER 18

On the following evening Ann Richards walked the promenade deck alone, in darkness. The hour was growing late, and the few passengers who were left aboard were turning in for the night, but her cabin still held the sultry heat of the day, and though the night was still hot and still, the open deck was preferable.

The *Dakota Queen* was feeling her way along beneath a sullen shower of stars that glowed like small red sparks in a black dome. The only light came from the turned-down lamps in the companionways. Above decks the white gloves worn by Al Coe, the second pilot, moved, handling the wheel like disembodied members in the dark pilothouse. The easier, lower reaches of the river were astern and navigation was becoming increasingly hazardous. The *Dakota Queen* was proceeding in darkness only because of necessity. All lights that might impede the pilot in spelling out the channel had been extinguished.

Heat lightning flickered occasionally. It lifted the curtain of darkness momentarily, giving glimpses that were almost terrifying of a vast sweep of land, brooding and primeval in its silence. These were the Great Plains.

There had been no poker game on this night, no singing or conviviality in the lounge. An aura of suspense and tension lay over the *Dakota Queen*. Even the pulse of the engine seemed to reflect that mood.

Council Bluffs, from which the steamboat had shoved off at mid-afternoon, had fallen below the rim of the plains before sundown and seemed ages removed—a part of another world.

There the boat had lost all but a handful of its paying passengers. For Council Bluffs and its sister settlement, Omaha, a-clang with the traffic of the newly built Union Pacific railroad, had been jammed with refugees and a stemmed flood of travelers who dared go no farther.

Indian war! White men were fleeing the plains, seeking

115

shelter in civilized communities as reports of the rising tide of tribal fury mounted. There were stories of settlements burned and of men and women scalped, of wagon companies wiped out and of Army posts beleaguered.

The bulk of the passengers had abandoned the trip then, and some of the deck and boiler-room crew had quit. Little more than a dozen passengers remained aboard. These were mainly miners and traders who had urgent reason for risking the journey in order to return to profitable enterprises in the Montana camps.

But Leila Ormsby was still a voyager. So was Sherry Dean. An Army major had personally come aboard at Council Bluffs to point out that the upper Missouri was hardly the place for women this summer. He had advised Walker Ormsby and Mead Jarrett to abandon the Fort Benton trip altogether.

But Jarrett had laughed at him. "We've bought fifty new repeating rifles, my friend," Jarrett had said. "And ten thousand rounds of ammunition. We're lining the pilothouse and the engine room with boilerplate that will stop any bullets and arrows the Sioux want to waste on us. I assure you we will dock at Fort Benton on schedule. We have freight that we are under contract to deliver, and an obligation to any passengers who have bought fare to Fort Benton. We rivermen aren't as easily stampeded as the Army, you know."

The major had bowed stiffly. "I trust you are right," he had said.

The loaded rifles were racked in the lounge and engine room, made ready for use. Supper had been a silent meal that night. Leila Ormsby, particularly, had scarcely touched her food. Ann wondered why Leila had not gone ashore at Omaha. The fact was that she had wanted to, but Mead Jarrett had angrily forced her to stay aboard.

"If you quit, then Ann Richards may give up, too," Jarrett had snarled. "We've got a fortune waiting for us, and I don't intend to let it slip through our fingers. Your scalp isn't worth any more to you than mine is to me. You're seeing this through to a finish."

Ann's throat was tight as she watched the river and the eerie glimpses of the region through which they were traveling. She wondered if her father was alive or dead. The Indian danger was only another weight on the burden of doubt that lay on her mind.

Her cabin had been searched a second time while she had been ashore at Council Bluffs to do some shopping. And her reticule had disappeared almost from under her hand at the supper table only a few hours ago. Later she had found it in her cabin, apparently untouched, but she knew it had been searched.

But the map was still in her possession, inside her bodice, next to her skin. She had not seen Bill Clay since that glimpse of him entering Leila's cabin the previous night. And Sherry Dean had not appeared on deck all day. It was plain to Ann now that Sherry was avoiding her.

Phil Howe had not appeared for supper either, although she had chatted with him on deck during the afternoon. His manner had been reassuring, friendly. She began to hope that Phil Howe was at least one person she could confide in if necessary.

She stood at the forward rail for a long time, thinking in circles. Finally she aroused, deciding she would turn in and attempt to sleep.

She moved to the larboard deck, heading for her quarters. She pulled up suddenly. Two men stood leaning on the rail amidships, smoking. They were in darkness, but were silhouetted against the subdued light that glowed from the aft entrance to the companionways, and she recognized them.

Phil Howe—and the man she knew as Bill Clay. Like herself they were taking advantage of the cooler air on deck. But it was their presence together that shocked her. She was in such a state of mind that her first thought was that now she could not even trust Phil Howe.

She started to turn, intending to retreat and wait until the way to her stateroom was clear, for she shrank from this meeting.

She halted again, staring frozen for a moment. A shadow had moved in that lighted entryway beyond the two men. Whoever moved there was between the lamp and the opening. But the shadow was only a blurred, unidentifiable shape.

Then, sharply outlined, she saw an extended arm, clutching a gun, and the shape of a man's head appear around the corner of the opening.

Someone was crouching there, leveling the weapon down the promenade at one of the two men who stood with their backs to this danger, unaware of their peril.

"Bill Clay—look out!" Ann screamed the warning shrilly, instinctively, her voice shattering the peace of the night.

The gun exploded. Its muzzle hurled a long lance of flame along the deck. The concussion hit her eardrums with heavy impact. But she saw that Britt—Bill Clay to her—had moved, leaping aside, an instant before the shot came. He had sent Phil Howe sprawling also with a thrust of his arm. She heard the bullet glance from a stanchion near where she stood.

Britt's gun was in his hand as he dropped flat. He rolled to bring it to bear on the point from which the shot had come. "Stay down, Doc!" he ordered tersely.

And over his shoulder he said, "Get in the clear, Miss Richards."

But the entryway at the rear was vacant. No shadow moved there against the soft lamp glow. The arm and the extended gun and the shadow of part of a man's head had vanished from the corner of the opening.

"He's—he's gone!" Ann said shakily.

Britt came to his feet. He moved down the deck slowly, warily, his gun ready. He edged into the lighted opening. The entryway was deserted. A narrow corridor led through to the starboard deck, and companionways led both above and below. Whoever had fired at him could have escaped by any of three routes.

Phil Howe appeared, also carrying a six-shooter in his hand. He looked questioningly at Britt.

"I'm all right," Britt said. "That one missed."

He walked back to where Ann stood. "Did you see who it was?" he asked.

"No," Ann said shakily. "I saw the shadow and then realized he was pointing a gun. But I couldn't make out anything more."

Mead Jarrett came running to the scene from forward, followed by Walker Ormsby. Other passengers were spilling from the cabins, rifles and six-shooters in their fists, shouting confused questions.

Britt lifted his voice. "It's all right, men. That wasn't an Indian attack. Just a little private target practice."

"Target practice?" a passenger howled indignantly. "This is one jumpin' hell of a time to brush up on yore shootin'."

Mead Jarrett was peering at Britt. "By all that's holy!" he exclaimed. "You! You, in the flesh! This is a surprise!"

118

Britt said evenly, "Hello, Mead."

Jarrett stood frowning at him, started to say something, then seemed to think better of it. He turned and began calming the passengers.

Britt waited while Jarrett and Walker Ormsby soothed the ruffled feathers of the aroused sleepers and herded them back to their quarters.

Phil Howe waited also. And so did Ann Richards. She was gazing at Britt curiously. He saw that she realized she now might learn more about him. He resigned himself to the inevitable.

Jarrett and Walker Ormsby finally returned. They gazed at Britt for a time, thinking. Jarrett automatically drew out his deck of cards and his fingers began manipulating them while he considered this problem.

"I hardly know what to say," Jarrett began at last. "I suppose, according to the law, we should put you under arrest."

"Arrest?" Ann exclaimed. "For what?"

Jarrett looked at her in amazement. "Do you mean to say you don't know this man? Why, this is Britt Cahill!"

Britt saw the shock of that build up in her as her mind grasped the full significance of that revelation.

"Br—Britt Cahill!" she repeated numbly.

"It seems that you've heard of him at least," Jarrett said dryly. "I recall now that you were away at school during the time the Cahills and your father were bucking each other. But you were aboard the *White Buffalo* the night Cahill's steamboat was lost, and you were in St. Louis when the fire . . ."

"Yes," Ann said, her voice a mere whisper. "But I had come aboard the *Buffalo* only at Independence. I had just arrived back from school and came upriver to join Dad. I—I never laid eyes on Britt Cahill in my life before—before tonight. At least to know that he was Britt Cahill."

Britt winced a little at the dead disillusionment in her eyes. Then she laughed wildly, almost hysterically. "But—but this explains everything!"

Suddenly she turned and ran to her stateroom a few doors down the deck. The door slammed and then there was silence.

Britt said nothing. He watched Mead Jarrett and Walker Ormsby. He had the distinct impression that his presence aboard had been no real surprise to them. That meant, of

119

course, that Leila had told them. He could understand that. After all, Walker Ormsby had been the one who had helped him escape from a lynch mob that night in St. Louis. Knowing that, Leila had seen no harm in confiding in her parent.

Walker Ormsby now said accusingly, "You place me in an embarrassing situation, Cahill."

Britt nodded. "I understand, Sir. However, it won't be necessary to place me under arrest. Or in confinement at least. I would hardly want to leave the boat. They say a man's scalp isn't safe ashore."

Mead Jarrett flashed his ironic smile. "On the other hand it seems to me you would prefer to take chances ashore rather than face the certainty of going to trial for murder by staying with us," he shrugged. "We, of course, will have to turn you over to the law at the first opportunity, Cahill. We have no choice."

"I would object to being put in irons, if that is what you are driving at, Mead," Britt said evenly.

A small and greedy interest began to quicken in Jarrett's ice-pale eyes. He glanced at Britt's holster. "I might overrule your objection, Cahill," he said softly.

There was a sudden, edged silence. Britt stood slack, his hand hanging near his gun, ready for any move. He had seen that lust in the eyes of one or two other men in the past and knew what it meant.

He said, "You've changed in the three years since you were a pilot for Zack Richards, Mead. That sort of thing grows on a man, doesn't it. It's like taking dope."

"What sort of thing?" Jarrett asked slowly.

"Killing. The urge to add another notch to your score. I hear you've grown very handy with a gun, Mead."

"Now, now," Walker Ormsby croaked in alarm, and stepped between them. "Let's keep our heads."

He looked at Britt, aggrieved. "You had no call to talk like that to Mead." He lowered his voice to a whisper. "I helped you once, Cahill. That was for my daughter's sake and against my better judgment. But I do not feel that I can shield you again."

Britt's gray eyes were flat—waiting. Walker Ormsby saw this and added hastily, "However, I am sure there's no need for putting a guard over you. After all, we're not policemen."

120

He turned to Jarrett. "We will think this matter over. I doubt if Cahill would attempt to leave the boat."

Jarrett shrugged. "Very well," he said. "I'll overlook that remark you made, Cahill—for the time being, at least. However, I feel that Captain Ormsby is permitting sentiment to sway his better judgment. Any attempt on your part to take sudden leave of us will be unfortunate. I will give orders to the deck watch to shoot you if you try it."

Jarrett regarded Phil Howe a moment with his cold smile. "You seem to have fallen into rather strange company, Doctor," he commented. Then he turned and walked away.

Walker Ormsby followed him, mumbling querulously, "A hell of a mess."

Britt stood for a time without moving. Then he looked at Phil. The young doctor's gaze was unreadable.

Britt said grimly. "So now you know."

"So now I know," Phil murmured. "Who was it that was murdered?"

"A night watchman for a steamboat company in St. Louis that was owned by Zack Richards," Britt said.

"Richards? Then . . . ?"

"Yes," Britt nodded. "He is the father of Ann Richards. You saw the effect on her just now when she learned that Bill Clay was really Britt Cahill."

"Then you and Miss Richards had met before tonight?"

"Once or twice recently. She knew me only as Bill Clay."

"Tell me more about this murder," Phil said quietly.

"A safe in the office of Zack Richards' steamboat company was robbed of around a hundred thousand dollars, mainly in gold. A fire was started to cover the murder and the robbery. The fire spread. It wiped out Zack Richards and it took half of the St. Louis waterfront before it was stopped. Zack Richards says he saw me leaving his boatyard, where his office and warehouses were located, just as the fire broke out."

"And was it really you he saw?" Howe asked in that same quiet tone.

"A man wouldn't put his own neck in a noose by admitting murder," Britt said. "Innocent or guilty, I would claim Zack Richards lied. You know that. Why did you ask that question?"

"Because I wanted to see how you answered it," Phil

said. "I am a little vain about my ability at judging a man's sincerity."

He laid a hand on Britt's arm. "You need a drink."

"Do you mean you'd be seen drinking with a known murderer?" Britt asked grimly.

"Let's put it this way," Howe said. "A man is entitled to the benefit of the doubt." He added thoughtfully, "And so is a woman."

He continued, "This fellow Jarrett is another proposition, however. Everything he said, every move he made tonight, was counterfeit. He wasn't as surprised as he tried to pretend at finding you aboard, for one thing. Tell me more about him, Clay—or Cahill, I should call you now."

CHAPTER 19

In her cabin Ann Richards heard the footsteps of Britt and Phil Howe recede down the deck and turn into the bar. She had listened to the faint, unintelligible murmur of their voices and had strained her ears to make out the gist of it, but had failed.

She finally made ready for bed, and climbed into the berth. She lay a long time, thinking. It seemed certain now that Phil Howe was allying himself with Britt Cahill.

In spite of that she felt that her own situation had improved. Britt Cahill was as good as in jail, for she had heard enough of the louder conversation with Jarrett to understand that Walker Ormsby and Jarrett meant to turn him over to the authorities at the first opportunity.

Her hand again went reassuringly to the map which she had pinned inside the bosom of her nightgown. There was no longer even a shadow of a doubt that Britt Cahill had been after that map the night he appeared at her dress shop. And that was why he was aboard the *Dakota Queen* now.

It was all plain enough. Cahill evidently was insatiably bent on hounding her father because of the sinking of his steamboat three years in the past. By common report she believed that he had already once bankrupted Zack Richards by murder, robbery and fire; also that he had escaped with a fortune in gold from her father's safe in that first vengeful blow, and still was not satisfied. She thought he meant to rob Zack Richards again.

Uneasily she found a flaw in that line of reasoning. Cahill's garb and appearance—everything about him—hardly fitted that of a man who had once been in possession of a hundred thousand dollars in gold. He looked as if he had led a hard, hand-to-mouth existence these past three years.

She went over in her mind the latest attempt on Cahill's life. Someone wanted him dead. For want of better explanation he believed that it was some mysterious partner of the pair who had previously tried to assassinate him before he had killed them in the fight at her shop.

Ann now doubted this. She intuitively felt that whoever was attempting to put Cahill out of the way had some other reason, some motive that Cahill did not understand, and which might have no connection with his knowledge of the sunken boatload of gold.

That assumption simplified her own problem, at least. She felt now that she had only Cahill—and possibly Sherry Dean—to fear. And Cahill, if he escaped death at the hands of this unknown foe, would eventually be in custody and facing trial for his life. Ann shuddered a little. That startled her, made her feel ashamed and almost disloyal to her father. Certainly Britt Cahill rated no consideration.

Sherry Dean, she reflected, might be a factor to consider, but she had confidence in her own ability to outwit any woman.

She finally fell into heavy, exhausted sleep. She was still asleep in the black hour just before dawn when the door of her cabin opened silently. She had bolted the door, but she did not know that the screws that held it in place had been tampered with so that they would yield under pressure.

A figure, wearing a flour-sack mask, entered the room, moved to the berth. A man's hand clapped over Ann's mouth, pinning her down. A hand ripped open her nightgown, exploring for the map—and finding it!

Ann tried to scream, but she was helpless, smothering, held down by a strength she could not combat.

She knew the map was being torn away, knew that her nightgown had been ripped from her shoulders until she was virtually naked.

Then a wadded cloth was forced into her mouth and tied.

She was thrown face-down on the berth and a gunnysack was yanked over her head with brutal force and lashed around her, pinning her arms.

In the next instant she realized the intruder was gone. It was many seconds before she could force out the gag, and it was minutes before she could find the strength and the breath to struggle.

She finally fought free of the gunnysack. She fell gasping, retching to the floor of the unlighted stateroom. The door stood open, and she could see the dark shoreline sliding past near at hand as the *Dakota Queen* followed a channel close to the river bank.

She drew her breath to scream, but halted. Screaming, she realized, was wasted effort now. No one above decks had been aroused by that brief, silent intrusion into her quarters. There was no sign of alarm from the deck. The only sound was the unhurried beat of the paddle wheel, and the clang of a fire door below.

A seething fury galvanized her. She came to her feet. "Damn—damn—damn him!" she choked.

She tore off the remnants of the nightgown and seized up a dressing gown. Then she fumbled for the big .45 that Britt had given her and found it still beneath the pillow on her berth.

Barefoot she raced from the cabin and ran to the starboard deck. The fury burned in her, and it was not until she reached the opposite promenade that she realized that the gown was flying open, trailing out behind her as she ran. But not even the deckwatch was in sight to appreciate that sight.

She angrily drew the gown about her, moored it down with the braided sash cord. Her bare heels hammering the deck, she continued racing vengefully to the cabin that Sherry Dean occupied.

She paused before the door an instant, placing an ear to the panel. She could hear nothing. The interior was dark.

She rapped on the door with peremptory knuckles, and then with the handle of the gun.

Sherry's sleepy, startled voice demanded, "What is it?"

"Open this door!" Ann commanded grimly. "It's Ann Richards. Open it or I'll shoot off the lock."

That brought swift motion. She heard Sherry's feet hit the floor. Then the bolt rasped and the door opened. Sherry

124

was wearing a silk night shift. A dim figure in the faint light, she stood peering out in amazement. "By the saints, darlin' . . ." she began.

Ann pushed past her, stepped inside, peering around in the darkness. "Come out!" she demanded. "I know you're here. Come out!"

"What is it, Ann?" Sherry implored. "In the name of heaven, have you gone daft? Who . . . ?"

"Light the lamp," Ann ordered.

"That I will do," Sherry said, her own temper beginning to flare in her voice. "That I will do indeed."

She moved about. A sulphur match flared and the lamp wick soon glowed and steadied. Ann walked around the stateroom, the gun in her hand, peering into the clothes cubby and back of the trunk and into the upper berth.

She wheeled on Sherry. "Where is he?" she demanded.

Sherry had watched this, and her own resentment suddenly faded. "Is it Britt Cahill you intend to shoot with that ugly weapon you are brandishing, Ann dear?" she asked gently.

"So you're brazen enough to admit that you know him by that name," Ann said.

"The whole boat knows it since the shooting earlier," Sherry said mildly.

"But you knew who he was long before that," Ann said.

"Yes." And Sherry offered no other explanation, nor any apology.

"Where is he?" Ann asked again, her voice frigid.

Sherry inspected her carefully. "He is asleep, no doubt in the cabin that is also occupied by the high-nosed doctor from Boston, Philip DeWitt Howe."

"Doctor Howe's cabin?" Ann was taken aback.

"Britt changed quarters once he was able to stand on his own feet," Sherry explained. "He never did feel, shall we say, comfortable here with a red-haired roommate."

Ann glared at her an instant. Then she turned and raced through the door and hastened back to the opposite deck. She found that Sherry was following her, pulling a cloak over her nightdress.

The first faint hint of dawn tinged the sky to the east. Ann reached the door of Phil Howe's stateroom, and once more she rapped until she brought a response. It was Howe's voice that answered.

She said, "Open up! I want to talk to you, Doctor."

The door opened and Howe, wrapped in a smoking gown, stood staring at her. "What is it, Miss Richards?"

Beyond him Ann saw the shadow of Britt in the background. Then Britt stepped into better view in the dim light at the doctor's' side. He had pulled on his trousers, but was bare above the waist. Ann, even in that moment of stress, saw that his chest was as brawny as his jaw. He had a six-shooter in his hand.

Ann tried to read their expressions, expecting to find signs of guilt, but it was impossible to see clearly in that dimness.

"How long has Britt Cahill been here?" she panted.

"Here? You mean in this cabin? Why . . ."

Britt pushed Phil aside and faced Ann. "What happened?" he demanded, his voice rough. "Why did you ask that?"

"A man broke into my cabin not many minutes ago, tore my nightgown from me and stole a certain letter from where I carried it," Ann said bitterly.

"You mean—the map?"

"The map," she raged. "And you were the man who stole it!"

There was a dead silence. Then Phil said, "I don't exactly understand what you two are talking about, but if something was stolen within the last few minutes from your cabin, Miss Richards, you are wrong in accusing Cahill. He has been asleep here for hours. I can vouch for that. He could not possibly have left my stateroom and returned without awakening me."

Sherry placed an arm around Ann's waist. "Darlin', you're all worked up. Let us talk this over, and . . ."

Ann jerked away from her. She stared wildly from Britt to Phil and then to Sherry. "You're—you're all in this against me!" she sobbed.

Then she turned and raced to her stateroom.

Britt met Sherry's gaze. "Now what is it to be, Britt?" Sherry asked sadly. "She's so alone—and in danger of her life."

Then Sherry also walked away, back to her own quarters.

CHAPTER 20

Council Bluffs was more than a week astern. The last tiny, isolated settlement, barricaded and fearful, was also past and receding into memory.

For days the *Dakota Queen* had seemed to hang suspended in an empty, alien world. The paddle wheel revolved, the wild and mysterious river came rushing endlessly to meet the prow, but there had been no real sensation of progress.

On either hand the plains had stretched vacantly to meet a far horizon that was formed by the empty, inverted hot bowl of blue-gray steel that was the sky. Buffalo grass covered the swells like the close-grown wool of an animal. Where it was ripening under the blaze of the summer sun the grass showed a yellowish-brown hue. Lonely buttes lifted tawny summits against the horizon and the flanks of wind-carved ridges and drying streambeds presented a bleached, bone-white tracery across the face of this land.

It was akin to the sea, limitless, impersonal, unconquerable. Each turn in the river had brought a vista that was exactly like the one just passed. And the river itself matched the land in its aspect of untamed ferocity. Fanged with rapids and snags, it rushed savagely between barren cutbanks as though fighting to escape from this hostile world.

Occasionally thickets of willows and stunted cottonwood had broken the monotony of the sterile cutbanks. But beyond, the loneliness was vast and pitiless. An eagle drifting high in the bowl of the sky, the far and primitive yammering of a coyote, the distant flash of the rumps of antelope, and once, far away, scattered brown-black dots that were buffalo, the advance guard of the northern migration. These things only accentuated the emptiness of the land.

Nothing human had moved in that vastness through which the *Dakota Queen* had labored as though on a treadmill.

Now, for the past day the outlook had been gradually changing. The steamboat was entering rougher country. Timbered ridges showed in the distance and the shores were losing their barren aspect and becoming increasingly wild with brush and trees. Mountain elk whistled at dawn. A big gray timber wolf had stared with yellow eyes at the steam-boat from a sand spit during the afternoon.

Britt walked to the foredeck, leaned on the rail as he finished a brown-paper cigarette. Twilight was at hand and that, at least, would bring relief from the stifling heat of the day.

His wounds had almost healed. The injury in his side gave him no trouble, but he still had to favor his left arm somewhat, though it was strengthening rapidly.

Sherry sat alone in the lounge, her head bent over a game of solitaire. That had been her only pastime lately, for there was no one now aboard who cared to match his skill against her at poker. The piano had remained covered since that night before the Council Bluffs arrival.

Britt could see Phil Howe at the bar, sipping his inevitable whiskey and mineral water. He spent the greater part of his time there now, though Britt guessed that he was not by nature a drinking man. Like Sherry, he had grown silent and uncommunicative toward Britt, keeping his thoughts to himself.

Ann Richards probably was in her cabin. She stayed close to her quarters, and had avoided Britt and Sherry and the tall doctor since the night the map had been wrested from her.

But she had not been able to escape meeting Britt face to face at times on deck or in the dining room, for he had the run of the boat. She had showed him nothing, neither fear nor scorn.

Occasionally she and Leila strolled the decks together, but it seemed to Britt they did not have much in common. Britt had seen Leila alone only once since the night he had gone to her cabin. He had talked to her on the top deck the previous night.

"Dad is sorry for you, Britt," she had said, "but he feels he has done all he can for you."

"And you only feel sorry for me, too, Leila?" he had asked.

"Now, you're trying to pick a quarrel," she had said petulantly, and had left him and gone to her cabin.

In any event Walker Ormsby still seemed undecided about his promise to turn Britt over to the law. There had been opportunity, for the *Dakota Queen* had stopped at Fort Lincoln, an Army post aswarm with preparations for the campaign against the Sioux. But nothing had been done.

Now, as he stood at the rail, he was thinking of that shadowy figure that had fired at him the night Ann Richards' warning had saved him. He had scanned every passenger, every member of the crew, attempting to see something in them that would connect them with the attempts on his life, without result.

Sherry swept up her cards, looked around with bored expression. She saw him on the foredeck and came walking to join him. She wore a cool, short-sleeved, simple cotton dress, and had her hair caught with a ribbon at the back in a ponytail style. She might have been a young, pretty miner's wife, shapely and demure. There was little of the flaming, rouged music-hall entertainer in her at this moment.

She placed her elbows on the rail alongside his, and asked, "What day is this, and where are we, pray tell?"

"Thursday," Britt said. "We passed the mouth of the Little Missouri during the day. We should dock at Fort Buford by mid-afternoon tomorrow. Jarrett will probably decide to keep going tonight, for the moon will be nearly full. The river is falling and he'll have trouble making Fort Benton unless he keeps pushing along."

He added, "But right at this moment he's aiming for a woodcutters' camp at String Creek. He's hoping the choppers haven't lit out for safety, for we're running low on fuel. String Creek should be showing up any minute."

"Fort Buford next ahead," Sherry murmured. "Then somewhere between here and there we should pass the place where Pete McLeod left Ann's father and the sunken mackinaw boat?"

Britt said levelly, "Yes."

Sherry was silent for a time. The course of the Missouri was directly westward at this point. The sun had been swallowed by the rims of distant ridges. Dusk was pooling in deep purple shadows on the brushy shore. The crests of ridges to the south were burning blood-red in the afterglow of sunset.

Jarrett was in the pilothouse, steering a channel that carried the steamboat within a short pistol shot of the gloomy shore. Sherry inspected this somber prospect and shivered a little in spite of the lingering heat of the day.

" 'Tis a place only for ogres and leprechauns," she murmured.

Still, the fears of the company in general had lessened as day after day had passed without the slightest sign of danger. It seemed that Mead Jarrett had been right. If there were Indians about, they apparently had no stomach for tackling a steamboat.

But, to Britt, the very desertion of the land was a warning rather than an assurance. He had a rifle leaning against the rail close at hand and his pistol was slung in a holster on his thigh.

He watched the shore, peering for some sign of the woodchoppers' camp. The chances were no more than even that they would find either fuel or men at the place when they located it, for it was probable that the Indian trouble would have sent them out of the country weeks ago. In that case it would be up to the crew and passengers to cut their own fuel, for the boiler supply was too low to carry the *Dakota Queen* the remainder of the way to Fort Buford.

Mead Jarrett impatiently pressed the whistle treadle, and the *Dakota Queen's* hoarse voice lifted a roaring challenge through the evening silence.

Britt frowned. Using the whistle was a needless display of bravado on Jarrett's part. Better in this region to proceed as quietly as possible.

The twilight deepened and the *Dakota Queen* cruised forward for another five minutes. Then Britt straightened and said, "There it is!"

A clearing showed ahead, where a tiny tributary joined the main river. A small pier jutted drunkenly from shore on stilts. On the bank stood a log shack and ricks of fuel, cut to firebox length.

Two woodcutters ran out on the pier, waving, and grinning from whiskered faces. Jarrett hit the whistle treadle again in triumph.

Britt saw Ann Richards step on deck from her stateroom. Gig Harney, the clerk, appeared, squirted tobacco juice over the rail, and hurried toward the forward companionway to go below where the deck crew was waiting to begin hurrying the fueling.

Jarrett was nosing the *Dakota Queen* to the landing. He rang the wheel into reverse, and the big steamboat quivered, her momentum slowing as she rode the boil of water from her paddles.

Gig Harney was saying as he passed Britt, "Looks like

there ain't been a Sioux this fur north this year. We'll be in Benton early next week an' . . ."

Something harsh and slim and as vicious as a snake drove its fangs deep into Harney's throat. The last words he ever were to utter were drowned in his own life blood. His eyes, rolling white, stared horribly at the thing that jutted from him—the feather-tufted shaft of a war arrow.

He reeled back a step, then pitched to the deck at the head of the companionway—dying.

A face that was painted half-crimson, half-orange, was visible above a clump of brush, jet eyes ablaze with fierce elation.

Britt drew his six-shooter, and fired, all in one flashing motion, even before Harney fell. The Sioux never lived to witness his kill, for he died as though struck down by a thunderbolt, so swift was Britt's retaliation. Britt saw the single eagle feather fly from its fastenings in the warrior's hair as the bullet tore through his skull. Then the painted face was gone, and there was thrashing motion in the thicket.

At the same instant something plucked at Britt's belt with a rough hand, twisting him partly off balance. Vaguely he understood that an arrow had glanced from the buckle without injuring him.

Other arrows were hissing like serpents. Their barbed heads were smashing into wood—and into flesh too, for men were screaming in pain aboard.

There was the sharp, nasal twanging of bowstrings in the dusk, and the heavy crash of rifles. Powder flame rippled from the brush, the flashes casting a sanguine glow over the scene.

Sherry Dean had dropped to hands and knees on deck, seeking what shelter the latticed rail afforded. An arrow had grazed her head, ripping the ribbon from its fastenings and her hair was flying about her in a coppery-hued tangle.

Britt saw Ann Richards race into the lounge and reappear with a rifle. She threw herself on her knees back of the rail, raised the gun and fired at some target. She levered in a fresh shell. It was evident that she knew how to handle a gun.

Britt shouted at her to take shelter in the lounge, but his voice was lost in the increasing tumult of battle that engulfed the boat.

The brush now spewed a swarm of screeching Sioux. There were scores of them—a big war party.

The tidal wave of Indians swept into the shallow water. They began wading to board the *Dakota Queen*. Arrows and bullets came in a steady, deadly hail from other warriors in the thickets.

A bearded miner raced to the foredeck, a rifle in his hand, to join in the fight. A bullet through the chest killed him before he could fire his first shot, and he plunged headfirst almost at Britt's feet, terrible surprise in his eyes.

Another passenger emerged from his cabin, and died in the door as a slug from a trade musket tore through his head.

Britt fired carefully, using the rifle now, picking his targets and scoring with each bullet. But the water alongside seethed with painted, howling Indians stripped to breechclouts.

Below deck the boiler- and engine-room crew had come into the battle and the Indians were beginning to pay the price. But their numbers were too great.

The two woodcutters had gone down in the first rush and had already been scalped. They had been allowed to live this long only because they had been useful in luring the *Dakota Queen* into this ambush.

Britt saw that Sherry Dean now had armed herself also from the gunracks, and was crouching beside Ann Richards, and shooting into the mass of Indians below. But it was also evident that she was unaccustomed to firearms for she was closing her eyes and flinching each time she pulled the trigger.

Britt realized that the *Dakota Queen* lay motionless, merely drifting idly in shallow water abeam of the shore. Her wheel was stilled, and the current was pushing her toward the dark thickets where she would soon go aground and be helplessly trapped in the midst of her attackers.

On the deck below he saw the chief engineer swinging an empty rifle as he fought to repel Indians who were now trying to gain a foothold on board. Then the man went down beneath a mass of Sioux who swarmed over the prow, and knives and hatchets hacked his body.

Britt raced down the companionway to the main deck. Here was hell in all its fury. The deck crew and engine-room

132

gang fought hand to hand with Indians all along the length of the boat. Gunsmoke lay in a choking cloud, through which the muzzle blasts flickered in smothered flashes of sullen crimson.

A stevedore fell with a hatchet buried in his skull. Britt saw a magnificently muscled Negro stoker, bare to the waist, swinging a ten-foot stoking bar like a scythe, clearing Indians from a space around him with this flail which broke legs and bodies, and sent warriors hurtling overside to drown.

A sinewy Indian, his bronze body ashine with grease and sweat, leaped at Britt out of this turmoil, a hatchet swinging. Britt parried the blow with his rifle barrel, then clubbed the Sioux to the deck with the stock.

He leaped over bodies on a deck that was now slippery with blood, heading for the engine room. He had to fight his way through the swirling mass, striking and slashing at Indians.

He finally reached the engine room. It was deserted. The throttle was in neutral. Britt seized the bar, moving it into reverse, feeding steam to the pistons. He felt, rather than heard, the wheel begin to churn, for the roar of battle was now a steady thunder.

He saw that the *Dakota Queen* was responding. The boat began to move, backing away from this deadly shore.

The screeching of the Indians rose to a higher pitch as they saw what was happening. A warrior appeared in the entrance to the engine room, a rifle in his hands. Britt killed him with his six-shooter.

He leaped over the body onto the deck. The *Dakota Queen* was moving slowly, but picking up momentum, recoiling from this ambush. But her progress seemed agonizingly sluggish.

Bodies of dead and wounded littered the deck. Other living men, both red and white and black, fought for its possession. At least a score of Sioux were aboard and scores more in the water alongside.

Somewhere Britt had lost his rifle. He now realized he was snapping the hammer of his six-shooter on empty shells. There was no time to reload. He seized up a rifle from the deck where someone had dropped it. The gun was empty too, but he used it as a club.

The man with the stoking bar had two arrows in his body,

133

but he was still on his feet. He had placed himself on the foredeck, guarding the companionway so that no Indian could slip above.

Phil Howe stood there with him, swinging a clubbed rifle. The young doctor's white shirt had been torn from his shoulders so that it hung about his belt in tatters. His teeth were bared, and his eyes were black and wild with the battle lust.

The *Dakota Queen* was gaining headway now, drawing clear of this evil shore, leaving behind the Sioux who had been unable to gain the deck.

The craft backed into deep water. The Indians who remained aboard suddenly became panic-stricken and gave up the fight. There were only a dozen of them left, and they turned and dived overboard, swimming frantically for shore.

Bullets and arrows continued to sweep the deck of the steamboat. A thrown hatchet killed a deckhand who had survived the worst of the battle. A spear skewered another.

Heartsick, Britt saw the Negro with the stoking bar go down, a third arrow quivering in his great chest.

A rifle kept cracking from the hurricane deck, picking off swimming Indians. That, Britt thought vaguely, probably was Mead Jarrett, indulging in his lust for killing from the comparative safety of his steel-sheathed pilothouse.

The *Dakota Queen* had now retreated almost to midstream. She was still on reversed wheel and still picking up speed. Jarrett had abandoned the wheel and there was no hand at the helm to guide the boat's course.

Realizing the new danger, Britt raced back to the engine room and eased off the steam, then moved the throttle to full ahead in order to check the boat's momentum.

But he was almost too late. The *Dakota Queen's* sternward progress slowed under the forward thrust of the paddle wheel. Then she struck. There was a jar that sent everyone aboard staggering. She heeled drunkenly to starboard, and hung in that position for long, breathless seconds. Then she slid clear and seemed to be floating freely again in deeper water.

Britt ran to the rail, peering overside. The steamboat had retreated out of effective range of the shore. A few shots were still being fired from the brush, but the bullets were falling short.

The *Dakota Queen* had backed almost to the north shore

and was swinging aimlessly in dangerous water where the current swirled over rock chains and recoiled from snags.

A panting, powder-marked man from the engine-room crew now appeared and raced to the throttle. "I'll take over," he gasped. "We're in trouble. We'll go aground here. We're in snag water."

Mead Jarrett evidently had remembered his duty now, for the whistle on the speaking tube shrilled. Jarrett's voice, high-pitched, began shouting orders. The engine bell began clanging.

The engine man moved the steam bar in response to the bell. The *Dakota Queen* steadied, seemed to take a deep breath. She was under control again.

Britt returned to the deck. He looked at the gray, stunned faces of the survivors. There seemed to be hardly a handful left alive on the lower deck. Here and there men groaned and some of them were in their last agony. The Sioux had come very close to wiping out the steamboat company.

Phil Howe was bending over the big stoker, seeking to check the rush of blood from the arrow wounds. As Britt reached their side the stoker smiled up at the young doctor and whispered, "Thet was a powerful bad fight, Suh." He died still smiling up at Phil Howe as though they shared a warm and friendly secret together.

Phil looked at Britt, his dark eyes now dull with protest. "I couldn't have saved him," he burst out hoarsely. "No doctor could have done anything for him, I tell you."

"Don't try to bear that burden, Phil," Britt said gently. "There was nothing anyone could do."

"It's—it's hard to see a brave man die," Howe said, and the protest was a pain in his voice.

"The women?" Britt asked.

Phil shook his head. "I don't know."

Britt raced above to the passenger deck. The carnage there was almost as terrible as it had been below. Only a few wounded men were in the lounge. With them were Sherry and Ann Richards.

Both girls had escaped injury and they now were beginning to do what they could for the wounded. They, too, had that stunned look in their faces and moved like sleepwalkers.

Britt hurried to the top deck. Mead Jarrett looked down from the pilothouse and asked, "How is it below?"

"Bad," Britt said. "Not many men left alive."

He found Leila crouched in the captain's cabin with her father. She screamed hysterically as he entered. She didn't seem to know him at first. She was glassy-eyed with terror. Walker Ormsby was in little better shape.

Britt lifted Leila to her feet, tried to soothe her, but she only kept babbling and weeping.

He turned suddenly and left them. He was remembering the way Ann Richards and Sherry had seized up rifles and fought alongside the men. But it was evident that Leila had hidden in her cabin. And so had her father.

He returned to the passenger deck only to meet a wild-eyed stevedore who came speeding up from below. The man moaned, "We're done fer! We're takin' water fast! We're sinkin'!"

Britt clapped a hand over his mouth. "Go on up and tell Jarrett," he snapped. "But keep it from the women."

He ran below and found two crewmen gazing into the trap that opened into the shallow hold on the foredeck. Britt knelt, peering. His heart sank. Water boiled among the cargo that was stored in the hold. That encounter with the reef had opened the *Dakota Queen's* hull.

He pushed the crewmen savagely into action. "Get tarps, oakum, clothing—anything that will help plug that hole!" he barked. "Hustle!"

He joined them. Between them they rounded up the material. Britt, moving with desperate speed, rolled wads of canvas and dropped them into the hold. The *Dakota Queen* already had taken more than a foot of water and was slightly down by the head.

Britt leaped into the hold. Exploring, he found the rupture where the river was swirling through. A plank had been sprung. He rammed the wadding in with a crowbar and deckmen rolled barrels of flour in on top of the improvised caulking to hold it in place.

That slowed the inrush of the river but did not stem it entirely. Britt suspected there was another rupture in the hull farther astern.

Walker Ormsby, pasty-white, had appeared. Mead Jarrett came hurrying from above. Jarrett had steadied the boat in mid-channel and turned the wheel over to a crewman.

Jarrett joined Britt. Full darkness had come now. By

lantern-light they studied the ominous swirl of water in the hold.

Britt straightened, peering around. The *Dakota Queen* was headed downstream, barely moving at steerageway. Silence held the river. He could hear the moaning of an injured man in the lounge above. The shores were black and almost imperceptible, for the river ran wide here, and moonrise had not yet cleared massive thunderheads that the heat of the day had left on the horizon to the east.

Only the reek of gunsmoke that still clouded the inner decks and the huddled bodies of the dead remained as a reminder of those desperate minutes they had endured. The shores seemed empty of all human life again, but Britt knew the Sioux were there in the darkness, following the progress of the boat, keeping it in sight.

Jarrett spoke. "How much time do you figure we've got, Cahill?"

Britt shook his head. "Not long. An hour at the most—if we're lucky. Probably less. She's sinking."

He added, "Go back to the wheel, Jarrett. We'll steam at full ahead as long as we can. That should leave the Indians behind. Once we're sure we've built up distance we'll sink her in deep water and take to shore and find a hideout."

Jarrett thought it over for a moment, then nodded. "That's the only chance we have," he shrugged. "Let's hope she doesn't sink too soon. At that, drowning would be better than other things that could happen to us."

Walker Ormsby had listened, not comprehending. "What's this about sinking in deep water?" he croaked.

"The Sioux don't know we're in trouble," Britt explained. "If we steam off into the darkness at full speed they probably will take it for granted that we're heading out of the country. They couldn't keep up with a steamboat for any length of time, even on horses, and I doubt if they'd even try. We want them to believe we're escaping out of their reach."

Walker Ormsby suddenly understood. "You—you can't sink my steamboat!" he wailed. "We'll beach her some place where . . ."

Britt eyed him icily. "If this boat is above water at daybreak tomorrow the Sioux will spot it sure. They'd hunt us down. None of us would live through the day. We have three women to think about. We've got to make the Indians believe we've gone downriver. And there's only one way. Sink the boat in a place where not even the funnels will show to give away the fact that we're still within reach."

Walker Ormsby began to mouth some frantic new objection, but Jarrett snapped contemptuously, "Shut up! Or is this damned boat worth more than our scalps?"

Then Jarrett hurried above to resume his place at the wheel. The engine bell clanged for full ahead, and the *Dakota Queen* began to pick up speed.

CHAPTER 21

Britt, moving fast, organized the company. "Lash down everything you can find that might float free, or stow it where it will go down with the boat," he told the handful of unwounded men he had rounded up. "We can't have wreckage littering the shore downstream tomorrow or the Indians will guess that the boat sank. Be ready to draw your fires and blow the boilers before she goes down. We don't want a boiler explosion to betray our situation."

He helped with the harsh task of consigning the dead to the river with weights tied to their bodies. Sherry Dean spoke a prayer as the bodies were slid overside. It was cruel, but the need of the living transcended the dignity of the dead in this desperate race against time.

Britt went above. Phil Howe was attending the wounded in the lounge. Ann Richards and Sherry were helping him. Phil's face was gaunt with the intensity of his task. He barked orders at the girls, and at the men, and cursed occasionally. He had donned a rough flannel shirt that he had found somewhere to replace the one that had been torn from him during the fight, but even this was bloodstained now as he worked on the injured.

Leila was in the lounge, pacing about with that wild look of panic still in her eyes. When she saw Britt she came rushing toward him. "We're safe now, aren't we?" she chattered frantically. "Mead said the boat is sinking. He lied, didn't he? You'll fix it, won't you, Britt?"

Britt gently pulled free of her fingers which clutched his arms. "Get a grip on yourself, Leila," he said. "We will have to abandon boat."

Leila buried her face in her hands and began to weep hysterically. Ann Richards came and tried to soothe her.

Britt looked at the bandaged men in the lounge. Some had only minor injuries, but others lay on blankets on the poker tables. "Four bad cases?" he asked Howe.

Phil shook his head. "Three now," he murmured. "One died a few minutes ago. And another poor fellow has only minutes to go. The others are in better shape. Only two will have to be carried."

Britt tallied their strength in his mind. Ten men, some of whom carried injuries, three girls and two seriously wounded men.

Leila was quieting now. Ann Richards left her and went back to the side of a dazed, moaning miner who had taken an arrow through his collarbone.

Sherry stood over another man who lay on a poker table. She was smoothing back his tangled, blood-matted hair, murmuring words to him that were like the soothing lullaby of a mother to a child.

Then Sherry's voice stopped, and she drew her hand away. She stood for a time, her head bowed in prayer, and finally pulled a blanket over the face that had stilled beneath her hand. The man was gone.

Britt walked to Sherry's side and placed his arm around her waist. She broke a little. She buried her face against his chest and sobbed silently. But only for a moment. Then she gained control of herself, and when she looked up at him her eyes were composed.

She drew away. "I am sorry," she murmured.

Britt brusquely addressed both Ann and Sherry. "It would be best if you dressed in men's clothes before going ashore. And Leila also."

Ann nodded. "We understand," she said quietly.

Britt knew what she and Sherry understood only too well, that the presence of three young women in the party would only increase the determination of the Sioux in case the *Dakota Queen's* survivors were discovered.

Britt carried with him the memory of that steady resolution in the eyes of both Ann Richards and Sherry as he hurried away to other tasks.

The *Dakota Queen* had only three small boats aboard. They were skiffs of the type popular on the inland rivers, each equipped with a double set of oars. Britt had the skiffs carried to the foredeck where he stocked them with goods, rifles, ammunition, blankets and cooking utensils, and with stout poles.

The *Dakota Queen's* race was about run. She was down by the head and Jarrett had slowed the paddle wheel for fear of driving her under.

Britt ordered the two wounded men placed in one of the skiffs.

"Take soundings," he ordered, peering at the river.

A crewman stood on the prow, threw the weighted measuring line and quickly drew it toward him. "Mark four!" he intoned.

"Only four fathoms," Britt murmured. "We need at least twelve. We've got to find a hole."

The line went out again. "Quarter, less three," the leadsman said hoarsely, panic showing in his voice.

Sixteen and a half feet of depth.

"Half twain!" came the next sounding. Then, "Mark twain!"

That was only some twelve feet of water.

"My God!" a stevedore breathed. "Look!"

The foredeck of the *Dakota Queen* was almost at river level. She had only minutes to live and they were in shallow water. If the boat sank here she would be a betraying monument. At daybreak her upper decks and stacks would be visible for miles above the river banks.

Then, "Six fathoms!" There was a rising, excited hope in the leadsman's voice.

Britt looked around. Ann Richards and Sherry had come down from above. They had Leila between them. All of them wore men's breeches and shirts and had their hair stuffed into masculine hats. They had helped themselves to the attire in deserted cabins.

"No bottom!" the leadsman yelled triumphantly. "Twelve fathoms or better! We're over a hole."

Britt ordered the paddle wheels into reverse to hold the logy steamboat over this deep area. He then had the boilers blown. Steam gushed from the valve. The wheel died as pressure faded, and the sinking boat drifted in darkness.

The fires were drawn. Then the skiffs were slid overside and men began tumbling into them. Mead Jarrett came hurrying down.

Suddenly the *Dakota Queen* began to sag sickly, wearily to starboard.

"Abandon!" Britt rasped. "Lively! She's going!"

He picked up Ann Richards bodily, lifted her into the skiff that contained the two badly wounded men, and did the same with Sherry. Howe also stepped aboard this craft.

Leila was with Jarrett and her father in another skiff that also carried two crewmen.

Britt was the last to leave the *Dakota Queen*. He shoved the skiff clear with a thrust of his legs as he came aboard.

And just in time. He seized up oars and began pulling frantically. Phil Howe followed his example.

The *Dakota Queen* heeled farther over. Her stacks seemed to loom menacingly above them. Britt braced his feet, dug the oars deep and fairly hurled the boat ahead—and clear.

The stacks broke free of their own weight from the capsizing steamboat and crashed into the river only a dozen feet astern of the skiff. Soot flew in a choking cloud and a wave of foam and solid water almost overwhelmed the small craft.

Britt's vision cleared in time to witness the last of the *Dakota Queen*. She lay on her side, her larboard decks tilted high, looming gigantically against the stars. Steam burst explosively from the river as the boilers went under. Heavy thuds marked the bursting of metal and pipes.

The upraised deck sank slowly, steadily, sliding beneath the surface. Then the *Dakota Queen* was gone, buried beneath the muddy Missouri, her grave marked by a raging boil of foam and surging eddies.

Britt and Phil continued to strain at the oars. Their boat was small and not meant to carry such a load. They were often in danger of capsizing as they were caught by unseen currents and eddies.

Near by a second boat was visible. Britt saw that it contained Jarrett and his party. It was a much larger craft and more riverworthy, and outdistanced the smaller skiff in the pull for shore. The third boat, which had contained four men, had vanished in the darkness.

Britt drew a sigh of satisfaction as they finally escaped from the current and reached shallow water. They were on the south shore, and he would have preferred to have been on the north side of the Missouri, with the river between them and the Sioux war party, but there was no help for it now. Any attempt to cross the river in small boats in darkness would mean certain disaster.

They drifted into the deep gloom of brush at the river's margin. Mead Jarrett's boat loomed up alongside and they waited there, listening and peering for the third boat.

But it did not appear. They began calling cautiously. No answer came.

After a time Mead Jarrett uttered an oath. "They'll never show up," he said. "They know they'll have a better chance of getting back to Council Bluffs if they're not handicapped by women and wounded men. So they've left us to shift for ourselves." He added, "Maybe they're smart at that."

Britt finally had to concede that Jarrett was right. The four men in the third craft had deserted them, or had met disaster in the current.

"What do we do now?" Howe asked.

"We'll head upstream," Mead Jarrett said.

"Upstream? But . . ."

"If the Indians happen to find that the steamboat sank, they'll hardly be looking for us upriver," Jarrett said impatiently. "Use your head, man. They'll search downstream, figuring we took to small boats, and would follow the easy way. We'll be bucking the current heading upriver, but Fort Buford is less than a hundred miles away, and we can make it in three or four days by traveling at night after the moon comes up. It's our best chance."

Britt was silent for a moment. Then he said, "I believe you're right again, Mead."

He saw Ann Richards twist around and peer sharply at him. The moon was beginning to clear the clouds now, and a faint luminescence lay over the river. But he could not make out the expression in her face. Then she quickly turned away again, busying herself with making one of the wounded men more comfortable.

He understood that she was gladdened by that decision. Somewhere between this place and Fort Buford she might find her father, or learn at least whether he was alive or dead. But she also surmised that it fitted in with Britt's own plans.

"I'll lead the way," Jarrett spoke. "We'll hug the shore, for the moon is coming out of hiding."

The two able-bodied men in Jarrett's boat had been deckhands aboard the *Dakota Queen*. Britt suspected that, like Jarrett and Walker Ormsby and Leila, these two had escaped damage by staying out of the thick of the fight with the Sioux.

Now these two bent to the oars and Jarrett handled the pole. They drove the skiff upstream. Britt and Phil followed. They soon found they were hard put to it to keep pace with the bigger, more lightly laden craft.

"Apparently it's up to us to stay with them or be left behind," Phil panted after a time. "Perhaps Jarrett also isn't too happy about having women and wounded men to worry about."

The moon cleared the clouds and sailed in a clear sky. Its light turned the river to rippling silver. They hugged the shadows of the brushy shore as best they could.

They had progressed perhaps a mile when Ann murmured tensely, "Listen!"

Britt had been hearing it, too. At first he had imagined it was the pound of his own heart. Now he knew it for what it really was.

Sound that was at first so vague it seemed to be felt rather than heard throbbed in the moonlight. At times it came in a deep, hypnotic rhythm. Then it would rise to a feverish, barbaric madness.

War drums. As they progressed ahead, the keening of squaws and the occasional wild outcry of many voices mingled with the staccato pounding of the tom-toms. Back from the river, perhaps half a mile, the red glow of campfires reflected against the sky. The drumming and the wailing and shouting became louder as they pushed nearer.

"Victory dance!" Britt murmured. "Warriors counting coup at the council fire and the Sioux women mourning the ones who did not come back from the fight."

He saw Sherry and Ann move close together like small children beset by the terrors of the unknown.

"At least it shows they think we're on our way downriver aboard the *Dakota Queen*," Britt said.

Slowly they passed by that danger point, the screeching and the wailing and the thunder of the drums seeming to fill all the night around them. Slowly these sounds fell astern as they fought their way upriver. Finally there was only the fading throb of the drums in their ears—and at last Britt began to wonder if that was only imagination, too, for it was a sound that a man carried in his memory—beating out its warning of death and torture.

Jarrett's boat had long since pulled out of sight and sound ahead. Britt and Phil fought the current. Often they missed disaster only by frenzied, heart-wrenching effort as the boat was swept toward snags and rocks over which the river boiled. Then they would work into quieter stretches of water again where progress was faster.

Britt realized that Phil was weakening, apparently unaccustomed to such physical toil. And his own muscles were protesting under the brutal exertion. His left arm, with its partly healed wound had to be favored whenever possible. But they made headway. The glow of the Sioux campfires faded in the distance.

They passed the embers of the woodcutters' camp where the Sioux had ambushed the steamboat. The ashes were fanned to a red glow by the stirring of the night breeze. The tang of burned gunpowder lingered here, mingling with the pitchy odor of burned logs.

They struggled onward for another two hours. Then Mead Jarrett's voice spoke irritably from the gloom of heavy brush on shore. "We've landed!" Jarrett called. "Where in hell have you been?"

They swung the boat to shore and made out Jarrett standing in the brush. Farther back, his party was groping in the moon-dappled shadows of a small clearing they had found a dozen rods back from the river's margin. They had pulled the bigger skiff into the thickets well out of sight.

Wearily Britt and Phil drove the skiff ashore. They carried the two wounded men to the site of the camp that Jarrett's party was making. Neither Jarrett nor any of his party offered to help with this task.

Phil Howe stumbled drunkenly. Abruptly his knees caved in and he sagged down almost at Britt's feet.

Britt uttered an exclamation. He bent, started to lift the young doctor, then paused abruptly. His hands had encountered caked, matted, half-dried blood.

"Damnation!" he gritted. "I had a hunch he wasn't acting right. He's wounded!"

Sherry came with a rush, uttering a little choked cry.

144

Phil tried to mumble something, but the words were unintelligible.

"There's a lantern in the boat, Sherry," Britt said. "Fetch it. I have matches. I want to take a look at Howe."

"Hold on!" Mead Jarrett exploded. "Are you loco, Cahill? Nobody shows a light here. We can't risk a lantern so close to that damned war village."

Britt ignored him. So did Ann Richards, for it was she who hurried to the skiff and returned with the lantern.

"Get blankets," Britt said. "Rig them on the brush so as to shield the light."

Jarrett uttered furious objections, but the two girls followed Britt's instructions.

Britt peered close at Phil Howe in the lantern light. He asked for water, and Ann, moving fast, found a pail among the camp implements and filled it at the river.

Britt carefully worked the blood-stiffened shirt free from Phil's body and came upon a hastily contrived bandage. Beneath that was an ugly gash. And Britt saw something else. His fingers gently explored the wound.

Phil had aroused a little. He winced and groaned under Britt's touch. "Just—just—a—scratch," he gasped. "Not much—much more than—a—a mosquito bite."

"That was quite a mosquito that bit you," Britt said.

"What—what . . . ?" Sherry asked faintly.

"Arrowhead!" Britt said tersely. "It's in the muscle under his armpit. He must have broken off the shaft. It's not too deep, but deep enough."

He added, his voice curiously low, "This fellow carried that thing for hours and never bothered to mention it. And I only thought he was just soft."

"What can we do?" Sherry choked.

"That thing has got to come out," Britt shrugged.

Phil looked up at him, a ghastly grin on his gray lips. "It looks like it's your turn to play doctor, Cahill," he said. "My bag is in the boat. You'll find all the tools you need. It won't be much of a job. I'll tell you how to go about it."

Sherry opened the medical bag. White-faced, she shrank a little from the glitter of the implements.

"Find the hypodermic needle," Britt instructed. "We'll give you a little shut-eye to make this as painless as possible, my friend."

Phil shook his head. "There's no morphia. I used—used it all—earlier. No laudanum left either."

There was a moment of utter silence. Then Ann Richards said softly, fervently, fiercely, "Oh, Goddammit!"

It was not blasphemy but more a prayer the way she uttered the word.

"My sentiments exactly," Britt commented. "Howe, you knew you'd need some of that stuff for yourself. You used it on the others knowing . . ." He let it remain unfinished, and made a helpless, angry gesture.

"Carve away," Phil mumbled. "It has to be done."

Britt looked up at the horrified faces of Sherry and Ann. He felt cold chills racing through him. Mead Jarrett and the others were staring from the background.

"Spread another blanket," Britt heard himself saying. "Then you young ladies will want to go away until this is over."

Only Leila Ormsby moved. She shrank hurriedly away from this, moving off into the darkness, a sick look in her face.

Ann and Sherry stood where they were. "You will need help," Ann said quietly.

"Yes," Britt said reluctantly. "I will. And thanks."

Britt laid out scalpel and probe and forceps, with Phil giving gasping instructions.

"Give him something in each hand to grip," Britt said to the girls. "Both of you help keep his arms spread. Kneel on his arms if necessary. This is going to hurt like hell. He may yell, but hold him down."

Ann broke small lengths from a cottonwood branch, thrust them into Phil's hands. Britt bent close with the scalpel. He saw Phil brace himself.

"You infernal, game, damned fool!" Britt grated. "This is going to hurt me as much as it does you."

Mead Jarrett moved up so that he would miss none of this. The inevitable pack of cards appeared in his hand. Beautiful fans bloomed and vanished magically. The cards seemed to have a will of their own in his quick fingers. A thin smile lighted his face, as though he anticipated enjoyment in Phil's suffering.

Britt looked up at Jarrett, and his gray eyes were cold as metal. Then he turned back to Phil, bent low, and the thin blade of a scalpel made its first thrust into flesh.

Ann Richards, ashen, tried to close her ears to the sounds that came from Phil. She let her gaze follow Jarrett's slim, sensitive fingers as they toyed with the cards. Even in that moment of great tension the thought came to her that Jarrett's hands were as graceful as a woman's—and far more deft.

Deft as a woman! That thought drove through her with sudden impact. Her gaze darted to Jarrett's face, a new, startled discovery dawning in her mind.

Britt's voice, rough and impatient, brought her back to the duty at hand. "Give me that long, curved pair of pliers," he was saying.

Ann handed him the forceps he wanted. Britt bent back to his task. He could almost feel in his own body the white hot agony that must be racing through Howe. But the young doctor refused to yell, though he could not suppress a strangled moaning.

Sweat streaked Britt's face. He heard Sherry's shaking voice repeat over and over, "Hail Mary, Mother of God, be merciful. Hail Mary . . ."

Ann wiped away the perspiration from Britt's eyes so that he could see to work.

Then Britt said with an exhausted sigh, "All right, I've got it." He had removed the arrowhead.

Howe had gone limp. Ann moved in with needle and suture. "I can do this better than you," she said to Britt.

And she sewed the jagged wound with swift, steady hands. Then she formed a bandage.

Presently Phil Howe's eyes opened sluggishly. Sherry continued to run a cool cloth over his forehead and across his dark, tangled hair.

"You're a damned butcher, Cahill," he mumbled.

"When the patient starts blaming the doctor, then the operation is a success," Britt said.

Sherry uttered a shaky little laugh that was more like a sob. She impulsively leaned toward Britt, ran an arm around his neck and kissed him. "Darlin', darlin'," she breathed. "You were wonderful!"

Phil gazed at them, a hopeless resignation in his eyes that were haggard and big in his unshaven face.

Mead Jarrett slid his deck of cards out of sight and spoke irritably. "Now, maybe you'll put out that cursed lantern.

147

Likely we'll have the Sioux about our ears at daybreak because of showing that light."

Britt picked up the lantern to snuff it. Just before he blew out the flame he saw Ann Richards' expression. She was again looking at Jarrett, a queer speculation in her face. Then the light died.

They made Phil and the other two wounded men as comfortable as possible. Jarrett offered to stand watch. The others turned in. Rolling up in blankets the majority of them dropped instantly into dead, heavy sleep. The strain of the battle and the long struggle upriver was hitting all of them, felling them almost in their tracks.

Despite his utter exhaustion Britt lay awake long after the others. He was remembering the way Ann had looked at Mead Jarrett, and he was puzzling over what it had meant.

Where was the map? By all odds it should be lost with the *Dakota Queen.* Of all the men who had died in the Indian fight it seemed only reasonable to assume that one of them had been the mysterious third party who had made the attempt on Britt's own life and had wrested the map from Ann Richards.

That meant that Ann's only hope now was that her father was still alive, and that, somehow, she would find him. But if he had died there in the wilderness, then that boatload of gold would probably lie forever buried in the river mud.

It came to Britt that if Zack Richards was dead, his own quest was useless. He could not choke the truth from a dead man. That murder charge would hang over him the rest of his life. He could never escape it, and sooner or later the law would take its toll of him.

For it was Zack Richards that he sought above all. The gold did not matter. In fact it had not mattered from the start. Zack Richards owed him the price of his lost steamboat. But even that was insignificant in comparison to his other need. It was exoneration that he wanted, above all— the right to walk among free men in his own identity as Britt Cahill.

The moon was striking full and clear into the little clearing now. The night chill of the high plains was making itself felt. Britt saw that Ann Richards and Sherry lay huddled for warmth under the same blanket.

Apparently, Britt reflected, Ann no longer mistrusted

Sherry. He pondered over that, wondering what had brought about this change in her attitude.

Phil stirred, mumbling wildly. He was fighting the Sioux again, in his fever, and he was living over once more the ordeal of having the arrowhead cut from his flesh. He thrashed about, kicking the blanket off him.

Britt heard Sherry's voice, soft as down. "Now! Now! You're all right, Philip DeWitt Howe. We're all here together and safe. There are no Indians. Lie back and sleep."

There was no scorn in Sherry's words. They were infinitely tender and soothing. Phil quieted and sank back to sleep. Sherry reached out and tucked the displaced blanket around him.

CHAPTER 22

There was no sign of danger at dawn, and the plains continued to remain vacant as the day advanced. They were forced to bide their time, for Britt and Jarrett had agreed that it would be wiser to remain in the hideout another day at least, in order to give the wounded a chance to gain strength.

Phil Howe recuperated rapidly. By noon he was on his feet. He was pale and shaky at first, but by mid-afternoon he began to feel more fit.

He examined his wound with a professional, critical eye, using Sherry's hand mirror. "Excellent!" he beamed. "Excellent! You evidently have missed your calling, Cahill. You should have chosen a career as a sawbones. And you stitch a very neat hand, Miss Richards. I am flattered to be the object of such surgical skill."

The other two wounded men improved also. One was a bearded, middle-aged miner named Hank Eilers, and the other, Sam Maxwell, was a leathery, slow-speaking Southerner. Eilers had a bullet-broken right arm, which Phil had set and splinted before the *Dakota Queen* had gone down. He also carried a lance gash in his chest muscles, but he was able to move about a little without help.

Sam Maxwell had taken an arrow through his collarbone and a deep hatchet slash in his right thigh. He was still too weak to move. Both of them owned claims in the Montana diggings and had spent the winter in St. Louis.

Eilers and Maxwell had vast respect for Phil Howe, for they knew that it was his surgical ability that had saved them. And they regarded Sherry Dean and Ann Richards with a gratitude that amounted to worship.

"I've heard o' Sherry Dean," Eilers confided to Britt, "but she ain't nothin' like the way she was painted. I was told she was a pure she-devil what sold herself for a price, an' used her shape to blind men so she could rob 'em at poker tables. That's a damned lie. Maybe she does gamble. But she plays strictly on the level. I watched her that night she sat in a game on the boat, and she asked no favors, though there was a couple of short-card sports that was tryin' to whipsaw her. Maybe she drinks. I wouldn't know about that. All I seen her take was a few sips o' champagne. Maybe she's got reason to drink. I've seen the way she looks at men. Some cuss did her a bad turn in the past, an' she don't trust nor respect the rest of us none at all. But she took care o' me 'n Sam last night like we was human bein's. She wasn't afeared o' dirtyin' her hands an' her dress on our blood like some others I could mention."

And Eilers added, "Ann Richards is cut from the same chunk as Sherry Dean. Did you see her usin' that Winchester durin' the Indian fight? An' she helped Doc Howe work on me an' Sam in that bloody lounge aboard the steamboat, smilin' at us, an' encouragin' us to be as game as she was. Both them gals has got sand clear down to their pretty toes. Any man that says a word ag'in either of 'em will have me to answer to."

Britt noted that Eilers did not mention Leila by name. She was sitting at a distance on the trunk of a fallen tree, preening her hair in sullen discontent. Heartened by the absence of any sign of danger during the day, she had calmed down and started complaining.

She blamed her father and Jarrett for everything that had happened. She made it plain she was uncomfortable and miserable. She had combed and recombed her hair half a dozen times, and still was not satisfied with the result. She had made it plain she resented the presence of Eilers and Sam Maxwell and considered it unfair that the party should be burdened with the responsibility of two wounded men.

Looking at her, Britt realized he was seeing her as a stranger, as a person he had never really known. That startled him a little, left a deep and empty regret—the regret of one awakening from a wonderful illusion into reality. For he saw now that the Leila Ormsby he had known was only a creature of his own mind. He had created her in his thoughts as he wanted her to be, not as she really was.

Leila saw his gaze upon her. She arose quickly, anxious for attention, and came walking to him, wearing her bright, inviting smile. "You've been ignoring me all day, Britt," she said chidingly.

"I'm sorry, Leila," Britt said.

Leila's smile vanished. She saw the remoteness in his expression. She saw the regret and the emptiness. She understood now. She visibly hardened. Something formed in her eyes that stirred an uneasiness in him.

Then Leila said savagely, "To hell with you—you murderer!"

She went back to the fallen tree, flounced down and began working on her long fingernails. Her father lay stretched on a blanket near by. Walker Ormsby's fine, broadcloth captain's uniform was muddy and brush-torn. He had hidden a whiskey bottle somewhere and had tippled from it steadily in secret, but it was empty now and there was no more to be had. He was beginning to shake.

Mead Jarrett sat with his back against a small tree, riffling his deck of cards. He was muddy, too, and needed a shave. He had laid aside his coat, for the day was breathlessly hot. He wore his shoulder holster, its leather harness offering a harsh and foreboding contrast against his fine linen shirt which was growing dusty and soiled. A rifle lay close by his side.

He dealt a hand of poker to imaginary opponents, the cards sailing with blurred speed upon a blanket spread before him. He picked up the hands, glanced at them and smiled, satisfied with the result.

Sherry and Ann Richards were preparing a meal over a tiny fire of dry cottonwood twigs that burned white and hot and lifted no betraying smoke. Jarrett watched them, boldly enjoying their shapeliness which was very evident in the masculine garb they wore.

Sherry became aware of this appraisal. She straightened, hands on hips, glaring at Jarrett with scorn—a temperish, full-bosomed young woman. "Your eyes, Mead, my lad," she said, "are a desecration."

Jarrett showed his dry smile. "Complimentary is the correct description," he admonished. "Don't tell me you don't like to be admired. You're a woman."

There was, Britt reflected, nothing soft or weak in Mead Jarrett. He accepted circumstances as they came and had his own unswerving purposes, his own secret thoughts.

Near Jarrett lolled the two deckhands. One was thick-shouldered, unwashed and unsavory. He had a stiff growth of black whiskers and matted, greasy black hair. One ear had been maimed in some brutal levee fight in the past, and the upper portion had been cut or bitten off.

The other, smaller, with hair the color of dusty hay, was of the same hard caste. This one was whittling on a stick. Both of them were ogling Sherry and Ann Richards. It was evident that they regarded Mead Jarrett as the leader of this party.

The lop-eared man laughed insultingly and made a remark to his companion. Britt walked across the camp, reached down, caught the speaker by his greasy hair, snatched him to his feet, then knocked him down with a fist that crashed to the jaw with the force of a mallet.

The other deckhand made a motion toward his gun, but thought better of it as he saw the cold blaze in Britt's eyes and the way Britt's hand hung close to his holster.

"Next time," Britt said, "I won't be as gentle if either of you speak out of turn."

Mead Jarrett sat riffling his cards, his cold, mocking smile unchanged. He dealt five cards face up to his mythical opponents. One of these cards landed at Britt's feet. It was the ace of spades.

"The black ace," Jarrett murmured. "That would mean that your luck is bad today, Cahill, if you're superstitious."

Britt turned and walked away from them. Ann Richards looked at him. "Thank you," she murmured. "I've been aching to hit that filthy person all day."

But it was apparent to Britt that the survivors of the *Dakota Queen* were divided into two groups and that there was no understanding between them.

Phil Howe had the same thought, for afterwards he said to Britt, "United we stand, divided we fall. However, if Jarrett lets his eyes roam over Miss Dean and Miss Richards again in that manner I may have to bring the issue to a head."

Britt looked Phil over, his eyes moving down the ragged doctor's lean length, resting at last on the holstered six-shooter that hung at his hip. Already that gun seemed to belong there. Philip DeWitt Howe's transformation was almost complete.

"Jarrett is chain lightning with a gun," he said. "If you brace him, shoot first and shoot to kill. You're too valuable to lose."

Phil laughed a little, an ironic hopelessness in his dark eyes. "I wonder which of us is the more valuable to Sherry Dean and Ann Richards," he said slowly. "I mean in the way of getting them safely out of this predicament we're in."

Then he walked away, favoring his injured side.

The long afternoon waned. The rumble of a distant thunderstorm broke the silence before sundown. Massive clouds drifted from the breaking storm, but only a few big drops of rain spattered the camp in the brush.

The sky cleared as twilight came. Darkness moved in, stifling hot again after the brief cooling respite from the storm.

Britt stood the first night guard at a lookout point a hundred yards downstream. This commanded a wide view of a curve in the river, and of the plains to the south and east.

Sitting on a deadfall, he watched the first stars appear. Occasionally, in this evening silence, the river telegraphed the throb of drums from far away. The Sioux were still dancing.

The heat lightning was at work again, playing above far ridges that leaped out from the blackness in mirage-like clarity, then vanishing again behind the hot wall of the night.

A step sounded in the thickets, and Sherry's voice gave soft warning of her approach. She groped through the darkness, guided by Britt's whispered directions, and finally he drew her down beside him on the deadfall.

The pulsation of the drums became audible again, then faded. He felt her shudder as she leaned against him.

Finally she said. "I'm sorry, Britt. And glad too."

Britt said nothing. He knew what she meant.

"I saw the way you looked at Leila this afternoon," Sherry said gently. "I heard what she said to you. I know

153

now you feel. We are two of a kind, Britt, as I've told you before. We build our own images and gild them with our loyalty. When those images crumble, we are left with nothing but dry and bitter dust in our hands. Empty dust."

Still Britt was silent. There was nothing to say.

"What are you thinking, Britt?" Sherry asked. "What are your plans?"

"Plans?" Britt felt futile impatience rise in him. "We've got to make Fort Buford with our scalps intact. What else? We'll start tomorrow night."

"Somewhere along the way is a sunken boatload of gold," Sherry said slowly. "And perhaps Zack Richards."

"I haven't forgotten," Britt said.

"Nor has Ann Richards. Zack Richards may be dead, but if he is alive she knows there is a man named Britt Cahill who is bent on vengeance upon him. Ann Richards has good reason to kill you, Britt, if it becomes necessary."

Britt twisted, staring. "You mean she would shoot me in the back to stop me?" he asked wonderingly.

"Not in the back. That is not in her nature. But she loves her father. She is the kind who protects those she loves. That is why it is unthinkable that you should drive her to such a thing. It—it would destroy her immortal soul, Britt."

Sherry's voice was quivering, pleading. She bent close and her lips pressed against Britt's rough cheek. "Be—be merciful to her," she said imploringly.

Then she arose abruptly to go. She halted with a little startled exclamation.

Britt turned. Ann Richards stood almost at arm's length, a vague shadow in the darkness.

Ann spoke hastily, confusedly. "I thought you heard me approaching, Cahill. I—I didn't mean to intrude. I—I'm sorry."

Britt realized that Ann Richards was taking it for granted that she had interrupted a love tryst. And now she had turned, and was retreating hastily through the thickets toward the camp.

Sherry snapped. "Damnation! 'Tis the luck of the Irish to be always misunderstood." Then she hurried after Ann.

Sherry's kiss was still cool on Britt's cheek. It had been a kiss of close affection, but only the kind of a kiss a sister would give a blundering and mistaken brother.

Somehow, Britt's mind turned to Ann Richards and her

warm and tempting mouth, with its softness and its capacity for passion. Amazed, he was aware of a blinding rush of wild and heedless longing for the touch of her lips.

He stood appalled, realizing where such fancies would lead him. He lifted a clenched fist to the night sky in grim self-condemnation, then opened it and let the invisible contents dribble from his empty hand.

In that moment he had discovered himself in the act of building another image, like the one he had created in Leila. A new image that was devastatingly beautiful and desirable, with the flame and fire of Ann Richards as its heart and soul.

And, inexorably, he had forced himself to smash it, and rededicate himself to the purpose that had been his sole guiding star for three years.

Ann Richards knew him as an accused murderer and the man who had ruined her father and who meant to ruin him again. Sherry had warned him that Ann Richards might kill him to protect her father. There was a gulf between them that could never be crossed.

He stood there for a long time, motionless, looking at the river and not seeing it. The moon came up and climbed into the sky. He was still standing there, lost in his thoughts, when a heavy step sounded in the brush. It was the surly, lop-eared deckhand he had knocked down earlier.

"I'll take over the watch," the arrival mumbled ungraciously.

Britt surrendered his position. He doubted if the man would stay awake long. However, he also doubted if it mattered. There was little danger during the night.

He made his way back to camp. Tiptoeing among the blanket-wrapped figures, he found his own bedding laid out in the shadows of the brush. Sherry and Ann Richards were near by, with Phil and the two wounded men sleeping just beyond them. Jarrett and Leila and her father and the other deckhand were stretched out on the opposite side of the clearing.

He rolled into his blankets. Presently he saw Ann Richards turn. He knew she was awake, lying facing toward him, as though trying to pierce the darkness to study him.

He wondered what were her thoughts, her plans. Again he felt that tumultuous longing to go to her, to learn if her lips really held that promise of peace and womanly fullness that was the antithesis of the emptiness that deadened his spirits.

She turned away, and a long time afterward he knew she had fallen into troubled sleep. Soon he was glad to feel sleep submerging his own chaotic thoughts, and then he surrendered to this forgetfulness.

Daybreak, gray and thin with the chill of the plains' dawn, was lighting the brush when he awakened. He lay there a moment, looking up at the colorless sky, and all through him was an intuitive, racing sensation of great danger.

He sat up. The opposite side of the camp, where Jarrett and the others had been asleep, was vacant! Even their blankets were gone.

Britt came to his feet and ran to where the skiffs had been pulled into the brush out of the river. Both boats were missing!

He sped back to camp. Ann was sitting up. "Look!" she gasped. "Look!"

She was pointing beyond Britt. Some distance from their hideout a column of smoke rose straight into the windless dawn, a black finger that could mark their location to the Sioux!

CHAPTER 23

Britt ran through the thickets toward this danger point. Above camp was an area where the river had receded from its flood channel, leaving a stretch of sand flats and pools of scummed backwater and flattened sapling growth. There were brushy islands against which driftwood had lodged.

It was one of these heaps of driftwood that had been set afire. There was little flame, for the tangle of damp logs and dead brush smoldered rather than burned, but it gave forth a thick, betraying smoke.

Britt began tearing the smoldering tangle apart, stamping out embers. Phil Howe came at a stumbling run, followed by Ann Richards and Sherry. The four of them worked frantically, kicking and beating at the debris, dragging smoking logs to a nearby pool of backwater, piling sand on others to smother the rise of the black column that marked their presence.

It was a race against the strengthening daylight. When the last curl of smoke was snuffed they looked at each other, grimy and panting.

"Jarrett!" Britt said, his voice husky. "Jarrett! He—they deserted us. And left this smoke sign so the Sioux would come to investigate. We may have got to it in time. Maybe not. There's no telling how far that smoke could have been seen in this light."

Every eye swung eastward. The Sioux village lay in that direction. Full daylight was coming now with a rush. The sky overhead was flushing to a peach color, carrying the reflection of the rising sun. Beyond the river the swells of buffalo grass were being washed with a warm pink hue. The flanks of lonely buttes and eroded ridges were crimson.

Something moved on a skyline. Britt watched it grimly, then relaxed. "Antelope," he said. "That's one good sign at least. There's no danger in sight from that direction—yet. Otherwise the pronghorn would be running."

He found the others looking at him, awaiting his decision. "We'll shift camp and find a hideout that will give us a chance to make a stand in case they come," he said.

They all knew their predicament. Handicapped by two wounded men, any movement in open daylight meant risking discovery. Situated as they were they could not hope to escape far on foot.

They hurried to the camp where Hank Eilers and Sam Maxwell were waiting anxiously. Jarrett and his party had made almost a clean sweep. All the food, except a smoked buffalo tongue, a portion of a bacon slab, a few pounds of flour and three cans of tomatoes, was gone.

Britt and Phil still had their rifles and six-shooters, which they had kept close at their sides while they slept. These guns were loaded, but the only additional ammunition was a dozen shells for the holster guns that Britt had carried in the pocket of his coat.

Ann Richards produced a third rifle. "I had it near me also last night," she said. "Jarrett and his friends didn't want to risk awakening us by taking our guns. And what food they passed up was what had been left over from the cooking yesterday and happened to be standing close to where we were sleeping."

157

Britt carried Sam Maxwell. The girls followed, helping Eilers along on his injured leg, and Phil brought up the rear with the blankets and the small pack of food.

They worked their way more than a mile upriver, keeping under cover until Britt discovered a dry coulee that came in from the south. He led the way up this wash until it narrowed to a defile a dozen feet wide between clay banks that were just high enough to hide them.

"This is as good as we'll find," he said.

The cutbanks would serve to stand off an attack. Westward their position was flanked by open flats for more than a mile. Eastward the situation was not as good. A low, rocky ridge jutted some two hundred yards away. It sloped toward the river bottoms, and tapered down to a swale to their left, but it cut off their view eastward and would offer cover to any danger approaching from that direction.

Phil examined Eilers and Maxwell with professional concern and decided that the activity of the past hour had done no serious harm. He scoffed when Sherry insisted on dressing his own injury, but meekly subsided when he saw the determination in her eyes. He seemed to think he had won a victory when Sherry decided that the wound was doing nicely.

"When do you estimate Jarrett and his crowd pulled out?" he asked Britt.

"As soon as they were sure we were sound asleep," Britt said. "That fire had been burning since midnight by the indications. They must have planned it all day, including setting off that smoke signal."

"But why?" Phil demanded. "I might understand them quitting us. They, of course, will have a better chance of saving their own hides. But why take both boats? And why this infernal treachery of trying to bring the Indians down on us?"

"They likely don't care to have us live to tell about it," Britt shrugged. "Deserting women and wounded men in Indian country isn't exactly a thing you'd want the world to know."

Ann Richards had been listening. Now she spoke, looking at Britt. "I think Jarrett had another reason also. He needed both boats to carry the gold that he hoped to find."

Britt wheeled, staring at her.

Ann nodded, and said, "Jarrett has the map."

158

"The map?"

"I am mortally sure of it," she said. "He is the one who took it from me that night in my cabin. At first I believed you were responsible, Cahill. And I believed Sherry was the person who had ransacked my belongings before that. The search had been done so neatly I suspected a woman. But the truth began to dawn on me only yesterday when I fell to watching Mead Jarrett's card tricks and his hands—his hands that are as slender as a woman's, and far more skillful. It occurred to me then that Jarrett was the guilty one."

She added hesitantly, "That—that is what I had intended to tell you last night when I came to—to where you were on watch. Now it is too late."

She turned to Sherry. "Forgive me, Sherry," she said, her voice humble. "I made myself believe the worst about you, even though in my heart I felt that I was wrong about you."

Sherry went to her, kissed her. "Do not be too quick in your forgiveness, Ann," she sighed. "There are other sins on my conscience."

Ann looked at Britt again. "I do not know how Jarrett learned about the map," she said tiredly.

Britt ran an arm over his forehead and eyes as though to brush away a terrible vision. "I know," he said, his voice heavy. "Leila! I told her about the map. It was that night in St. Louis, just before I was shot. I was in love with her. I trusted her. I told her that I meant to follow you until you led me to your father."

Ann Richards' eyes were dark with brooding, big with a fierce regret. "Why do you hate my father, Cahill?" she burst out.

Britt did not answer.

"Is it because our steamboat sank your *Northern Star* that night three years ago?" she demanded. "Don't you understand that no one regretted that accident more than Dad?"

"Accident!" Britt said jeeringly. "Zack Richards sank my boat deliberately!"

"Oh, no! You can't really believe that?"

"He could have missed us if he had rung his wheel into full astern," Britt said, his voice harsh. "But he came on at full steam."

"But—but . . ." she protested wildly, "Dad wasn't at the wheel! Mead Jarrett was in the pilothouse."

"Jarrett?" Britt exclaimed disbelievingly.

"Jarrett worked for Dad at that time, as you must remember," she said, the words pouring from her excitedly. "He was second pilot on the *White Buffalo* on that trip to Fort Benton and back. I was aboard that night. I had just returned from school in the East and had joined our boat at St. Joe. Dad had been on duty all evening while the fog was so heavy. He was worn out, and the fog was breaking up. He believed it was safe to turn the wheel over to Jarrett. After all, Jarrett was an expert pilot also."

"Then why didn't Jarrett act to . . . ?" Britt began.

"He testified at the inquiry that he didn't have time," Ann interrupted him. "He said our boat emerged from a bank of fog and found your *Northern Star* broadside of the channel and directly across our course. Jarrett said you apparently had become confused in the fog."

Britt stared, astounded. He wanted to doubt her words, but her sincerity was too evident. He had taken it for granted that Zack Richards had still been in the pilothouse at the time of the collision. After escaping from St. Louis he had never learned what had transpired at the inquiry into the sinking, for he had been out of touch with events for months while he remained in hiding from the law.

"Jarrett lied," he finally said slowly. "He was the one who was off course. And he could have avoided sinking me if he had only . . ."

The words trailed off futilely. He believed he knew what Ann Richards was thinking. It was only his word against Jarrett's, and his was the word of a man accused of murder and robbery, and of committing arson to conceal the crime.

Even if Jarrett had been at the wheel, he probably only had been following Zack Richards' orders. Zack Richards likely realized there was less chance of suspicion being directed toward him if the collision came when he was not at the helm, and in Jarrett he had found a man with the cold nerve to carry out his plan.

To give the devil his due, Richards may only have intended to remove Britt as a competitor by sinking his boat in what would be listed as an accident. The complete disaster and the heavy loss of life probably had not entered into his calculations.

Normally a steamboat would have stayed afloat long enough to be beached. But the *Northern Star* had gone down in deep water, carrying scores to their deaths, and Zack Richards had found himself in an unexpected and unnerving dilemma. He faced prison, or even the gallows, if it could be proved that the sinking was deliberate.

In that situation Richards snatched at the chance offered by the murder and fire to make sure Britt would be discredited. He had been ruined financially by that series of events, but he had salvaged something out of it, too, by seeing to it that Britt would never dare confront him and accuse him. He had at least saved his personal reputation, while making a fugitive of Britt.

This accusation arose to Britt's lips. But the look in Ann's eyes stopped him. He saw again the strain that was wearing on her, the lines about her eyes and mouth. He found himself suddenly wanting to smooth away those marks of doubt and discouragement.

"Cahill," she said, the words shaking, "you are more than welcome to the gold if we find it. But whatever you believe about my father is—is wrong. You cannot—must not fight each other. You both are violent, determined men. You both might—might die."

She choked up. Sherry took her in her arms, murmuring to her soothingly.

"Mead Jarrett is the man you have to worry about first," Britt reminded her. "He is a determined man, too. Would you prefer that he find the gold and your father—rather than me?"

Ann gazed at him, torn by doubt and indecision.

"You must have studied that map," Britt went on. "Have you any general idea as to where that mackinaw boat might have sunk?"

She drew free from Sherry's arms. "Yes," she said. "Dad's instructions said the place was on the south shore of the river a day's journey by small boat from Fort Buford, and just below where a tiny stream, blocked by beaver dams, joins the main river. He said rivermen call this stream the Beaverkill."

"The Beaverkill?" Britt said.

"The map itself marked the exact spot where the boat lies," she went on. "There are bearings to certain landmarks and sightings that were too detailed to remember. Evidently

161

the boat would be very difficult to locate without the most minute instructions."

Phil Howe had been listening. "I don't know what this is all about, Cahill," he said, "but I gather there is a sunken boat involved with treasure aboard, among other things."

"I'll tell you all about it later, Doctor," Sherry spoke. "Britt, you seem to have heard of the Beaverkill?"

"It joins the Missouri about fifty miles upstream from here by the way the river flows," Britt said. "But it is little more than half that distance by land. Maybe thirty miles, at a guess. You see, the river swings north from this point in a big fishhook curve, then veers south again in a series of loops. If we could cut directly across the neck of these curves we might reach the Beaverkill ahead of Jarrett."

There was a silence. Thirty miles might as well have been a thousand at this moment. With Maxwell helpless, and Eilers too weak to stand a fast march, and with the Sioux to consider, it seemed hopeless.

Britt voiced his thoughts aloud. "Jarrett and his party probably did fifteen or twenty miles last night. Maybe more if they risked traveling after daybreak. They'll have their troubles, handling two boats, but then this particular stretch of river is a little easier for small boats, and they should make fair headway. They'll have to hole up and rest during the day, and then set out by moonlight again tonight. The chances are they'll be near the Beaverkill tomorrow morning."

Ann's pallor deepened. But she kept her emotions under rigid control.

"We'll move on tonight," Britt said reluctantly. "That's the best we can do. Travel in daylight, afoot, would be suicide. There're bound to be Sioux hunting parties around."

"Of course," she said wearily.

The sun was up now. Britt eyed the ridge to the east which placed them at a disadvantage. "I'm going out there a way, so I can get a look-see at what lies in that direction," he said. "That war village is still too close for comfort."

Phil joined him, and they crawled through the sage and bunchgrass and past areas of prickly pear and finally reached a vantage point among wind-worn rocks on the crest of the ridge a long rifle shot east of the dry wash.

This gave them a wider outlook, although the country eastward was broken by other ridges and buttes that cut off a long view in that direction. Directly before them, the hog-back ridge on which they lay slanted down to a brushy, rock-studded draw that was more like a basin and nearly half a mile wide.

Time dragged. The sun began to beat down. Whenever they moved to more comfortable positions among the rocks they were careful not to skyline themselves.

After two hours Ann Richards emerged from the wash and came crawling toward them, her rifle on her back, thrust through her belt. She brought a tin of water that eased their dry throats.

"Three pairs of eyes are better than two," she said, looking at Britt like a little girl who expected to be reprimanded. "I couldn't stand it—the waiting. I had to come out and see for myself."

She wriggled into a vantage point between them. Phil patted her hand and grinned. "You at least add beauty to our little party," he said. "But you'll find this monotonous also. All I've seen so far is a magpie, and some kind of a small ground animal that keeps popping out of the rocks down there. I almost wish something would happen to . . ."

Britt made a warning gesture, and reached for his rifle. Phil and the girl tensed.

Something moved among the brush in the basin to their right, and a considerable distance away. Britt glanced at them with a taut smile. "Only an elk," he murmured.

The elk, a young bull, moved steadily across the draw, its course bringing it nearer, and finally vanished off to their left in the direction of the river.

"Figuring on finding a mudhole during the heat of the day," Britt said.

Another long, slow hour wheeled by. The deer flies had found them now, and eye gnats danced before them. Britt was always keenly conscious of Ann Richards' nearness. She had fixed her hair into two tight, plaited coils which were pinned down on either side at the back of her head, and wore a blue bandanna about her slim throat to offset the blast of the sun. She lay on her stomach, propped on her elbows, wriggling now and then to a new position on the rocky ground. Some insect aroused her to consternation, and she pulled up a trouserleg, slapping vigorously. She said apologetically, "I thought it was a big bug."

The sun was relentless. Heat reflected from the rocks. Then

Britt suddenly again breathed a word of caution, and all three of them froze.

Something had moved again in the brushy basin where the elk had appeared. This time it was not an elk.

"Don't move!" Britt murmured. "Keep your heads down."

Lying flat, peering between rocks, they watched an Indian ride into view. Then another and a third. One was leading a riderless pony. Two wore only breechclouts. The third was bare to the waist, but had on heavy buckskin leggings. They all carried rifles, and two also had bows and quivers of arrows slung on their backs.

"They're trailing the elk," Britt whispered. "They're hunting meat right now, not scalps. But they'd prefer scalps. Don't move. Don't . . ."

A new thought stirred him. "If we only could get our hands on those horses!" he breathed longingly.

Phil and the girl looked at him, a sudden excited hope in their eyes.

But the three Sioux were too far away, and they were riding toward the river, following the trail of the elk. They were just within long rifle range, but soon would be out of sight. It would be hopeless to attempt to race after them on foot. That would only reveal their presence. The mounted Indians would be sure to scatter to cover, and one of them would surely ride to the main village with news that scalps were to be had for the taking.

Suddenly Ann laid aside her rifle, and began crawling away, staying on the far side of the ridge from the draw through which the Indians were riding.

"I'll try to decoy them within reach," she whispered over her shoulder. "Follow me, but not too close."

Britt grasped her plan. And so did Phil. Britt opened his mouth to order her to return. But she had now come to her feet, and was running downward along the slant of the ridge, heading to the point where it tapered down to meet lower ground to their left.

He looked at Phil helplessly. Then he picked up her discarded rifle and his own. They retreated off the skyline and went hurrying after her.

CHAPTER 24

The point toward which Ann was heading was an arm of the bigger draw through which the three Sioux were riding, following the spoor of the elk.

As she ran, Britt saw her loosen her braids, tearing them free with frantic fingers. Her hair, a lustrous rich amber cascade, streamed out free to fly in the hot sunlight.

Thus, with her hair loose and proclaiming that here was a woman, she emerged from the shelter of the ridge and Britt knew she must now be in view of the Indians who were off to the right and hidden from him and Phil by the arm of the slant which they were still descending.

Ann did not look back. Britt knew that she was fully aware of the danger she was inviting. Now she began simulating utter exhaustion. She moved at a stumbling walk, fell, then arose again. She staggered on for a few more yards, then pitched forward on her face and lay there among the thin brush in the open draw.

Britt dragged Phil down to hiding in a litter of boulders, and they crawled ahead until they were little more than fifty yards from where she lay. Her position was slightly downhill from them.

"She knows they've seen her," Britt murmured. "Maybe they won't come this way. Maybe they'll suspect it's a trap."

Minutes passed and no sound came. Britt felt the suspense build up in him until it constricted his throat.

Ann stirred. She dragged herself to her feet, made a few uncertain steps, then fell again. Never did she look eastward—in the direction the three Sioux had been. Britt knew that required a supreme effort of will. She was playing a role, acting the part of a lost woman who had wandered for miles and now was at the end of her strength. She did not want the warriors to know she was aware of their presence. She wanted them to believe she was too spent to see or know anything. She was placing before them a prize that would be hard to resist, the chance to make a captive of a young woman.

Britt knew that his mouth had turned leather-dry. He could hear the drumming of his own heart. If the Sioux guessed that she was only a decoy they would undoubtedly put a bullet in her as she lay there.

Then came a faint sound, the rattle of a turned pebble. Britt and Phil tried to make themselves smaller, hugging the hot hillside against which they lay. They did not dare lift their heads, but from Britt's position he had Ann's location in sight, though she was hidden amid the small rocks and bunchgrass.

Another scuffing sound came, startlingly near. Then a figure darted to cover of a boulder only a stone's throw away, and between Britt and the girl's position. It was the warrior wearing the leggings.

The trap was working. Britt glimpsed a second Indian moving from cover to cover farther away. Presently he sighted the third Sioux, following the same tactics.

The three were afoot. Evidently they had left their horses the instant they had sighted that staggering figure. They had spread out and were closing in from three points. And they were almost sure now, for they were becoming less wary as they converged on where the girl lay.

Now competition entered into the stalk, and the three, each anxious to be the first to claim this prisoner, abandoned all caution and left cover and ran toward Ann at full speed, their eyes alive with wild elation.

Britt and Phil came to their feet, their rifles in their hands. "Hola!" Britt barked.

The three Indians were almost at Ann's side. They halted, twisting and staring, with a consternation that was almost ludicrous, at the two gaunt, unshaven men who stood among the boulders so near at hand.

The helplessness of their position came to them and they froze, waiting for bullets to tear into them.

Ann got to her feet, ran to join Britt and Phil. She picked up her rifle and lifted it, covering the Indians also.

"Drop your guns," Britt snapped. He did not know the words in Sioux, but his meaning and his gesture was plain enough to them.

Their eyes flickered about, seeking some solution. Then one of the pair in breechclouts turned with a screech, and attempted to run for cover.

To let him escape meant death sooner or later for all of them. Almost regretfully, Britt squeezed the trigger. But he shot low. The advantage was all in his favor at the mo-

166

ment and he could not bring himself to kill the running warrior.

The bullet knocked a leg from under the Sioux, and its force whirled him around. He fell, turning a partial somersault, then lay limp and moaning.

Britt swung his rifle back on the other two. "Drop your guns!" he said again.

These two seemed to comprehend now that this grim-faced, wide-shouldered white man did not want to kill them. That seemed incredible to them, for that was not the way white men usually acted toward them. But now they released the rifles. They stood tense and straight and proud—waiting.

Britt and Phil ran to them, keeping them covered, and stripped them of their bows and slung arrows, and of the scalping knives each carried. They were young. Britt judged they could hardly be more than eighteen.

The wounded Sioux was older by four or five years by appearance. He lay with eyes dulled by pain, the shock of the bullet paralyzing his mind.

"Losing too much blood," Phil pronounced. "I've got to stop that hemorrhage." He took Ann's bandanna neckerchief and formed a tourniquet.

The shot had brought Sherry from the coulee. Hank Eilers, using a stick for support, came hobbling after her.

Britt pushed the two young braves into a sitting position against a rock and turned them over to Phil and Sherry to watch.

Then he headed at a run for the bigger swale to locate the horses. He found that Ann was following him.

"I can help," she panted.

Her hair was still flying loose. Again Britt felt that overpowering desire for her. Again he conquered it.

The Sioux had tied the animals in hiding among scrub cedar. Britt approached them warily. They began to snort and shy away, but finally allowed him to walk up to them.

He saw now that three carried Army brands. They were cavalry horses the Sioux had acquired in battle or raids. The fourth and wildest, which had been brought along to pack the expected elk meat, was a wiry Indian pony which objected to white man's scent. But it, too, calmed after Britt talked to it for a while.

Leading the horses by braided rawhide picket lines, Britt

and Ann returned to where the others waited. Phil had finished with the wounded warrior, who now had a bandage on his leg, and was becoming aware that he was a captive.

"An ugly wound," Phil said. "But he should recover if he is careful. However it will be some time before he'll be performing any war dances."

Hank Eilers, his bearded face hard, fingered his rifle, rocked back the hammer. "If'n you ask me, I say the only thing to do is put a slug in 'em," he said harshly.

Britt pushed Eilers' gun down. "That isn't necessary," he said sharply.

"What else is there to do?" Eilers demanded.

"Tie 'em up and leave them here," Britt said. "The tribe will miss them sooner or later and will trail them here and take care of them."

"And they'll find us, too," Phil reminded him grimly.

"We're pulling out—at once," Britt said.

"In broad daylight?"

"But we have horses now," Britt said. "We've got to chance it. In fact we have no other choice. We can't hang around here any longer. We've got to hope we don't bump into any more Sioux hunting parties. We'll have to make tracks and put as much distance as possible between ourselves and this spot before trailers show up here to find out what happened to these fellows."

He added tersely, "If we're lucky we may be able to head off Jarrett. We might be able to make it to the Beaverkill by sunup tomorrow. I doubt if Jarrett will be far ahead of us."

He saw Ann Richards' head lift, a new life in her eyes. Then her glance came to him, and the hope that had flared in her was replaced by something else—dark and brooding.

"But Maxwell can't ride . . ." Phil began.

"That Indian pony has been broken to pull travois," Britt said. "See the rub marks on its flanks?"

"Travois?" Phil questioned blankly.

"That's an Indian rig of dragpoles pulled by a pony," Britt explained. "We can rig one and fit it with a frame to which we can strap Maxwell. The rest of us can make out with the other three animals."

He looked around, searching their faces for their thoughts. "We'll have to be careful until dark, staying to cover and scouting ahead," he said. "That will make slow

168

going. We'll have to gamble that the Sioux don't hit our trail too early in the game. If we're still alive at nightfall we'll have a fighting chance. We'll keep going after the moon comes up. If we can make it to the Beaverkill by daybreak we can stake out. Jarrett will be arriving there eventually. I imagine you know why. Sherry told you the story, didn't she?"

"It was a rather astonishing tale," Phil nodded. "It cleared up several matters that have puzzled me."

"Jarrett has two boats," Britt said. "Boats leave no trail. With a boat in our possession again we ought to be able to shake off the Sioux if they trail us, and make it to Buford."

"I doubt if Mead Jarrett will welcome us," Phil remarked. "The boat will be had only for the taking."

"Let's quit palavering and start moving," Britt said.

He hurried away toward the river. After some time he returned, dragging two straight, stout lengths of cottonwood, still green enough to be supple. With a scalping knife he advanced on the Indian who wore the buckskin leggings. The warrior stared somberly, expecting death.

"It's only your britches I want, Mister," Britt said.

He stripped the owner down to his breechclout. Then he cut the leggings into strips. Using these for bindings, he formed a travois frame, lashed a blanket to it and made a harness from strips of blankets and picket ropes.

"Let's hope it holds together for a day's travel at least," he said.

He bound the prisoners hand and foot with the remainder of the buckskin lashings, then tethered them to trees so they could not help each other.

"Even if they're not found," he said, "one of these thunderstorms is sure to pass this way, maybe this afternoon. They'll work free after it rains."

"After it rains?" Phil questioned.

"Buckskin stretches when wet," Britt explained. "You noticed that I softened it a little with water to make it pliable to tie them up. It will tighten up on them as it dries, and hold them like iron, but it will stretch like rubber if it gets a real soaking."

Phil looked at him with a quizzical smile. "You are a merciful man, Cahill," he observed. "You could have killed that one who was running. You had every reason to do so. No doubt he was one of those who fought to take our scalps

169

at the steamboat. I never saw a prettier wing shot than the one that brought him down."

"Meaning what?" Britt asked absently, busy with a final strengthening of the travois frame.

Phil's glance traveled to Ann Richards, who was within earshot. "Meaning that you're supposed to have murdered a man in cold blood for profit, Cahill," he said. "It doesn't add up."

Sherry sniffed. "Why, Doctor Philip DeWitt Howe," she said bitingly. " 'Tis common sense you are beginning to show, or do my ears deceive me? Could it be there is something in you besides thin blue blood and stuffing?"

Wholesome anger poured color into Phil's face. He swung around and advanced on Sherry. She saw the look in his dark eyes, and backed away in sudden apprehension. "Now —now—don't you dare . . ." she chattered in a panic.

"I've stood your scorn long enough," Phil gritted. "It is you who has been the snob! You need to be taught a lesson."

"Hold on!" Britt protested. "You'll pop those stitches, Phil!"

The young doctor was too angry to heed. Sherry tried to flee, but he overtook her. Sherry kicked and squawled, but he swung her off her feet, laid her across his knee and applied the palm of his hand vigorously. It was a very sound spanking that he administered.

"There!" he panted, releasing her.

Sherry rubbed her injured anatomy, tears of pain on her cheeks. She yelled furiously at Britt, "And what kind of a man are you, to let this brute humiliate a lady?"

"Lady?" Phil jeered. "Since when did a little flannel-mouthed mick named Mollie O'Toole earn the right to call herself a lady?"

Sherry stared, shocked into silence. Her glance darted accusingly to Britt.

"No," Phil snapped. "Cahill didn't tell me. It happened that I was one of the few wedding guests who showed up on the groom's side of the church one day in Boston when a bride was left jilted at the altar."

There was a long moment of absolute quiet. Sherry stood gazing at him, a trapped despair in her eyes.

"That was the first time I had ever laid eyes on Mollie O'Toole," Phil said, breaking that quiet. "I did not see her again until I happened to visit Pierre's gambling house in

St. Louis one night recently, and listened to the singing of Sherry Dean. I learned that Sherry Dean was leaving for Montana at the conclusion of her engagement there. That —that was one of the reasons why I was also aboard the *Dakota Queen.*"

He turned to Britt. "I shouldn't have done that, I suppose," he said in a strained voice. "You had a right to kill me for doing it, Cahill. I know how it is between you and— and Mollie O'Toole. I wish you both all the happiness in the world."

Then he walked away. Sherry stood staring after him, a strange bafflement in her eyes. Britt saw something of that same futility in Ann Richards' expression. Then Ann turned away also, busying herself with some task.

After that they worked in silence. They placed Sam Maxwell on the travois, made him as comfortable as possible. Britt lifted Ann and Sherry on one of the horses to ride double. He helped Hank Eilers onto the pad saddle of the second animal. Both Eilers and Maxwell were in for an ordeal, and he told them to call a halt whenever the going became too tough.

With a final inspection of the captives' bonds, he said, "All right."

He guided the way on foot, and the four horses stirred reluctantly into motion. Phil, mounted bareback, led the pony which dragged the travois.

Britt knew they were leaving a trail that could be followed with ease. Putting distance between themselves and the Sioux was their only hope.

But progress was slow, for they could not follow the easiest route, but were forced to veer and zig-zag in order to take advantage of what cover they could find to hide them.

Britt scouted well in advance, moving at a half-trot, crawling to each rise to survey the next stretch of country before beckoning the cavalcade ahead.

The land grew increasingly rough, broken by ridges and coulees and buttes from which danger might appear at any moment. As they labored westward the river left them, its brushline vanishing into the run of the country as it swung northward on its long loop.

The blazing sun was a savage enemy as the afternoon advanced. The sage-covered flats baked in that fierce blaze.

The ridges reflected the ovenlike heat. Prickly pear growing in phalanxes in favorable spots forced tedious detours.

Sam Maxwell was suffering, for no amount of care could spare him all the jolting of travois travel. But he was tough, and insisted that he was all right.

The girls rode limp, their hair and eyelashes gray with the dust that was powdering ponies and human beings until they were the same hue as the harsh land. Phil Howe was tight-lipped, evidently feeling the pain of his arrow wound, but refusing to offer any complaint.

Britt told them that the heat offered one factor in their favor, at least. All game should be bushed up now, and that meant that hunting parties like the one they had captured would likely have returned to the village.

But he was wrong. He discovered his error not many minutes after he voiced this bit of optimism. He had climbed to a saddle on a steep, rock-toothed ridge, and crawled to peer ahead without skylining himself, when he suddenly flattened—every fiber in his body jangling with shock.

A mounted Indian was ascending this same ridge from the opposite side, and was heading for the saddle in which Britt lay. And he was already less than a pistol shot away.

Britt slid to hiding back of a slab of rock. He was certain he had not been seen, for the oncoming rider's attention had been diverted northward at that moment.

He chanced another glimpse. This Sioux was a mature, tall, powerfully muscled opponent. Mounted on a handsome, roan buffalo pony, he wore an elkskin vest which was decorated with the teeth of elk and grizzly and bore painted medicine signs. His leggings and moccasins must have cost some squaw many patient days in the making. He rode a pad saddle, with a carbine in a scabbard, and had a sheathed knife at his belt. His medicine bag hung about his neck. The scars of the sun dance were visible on his chest where the vest hung open. Hawk-nosed, fierce of eye, here was a warrior of pride and many ponies. A fighting man who had proved himself in battle.

Britt twisted, looking back. His own party was in plain sight, toiling up this slope toward his position, but still some two hundred yards down the slant.

Discovery was certain, and within seconds, for he could already hear the Indian pony's unshod hoofs scuffing rocks near at hand. The Sioux was certain to come upon him in a moment or two, following the same easiest path Britt had been tracing He would sight the party below, and would undoubtedly wheel and ride to bring other tribesmen down upon them.

Britt guessed that the Sioux was searching for the three who lay bound and tied half a dozen miles east. But there might be other Indians close and any gunshot would bring them.

All these thoughts whirled through his mind in those fleeting moments as the Sioux came riding steadily upon his position. Then the pony and the warrior loomed above him and he had only one choice. He sprang to his feet, his six-shooter poised, hoping he could club his man with the barrel. But the Sioux had glimpsed him just before he arose, and that cost him the greater part of the advantage of surprise.

The warrior reacted swiftly. A yell rose to his lips. He made an instinctive move toward his carbine, but gave that up instantly, realizing he did not have time to bring it into play. For Britt was upon him. The Sioux snatched out his knife instead.

The pony reared, striking at Britt with frightened front hoofs. That deflected Britt's leap. He swung at the Sioux with the muzzle of the gun, but missed. He stumbled, but managed to grip the warrior's leg as he fell, and dragged the Indian with him to the ground.

But he was at a deadly disadvantage now, with his opponent on top of him and braced on a leg and a knee. The Sioux drove his knife at his throat, but, fighting for his life, he managed to lock the fingers of his left hand on the sinewy wrist as the blow descended, halting the thrust.

At the same instant the warrior grasped Britt's gun arm, holding the weapon away so that it could not be used against him.

They remained in this position for long, heart-straining seconds, muscles swelling, veins bulging on their jaws and temples, matching their strength, with death as the penalty for weakening.

Britt, clawing with his feet, swung them around, and found leverage against a boulder for his leg. He twisted suddenly, throwing the warrior off balance. They rolled and Britt wrested his right arm free.

Momentarily he had his chance. He realized it was his

last chance, for the hectic events of the day—and indeed all that had happened in the past weeks, bore down on him now, and he knew he could not hold that knife away from his throat in a second test of strength.

He swung the heavy, seven-inch barrel of the gun, bringing it crashing down at the base of the warrior's neck. He gethered all of the last of his fading endurance in that blow, gambling to win or lose on that one final effort. And it was enough, for he heard bone crunch and snap.

The warrior went limp in his grasp. Then he toppled aside, a strange, whistling sigh issuing from his mouth. Then he was dead. That blow had broken his neck.

Britt lay beside his opponent, too spent to move. He heard running feet and voices. Phil loomed above him, and then the faces of Ann and Sherry.

Phil knelt beside him, straightened his cramped legs, and stood to shield him from the sun. Presently he felt his tortured lungs begin to subside. There was the taste of blood in his mouth, his own blood from the tremendous exertion.

He turned his head and looked at the Sioux. There was a vast regret in him that the warrior had had to die.

Ann, who was kneeling beside him, must have seen this, for he felt her hand touch his own in a soothing gesture. "You—you had to do it, Cahill," she said.

CHAPTER 25

They took cover, watching the country. No other Sioux appeared, and after an hour Britt gave the signal to proceed.

At dusk they found a small stream and rested there until the moon was bright. Then they pushed on again. They had lived through the day and that strengthened their resolution.

Darkness brought relief from the pitiless heat, but it brought other problems too. Unable to sight clearly their route ahead in the moonlight, they found themselves at times in blind draws, or confronted by impassable ledges that necessitated backtracking and painstaking searching until a feasible path westward was found.

Still they slowly, grimly built up the miles. The horses began to tire, and the girls and Phil were walking the greater part of the time to spare the animals. Sam Maxwell fell into a stupor of sheer pain and exhaustion, and Eilers rode like a collapsing bag on his horse.

The slow swing of the moon and the stars marked the march of the hours. Midnight came and passed. They halted once, and ate the last of their food. Then they struggled ahead once more.

Ann stumbled again in the darkness and fell. Britt lifted her to her feet. She leaned against him, surrendering for a moment to her weariness and to all the doubts and emotions that tore at her. She remained thus, her body touching his, dependent on his strength. Then slowly she straightened and drew away. She said, "I'm sorry, Cahill—for—for everything!"

She moved ahead again, leaving Britt once more with that emptiness, that knowledge of both her nearness and her remoteness.

Daybreak was not far away when Britt, who was leading the way, lifted his head. He waited for a time until he was sure. Then he said, "Smell it? The river! We're nearing it again. We've crossed the neck of the bend!"

The rough and wild land was lifting its shaggy, gray-green bulk into the full presence of daylight as they topped a rise and saw the glint of the river in the distance. They pulled up, staring.

The main channel of the Missouri was still some two miles away. It was flanked by a brushy, swampy bottom land nearly half a mile wide. Islands and humps of higher land rose above this area and were thickly grown with willows and wild currant and chokecherry and cottonwood. Backwater still veined this maze, for the river had not yet receded to its mid-summer ebb.

The brushline of a tributary stream joined the river just to their left.

"That," Britt said, "should be the Beaverkill."

He saw the look in Ann's eyes as she inspected this wild river bottom. Here, within her reach at last, after all these weeks, was perhaps the answer to whether her father was dead or alive.

Then her gaze swung to him and he watched dread form in her expression. Almost as clearly as though she had spoken, he knew that she was seeing that this might also be the end of the trail he had followed so relentlessly.

Gazing at the labyrinth that confronted them Britt could

understand why Zack Richards had taken pains to map the location of the mackinaw boat in painstaking detail. No doubt, at the time the boat had gone down, the river, high with the spring runoff and choked with ice, had covered the greater part of this flood channel. The boat probably had been crushed by ice, and had sunk somewhere in the backwater during the flood. Without exact instructions a man might search for a lifetime and never find what he sought.

Silent now, they moved forward again, heading for the brush. Britt knew the same question was in all their minds. Had they won the race to intercept Jarrett?

And even if they sighted him they were all realizing that the chances of commandeering at least one of the boats were banked steeply against them. The Sioux would certainly be on their trail before the day was far advanced. Exhausted, the horses spent, they would have little chance of making it to Fort Buford on foot before being overtaken.

They were near the river brush when Britt halted, pointing. Nearly half a mile to their right a higher ridge reached out into the river bottom. It was studded with rocks, and carried a stand of bigger timber than the surroundings and extended to the main channel of the Missouri.

From beyond that hogback a thin puff of smoke was rising. Its color was gray-white and almost imperceptible in this gray dawn light.

Even as they watched, it faded, and then there was nothing. "Cook fire," Britt said, a throb of vast excitement in his voice. "Somebody just snuffed a fire with water."

"Indians?" Phil asked quickly.

"White man's fire," Britt said. "No Indian would be that careless."

He added with fierce, positive conviction, "Jarrett and his party."

They prodded the horses into motion and made their way to the brushy river bottom. They found a stopping point and lifted Sam Maxwell from the travois to a blanket bed.

Britt and Phil picked up their rifles and made sure of the action of these guns and also their .45's.

"We've got to take it slow and careful," Britt said. "We'll first locate the camp. If it really is Jarrett, then we'll figure out what to do. Sound carries a long way at this hour. If they hear us before we want them to they'll be ready for us."

Sherry, ashen-lipped, said, " 'Tis a long way from Boston that you've come, Philip DeWitt Howe. I pray that you live to see your home again."

Phil looked at her, a sudden, shining startlement in his face. He abruptly walked to her, took her in his arms and kissed her. "At least," he said roughly, "you'll have that to remember me by, Mollie O'Toole."

Then he released her. "You have all the luck, Cahill," he said. "Lead the way."

Britt hesitated. Then, realizing he had nothing to say, he moved off through the thickets, heading in the direction of that smoke sign they had sighted earlier.

The area was half water, half land. At times they traveled on dry sandbars or the higher islands. And then they would be laboring through bogs where they sank to their thighs in oozy mud. The Missouri had only lately surrendered some of these lowlands.

Twice they were confronted by sloughs through which they were forced to wade to their armpits, holding their weapons above their heads.

To their left the main river began to glint nearer at hand through the brush and timber. The ridge which held the secret of that puff of smoke began to loom up also, and Britt moved slowly, using every possible cover to mask their approach.

Now, faint sounds began to drift to them, the rasp of oarlocks and the occasional hollow thump of feet on a boat bottom. He and Phil looked at each other grimly. There was no longer any doubt that they had Jarrett and his party to contend with.

Then a man's voice came in an exultant yell. "I got it! I got it! God! Look! Look!"

Another voice spoke sharply. "Quiet, you infernal fool! Quit that screeching!"

The second speaker had been Mead Jarrett. The speakers evidently were still some distance away and beyond the ridge, but the words had carried clearly in the morning silence.

Britt nodded and he and Phil moved ahead and reached the ridge. It was broad, and lifted to an elevation of twenty or thirty feet above the lowlands. Crawling through brush and timber they made their way to the crest and peered cautiously.

Beyond the ridge lay a sizable slough more than a hundred yards wide. Near at hand and below them on the shore of this backwater was an overnight camp that had been recently used. Cooking utensils and blankets still lay there near the water-drenched ashes of a fire.

On the far side of the slough the two skiffs floated in shallow, reed-grown water among stumps and deadfalls. Mead Jarrett stood erect in one boat which he held in place by means of a pole driven in the slough bottom.

With Jarrett in this boat were Walker Ormsby and Leila. The other craft lay only a dozen feet away, and with it were the two deckhands. One was standing in the boat, but the other was in the water which came only to his waist.

The man in the water was the lop-eared deckhand. He was dribbling a little stream of something from one hand to another and his unshaven, ugly face was aflame with a wild, hysterical delight.

For the first rays of the rising sun were striking through the timber now and catching the hue of that sand-like material. It was not sand! It showed a dull brassy color in that light. Gold! Coarse, raw gold!

"All right," Jarrett said in his cold voice. "Quit playing and get the rest of it. And be careful. Those buckskin pokes are rotten and will burst like that first one. Here's a blanket. Slip it under each bag before you try to lift it. Then hand them up to me."

The man in the water took a blanket, ducked partly beneath the surface of the river and scrabbled around for a time at some awkward task. Then he brought up a blanket, dripping mud and water, which was wrapped around some weighty object, and Jarrett swung it aboard.

The operation was repeated again and again. They were recovering Zack Richards' gold hoard. The man in the water was standing on the mackinaw boat where it lay in the shallow backwater, and he was retrieving the rotting buckskin pokes, loaded with treasure, from the mud-filled hull.

"We'll wait until they come ashore," Britt murmured to Phil.

Behind them, and off to their right, a man appeared without sound from the thickets. He was a wild-looking figure, with matted, graying beard on a deeply lined, powerful face that was marked by suffering and privation. His clothes were in rags and he was hatless, his gray hair a fierce tangle about his ears. More than six feet tall with gaunt, wide shoulders, he now held a notched stick, which he used as a crutch at times for his left leg, which had been broken not long in the past and was not yet strong enough to permit him to place his full weight on it for any length of time.

Zack Richards had a six-shooter in his hand. He seemed as much a part of this wilderness as the brush from which he had emerged.

He recognized Britt now. The surprise of that showed in his dark, sunken eyes. At first he was puzzled. Then Zack Richards' mouth thinned as his mind raced back three years to that night in St. Louis when he had seen his steamboats and his warehouses and all the accumulation of his life go up in flames.

Implacable rage flared, and he lifted the six-shooter, bringing it squarely to bear on Britt.

Neither Britt nor Phil Howe was aware that death looked at them over the sights of that gun, for they were absorbed in watching the scene across the stretch of backwater.

Only a man of iron could have survived the two months that Zack Richards had endured in this wilderness on the Missouri River. He and Pete McLeod had salvaged only a rifle and a holster gun and a little food when they had swum ashore through the ice floes from their crushed mackinaw boat the day of the disaster after the fight with the Sioux.

Pete McLeod had taken the rifle when he set out for Fort Buford to bring provisions and horses. He had left the pistol with Zack Richards, along with some thirty rounds of shells that had been in a watertight case.

Helpless because of his bullet-broken leg, Zack Richards had nearly starved after the food that McLeod left had given out. There were days when he had been raving and delirious, and nights when he had placed the gun to his temple and tried to steel his will to pull the trigger.

But the fierce desire to live had prevailed and carried him through. He had managed to shoot a beaver and its nourishing meat had brought him back from the brink of death. He had cared for his own leg, made his own splints and bound them in place with tough, pliable roots and strips from his own clothing.

During that time he could only speculate on McLeod's fate. He knew McLeod was dead, and took it for granted

179

that he had fallen victim to the Indians He wondered if it
had happened on the trip to Buford, or whether McLeod had
died on his way back with the provisions for which he
had made the journey. If McLeod had lived to reach the
trading post he would have undoubtedly mailed the letter
and map that Zack Richards had addressed to his daughter
in St. Louis.

That was the one hope that had helped buoy him up all
these weeks. He knew that if Ann had received that letter
she would turn heaven and earth to find him.

He had finally managed to kill a doe that wandered within
reach of his .45. That had been the final turning point in his
fight for survival. He still had venison jerky which he had
dried in the sun. And he still had a scant dozen shells for his
gun.

Always there had been the danger from Indians. Each
time he had fired a shot to bring down game he had expected the report to bring the Sioux also, but luck had been
with him.

Several times, from the river's margin, he had tried to flag
down passing steamboats, or mackinaws carrying men downriver, but he had been ignored. All craft were now wary of
being lured into Indian ambush.

Now, suddenly, two small boats had appeared, landing at
daybreak on this point of land that overlooked the spot
where his gold-laden mackinaw had gone down.

He had recognized Mead Jarrett and Walker Ormsby and
Leila instantly. The lop-eared man and the other deckhand
were strangers to him. He had not made his presence known
at once, for these weeks had instilled an animal-like caution
in him. And there had been something in their attitudes that
had made him uneasy, and had warned him to go slow.

He had watched Jarrett search the area warily, a gun in
his hand, and he realized that Jarrett was seeking some sign
of his own presence or fate here. But he had made his own
hidden camp on the main shore some distance away, and
had been careful to leave no trail that a Sioux might find.

Jarrett, unable to discover any evidence of anyone having
been on this point of land, had at last given up the effort,
deciding that Zack Richards was either dead or had made his
way out of this region.

Afterwards Zack Richards had crept up on the camp they
had made to cook a meal. And he had heard them talking

about gold—his gold. He had seen Jarrett and Walker Ormsby and Leila studying a paper.

The map! The map he had drawn with such care as he lay desperately wounded and suffering, while McLeod made ready for the journey to Fort Buford. The map that had been intended only for the eyes of his daughter! Somehow it had fallen into the possession of Mead Jarrett.

And so he had waited, biding his time, while Jarrett began recovering the gold from the slough.

And now, even more amazingly, two more men had come out of the wilderness to this spot that only he had inhabited for weeks. One of them he did not know. The other, Britt Cahill, was the man who had ruined his steamboat company, and was wanted for the murder of his watchman the night of the fire.

Zack Richards kept his gun trained on Britt's back for long, deadly seconds while he debated what all this meant. This bitterness, which he held toward Britt, was greater even than the anger that seethed in him at the way Mead Jarrett was so casually helping himself to the gold that he had taken from the earth at the expense of two years of unceasing toil.

He started to speak, to bring Britt around facing him, for he found that he could not force himself even now to shoot him in the back without giving him a chance.

Then he realized that this was not the time, for there was Jarrett to consider. Soundlessly he retreated into the thickets, melting away among the foliage and merging with it in his stained, ragged garb. He waited there, watching from hiding, his gun still in his hand and ready.

Then he crouched down tighter in his covert as he heard something else. He watched another figure come moving cautiously through the brush, mounting the ascent toward where Britt Cahill and the other man lay.

This arrival wore man's garb, but Zack Richards saw that it was a young woman. She was muddy, and evidently had followed Cahill. She had a rifle and she moved to Cahill's side and lay there, joining in watching Jarrett's party in the boats.

It was then that Zack Richards recognized her. He came partly to his feet, staring in utter disbelief. He again drew his breath to shout out, but strangled it back in time. This was his own daughter, Ann! He froze there, gazing at her. Then he decided to wait a little longer before making his presence known and exacting his vengeance on Britt Cahill.

CHAPTER 26

Britt looked at Ann and pointed silently toward the boats. He heard her draw a little sighing sound as she realized what was happening.

The recovery of the gold was completed. The notch-eared man was breathing hard from his grampus-like exertions, the sound carrying clearly in the stillness.

"Make sure," Jarrett said impatiently.

"I tell you there ain't no more, Mead," the man snarled. "We got every last ounce o' it. There ain't nuthin' left in thet hull but mud. An if'n you don't believe me, git yore own fine feet wet an' take a look-see fer yoreself. Me, I'm climbin' out. That water's cold."

The man started to pull himself aboard the boat in which his companion stood.

Mead Jarrett, without a word, drew his six-shooter from his shoulder holster. As precisely and casually as he would shoot at a target he killed both of the deckhands with two bullets.

He shot the one who was standing upright in the boat first. The bullet pitched the man overside. Even before the body hit the water Jarrett killed the lop-eared deckhand whose back was turned to him as he was trying to lift himself over the gunwale into the skiff.

The lop-eared one's breath exploded from his lungs. He twisted around, staring up at Jarrett with a startled, wild expression. He tried to say something, but blood choked his throat and lungs. Then he slid back into the water, writhing in agony. Slowly that stilled, and slowly he sank from sight.

His companion floated face-down on the opposite side of the skiff, crimson bubbles rising around him. Then his body, too, gradually sank, merging with the muddy hue of the water. Then he was gone.

Britt lay stunned by the enormity of this cold-blooded double murder. He heard Ann utter a rasping, terrified sound. Horror held Phil Howe motionless.

Leila Ormsby and her father also sat frozen in the boat,

staring unbelievingly at the water where the two men had vanished from sight forever. Jarrett, with his swift, strong fingers, punched the two empties from the gun, reloaded, and flipped the gate back in place.

He said in a voice of thoughtful concern, "I trust there are no Sioux within hearing distance of those shots. But we have the boats. We will move to the north shore at once. I doubt if any hostiles are on the other side of the river."

Leila screamed then—wildly, horribly. Her thin, long face was snow-white. She recoiled from Jarrett, scuttling crabwise away from him to the prow of the boat where she pressed close against her father. Walker Ormsby also sat fearstricken, the purple veins standing out against the shroudgray hue of his skin.

Leila's screaming kept running up the scale until it was like a physical blow on Britt's ears.

Jarrett stepped along the boat, slapped her savagely across the mouth. "Stop it!" he said in that icy voice. "Stop it, I say!"

Leila's screaming died, crushed by utter terror. She merely lay there now, huddling against her father, staring at Jarrett in almost hypnotic dread.

Jarrett moved to the oars and swung the skiff to overtake the second boat which was drifting slowly away.

"There was nothing else to do," he said in that same conversational voice. "You wouldn't have wanted to split the gold with them either, and you know it. They deserved nothing. Grab the painter of that boat, Captain. We'll tow it to shore, gather up our camp outfit and get out of this place. We'll be safe at Fort Buford in two or three days."

Leila still stared at him with that frozen fear in her pale eyes. Walker Ormsby mechanically obeyed Jarrett's instructions and caught the painter of the drifting boat with numb hands.

Jarrett rowed ashore, stepped out and pulled both craft a few feet on the bank. He spoke impatiently to Leila, who still crouched rigidly in the boat. "Come ashore, my dear, while we rearrange cargo. We'll divide up the gold between the boats. Then they'll handle better."

Leila, moving like a sleepwalker, stumbled to dry land. Walker Ormsby followed. It was evident they both expected to suffer the same fate as the deckhands.

183

Mead Jarrett's handsome face wore a small, mirthless smile. He was enjoying their fear of him.

Britt arose, stepped into the open, his six-shooter in his hand. "Jarrett!" he spoke, his voice flat.

Jarrett whirled and stared for an instant at Britt and at Phil Howe and Ann Richards in utter incredulity.

Then his sharp mind accepted the situation and acted instantly to meet it. Even before Jarrett moved, Britt saw what was going to happen, and realized his own mistake in appearing prematurely. He should have bided his time a moment or two longer.

For Leila stood only a few paces from Jarrett, and already he had glided to his right so that she was now between him and Britt. Shielded thus, Jarrett retreated swiftly toward boulders and brush a rod behind him.

Britt did not dare fire. Leila, realizing her danger, stood frozen, staring at Britt's gun. Britt heard Phil utter an exclamation and begin shifting quickly, evidently intending to draw clear of Leila in order to bring Jarrett into a clear line of fire.

Beyond Leila, Britt saw Jarrett's gun swing up. He dived aside in a twisting fall as Jarrett fired. The bullet must have passed within inches of Leila's body, but Britt had made his move at the exact time, and the slug missed him.

He rolled, followed by another shot that kicked dirt over him, and reached shelter back of a foot-high ridge of moss-covered bedrock that jutted above the surface.

He was yelling to Phil to take cover even as he moved. Jarrett's gun crashed a third time and Britt saw the young doctor pitch forward sickly on his face, roll over on his side. Then Phil Howe's body lay still there. Jarrett's bullet had found him.

Britt lay flat, his body barely sheltered by the finger of rock that had saved his life. Turning his head he saw Ann crouching back of a boulder near by.

Jarrett had backed now to the boulders and brush to the left of the camp his party had made, still keeping Leila between him and Britt. Leila now aroused from her paralysis of fear and turned and ran to the right.

This was what Britt had been waiting for, and he fired twice. But Jarrett had anticipated that, and had gone to cover, and was momentarily out of sight.

Britt left his position and raced to take shelter of a tree.

Jarrett fired again and he felt the tug of a bullet at the collar of his shirt. Then he found the protection of a sizable cedar trunk.

Silence came for a moment. It had all happened in blurred seconds. Walker Ormsby cowered near the boats, gibbering in fear. There was no fight in him. Leila had run off into the thickets to the right.

Phil Howe's body lay in the open, motionless, apparently dead. A streak of blood showed on his temple just where his thick, dark hair began.

Ann still huddled back of a boulder fifty feet to Britt's right. She was looking at Phil. Then her eyes turned to Britt, and they were dull and blank with sorrow.

Someone was racing through the brush toward them. A woman's voice called frantically. It was Sherry, who had followed their trail through the swamp.

Sherry burst into view. Britt shouted a warning at her, but she did not even look in his direction. She had seen Phil's body. She screamed, and the sound was that of utter desolation.

She ran to where Phil lay. She knelt, huddling over him, rocking in grief. "And now 'tis Boston you'll never see again, Philip DeWitt Howe," she moaned. "And you died, thinking I despised you. I loved you. Me, Mollie O'Toole! I dared love the fine and wonderful gentleman that you are. And now you're gone, and there's nothing left in the world for me."

Mead Jarrett could have shot Sherry. And Ann also, for she left shelter now and hurried to Sherry's side. But Jarrett must have known that he had no bullets to waste, for he let them live.

Instead, Britt glimpsed the gambler darting deeper into the timber. Jarrett's purpose was to flank him, or drive him into the open. Britt followed his quarry's tactics, keeping pace relentlessly with him, never giving him a chance for a certain shot.

"No, Cahill!" Ann's frantic voice came. "He'll trap you—kill you!"

Britt did not answer. He kept moving, leaping from boulder to tree, from deadfall to brush clump.

Jarrett sighted him and fired over the rim of a boulder. The bullet ripped bark from the tree that sheltered Britt.

Britt's gun flamed instantly, and his slug nicked the boulder's rim an instant after Jarrett had dropped out of sight.

Jarrett retreated with greater wariness. Presently they traded shots again—and again their bullets missed only by fractions.

"Damn you, Cahill!" Jarrett spoke, and for the first time the tinny pitch of panic showed in his voice. "Who's the killer now?"

Britt pushed fresh shells into his gun. "You can always come out with your hands up, Jarrett," he said.

Jarrett's answer was three fast bullets that raked Britt's position. But once more a tree shielded him.

Jarrett darted to a new position. Britt followed.

It was a creeping, relentless duel, fought in the dappled shadows of the brush and timber—with death the penalty for a wrong move.

Jarrett's strategy now was to break past Britt and make toward the camp from which he had been driven. For he had made his mistake when he had first retreated in this direction. He was trapped on this narrowing spine of land which jutted to the margin of the main river. Already the Missouri's surface was glittering in the sun only a hundred yards away. Soon he would be able to retreat no farther.

But always Britt outmaneuvered him and herded him inexorably toward the river, toward the inevitable moment when he must come to bay.

There Jarrett would have to make his stand or surrender. And he would never surrender. That was the one thing that was certain in this duel to a finish.

Jarrett realized this now. The brush and timber were thinning and the river was near at hand. He made his last rush, heading for an outcrop of boulders that were overgrown with chokecherry and currant bushes, and guarded by a small clearing.

It would be a strong position, unassailable for a lone opponent, once Jarrett found a vantage point in that tangled litter.

Britt saw this and responded instantly. He burst from the brush thirty yards away even as Jarrett was making his run to this refuge. Jarrett fired twice at him, but the gambler was moving, too, scrambling over boulders, seeking a crevice to shield him. One bullet grazed Britt's side, the other missed.

Then Britt had covered the open ground, and was among

186

the brush and boulders too, scarcely thirty feet from where Jarrett had ducked out of sight.

Britt did not stop. He had the advantage of momentum. He vaulted a rock, circled another and drove ahead, crashing through the brush.

And then Jarrett, his cold nerve shattered at last, made his final mistake. Like a flushed rabbit he broke from the shelter he had taken only a dozen feet ahead.

Britt saw the gambler's frenzied eyes, saw the way his lips were peeled back from his white teeth in that moment of decision, saw the disorder of his blond hair.

Both their guns roared at this range that was almost point-blank. Jarrett missed again—for the last time in his life. He missed because he was shaken by panic.

Britt's shot did not miss. Jarrett's body was driven violently back, his head rolling sickeningly limp on his spine. Britt had a brief, terrible glimpse of a small circle that had been punched in the gambler's throat.

Jarrett pitched backwards over a boulder. He rolled in a half somersault, then straightened, and lay twitching convulsively for a time.

These throes faded, and Mead Jarrett was dead at Britt's feet. The bullet had torn through his throat, and had shattered his spinal cord.

Britt became aware of the wheezing of his own labored breathing. The reek of powder smoke was in his nostrils and dry as acid in his throat. Numbly he began to realize he was alive—almost unscathed. A thin trickle of blood ran from a bullet graze on his forearm. And an instant before, he had given himself up for dead. He had never dreamed that Jarrett would miss at that close range.

He began to shake. His knees were as soft as new putty. He now heard Ann Richards' voice calling his name.

She came running from the thickets into sight and saw him standing there. She cried wildly, "Cahill! Oh, Cahill . . . !"

Then she fainted, sagging to the earth with a small, moaning sigh.

That aroused Britt. He turned away from Mead Jarrett's staring, dead face, and walked on unsteady legs to her side. He knelt, gazed down at her face for a time. Presently he lifted her in his arms and carried her through the brush back toward the point where the fight had started.

She stirred. Her eyes, very dark with her memories, looked up at him. For a time they gazed into each other's thoughts—into their hearts. Her lips, ashen and cold, came nearer. Britt kissed her, holding her fiercely tight against him, feeling her mouth respond on his.

And both of them knew that this could not be, that this kiss was something that must not happen—should never have happened.

Britt drew away then, and she lay in his arms looking up at him, with this knowledge a barren and bitter thing in her gaze.

"I can walk now—alone," she said.

And so Britt placed her on her own feet, and she moved apart from him.

They walked in silence back to the camp. As they came into view of the boats, Britt's head lifted and Ann uttered a cry of thankfulness.

Phil Howe was sitting up. Sherry held him, his head against her breast. Her face was radiant with gratitude and the glory of a woman who had found her soul given back to her.

"The bullet," Phil said shakily, "only barked my skull. Slight concussion is my diagnosis. Knocked me out for a few minutes."

Leila and her father sat apart. They looked at Britt dully. They did not have to be told that Mead Jarrett was dead.

Then Zack Richards stepped from the thickets a dozen yards from Britt. He had his six-shooter in his hand.

"Ann!" he said.

Ann turned, stared at the bearded, ragged figure. "Dad!" she choked. "Oh, Dad! You're—you're . . ."

She started to rush toward him. Then she remembered! She halted, swung around and looked wildly at Britt.

Britt stood gazing at Zack Richards, and all the injustice of what he had gone through was back in his heart, all the memories of his three years as a fugitive, all the bitterness.

"Why did you do it, Richards?" he asked, his voice a monotone. "Why did you lie about me?"

Ann stepped in between them. Tears were streaming from her eyes. "No!" she sobbed. "No! This can't happen. Don't shoot, Dad! Don't fight him. I—I couldn't bear to have you two—you two . . ."

She could not go on. Britt made no move toward his gun.

For three years he had looked forward to the day when he would meet Zack Richards face to face, choke the truth from him, then put a bullet in him. And now that day had come, and he could not go through with it. He could not kill Zack Richards. He could not bring that grief on the girl he had held in his arms so recently.

Zack Richards' sunken eyes were fiercely, keenly alive. He looked from his daughter to Britt and back again with a growing perplexity.

"Lie?" he demanded, his voice rusty from long disuse. "What do you mean by that, Cahill? I should kill you. You ruined me that night in St. Louis and murdered my watchman. Maybe you figured you had reason to burn me out and rob me. I could understand how you felt about the loss of your boat. But murder is something else. And now I find you fighting to the death with another man for gold that belongs to me. What is this that you say I lied about?"

Britt laughed harshly. He wheeled abruptly to walk away from all this, to escape from this situation that he felt he could never solve.

Something halted him. Walker Ormsby had come to his feet a short distance away. Ormsby was staring at Zack Richards, and there was a terrible and sick fear in his face.

Britt watched this expression. Ormsby, moving like a man in a nightmare, suddenly turned and headed in a blind, stumbling run for the brush.

Britt overtook him in long strides, grasped his shoulder and swung him violently around. Clutching him, he stared into Walker Ormsby's eyes, seeing the small soul of the man, seeing his treachery and duplicity.

For a long moment Britt stood motionless, gazing at this big, broken hull of a man. And his mind was racing back three years to that night in St. Louis.

"Walker," he said softly. "You were the one who told me that Zack Richards had gone to the police with the story that he had seen me there at his boatyard when the fire broke out."

There was a silence, broken only by the broken, terrified wheeze of breath in and out of Walker Ormsby's throat.

Britt's eyes swung to Leila. She had come to her feet also, and in her face was the same panic that gripped her father.

"Instead, it was you who went to the police, Walker," Britt said, his voice thin. "You were the one who accused me of

189

murder and put lynchers on my trail. You! You and Jarrett."

Ann came with a rush toward him. "Cahill," she choked. "I took it for granted that you knew it was Walker Ormsby. I—I never dreamed that this was why you—you held such hatred toward my father."

Britt shook his head dazedly. "Why was I so blind?" he said, his voice hoarse. "It was all plain enough, if I only would let myself see it."

He still gripped Walker Ormsby. "You and Jarrett," he said in a monotome. "You two worked together. Jarrett sank my steamboat that night. Maybe it was only because he had the lust to destroy. Maybe he had planned that as the start of this whole thing. Either way he saw his chance to make a stake for himself by robbing the safe in Zack Richards' office and placing the blame on me. He needed help and knew you were a man of the same stripe at heart, and you two got together on the scheme. Jarrett did the robbery. You wouldn't have the guts for that. He killed the watchman, then set fire to the place. You took care of the rest of it."

His hands tightened on Walker Ormsby's throat. "You knew I was in love with Leila, and that I would trust you. You stampeded me into escaping from St. Louis, instead of staying and facing the charge, for you knew that if I learned you were the man who had lied about me I would probably guess the truth about the whole affair. And then, when I showed up alive that night in St. Louis a few weeks ago, Jarrett shot me, because he never wanted me to confront Zack Richards and compare notes. And he tried again to kill me aboard the *Dakota Queen*. It was Jarrett who shot at me from that entryway."

Britt was shaking Walker Ormsby as he would a stick, and his fingers were clamped like steel bands on the man's throat.

He became aware that Ann was struggling frenziedly to loosen his grip. She was pleading desperately, "Don't—don't, Cahill. Don't kill him! He isn't worth it! He isn't worth it!"

Britt came back to sanity. He released Walker Ormsby, and stepped back. Ormsby collapsed on the ground, slobbering and whimpering in self-pity.

Zack Richards looked at him and said, "Ormsby, I'll see to it that you stand trial for what you've done."

Britt ran an arm over his face as though to wipe away hideous memories. His eyes swung to Leila, seeing her colorless face which held fear and vindictiveness and defiance, but no shame. He turned his back on her.

He looked at Zack Richards. "For three years I wanted to kill you, Richards. Thank God, I was spared that, at least."

Ann spoke huskily. "And I, too, will always thank God."

She moved to him. She placed her hands on each side of his face, and stood gazing up at him for a long time, her eyes warm with the same radiance that Britt had seen in Sherry.

She said softly. "I thank God, too, that I was wrong when I believed you and Sherry were meant for each other. I thank God that it was Phil that Sherry loved. I was so jealous of her, because you and she were always so close, so understanding of each other. You two were always so much alike. I loved Sherry like a sister, and I loved Phil like a brother. But that is not the way I feel toward you, Cahill."

She rose on tiptoe, brought her lips fiercely against his. His arms went around her, bringing her against him, never wanting to free her. She began laughing and crying as she kissed him, saying little wild things to him.

Phil Howe and Sherry watched this, and looked at each other, smiling.

Zack Richards spoke finally. "Seems to me we better move out of here, and try to cross the river. Lots of shooting lately in these parts. Some Sioux might show up to take a look."

Sherry exclaimed. "Wait! By the saints! A steamboat!"

A sternwheeler was rounding in sight on the river, bound upstream. She carried the Army pennant at her staff. As she drew nearer, Britt saw that she was loaded with troops—reinforcements for Army posts in the upper country.

Sherry and Phil and Zack Richards ran through the timber to where the ridge overlooked the river, and began waving and shouting. Britt, with Ann's firm, small hand in his, followed. Together they watched the packet veer toward them, and come edging in for a landing to pick them up.

Britt thought of Hank Eilers and Sam Maxwell, who must be waiting in a fever of anxiety in the camp on the fringe of the river bottom. And he thought of the gold in the skiffs that belonged to Zack Richards, and which must be loaded.

But what he said was, "We'll be in Fort Buford by tomorrow. And by tomorrow night you'll be a bride, Ann."

"I can hardly wait," Ann said, and looked at him, her eyes gay, impudent, her thoughts all for him.

"Nor can I," Sherry said, kissing Phil. " 'Twill be a double wedding. Imagine the likes of Mollie O'Toole marrying a man with the name of Philip DeWitt Howe."

Behind them, Leila and her father stood, almost forgotten, as the steamboat dropped its stageplank in the brush of this wild shore.

THE END